COMBATANTS
THAT SPAN

DANIEL JACKSON—c
on Earth, is now a hero to a people in need of technology and education. Torn between his new bride and a movement he cannot resist, his unique knowledge of the StarGate may be his undoing. . . .

JACK O'NEIL—leader of the rebellion that destroyed Ra and stood firm against Hathor, finds himself faced with war of a very different kind . . . when old friends become new enemies, and control of the StarGate may cost him his command, his life, and his men. . . .

SHA'URI—anxious to help usher in a new era for her suffering people, has staked everything she believes on the promises of her new allies from Earth. But the growing strife between her and her husband, Daniel, may destroy a great deal more than their marriage. . . .

SKAARA—having earned his militia leadership in the war for freedom, must now hold his fragile army together although waves of violence buffet the new ship of state at every turn, and the future seems doomed. . . .

HATHOR—enraged at her failure to crush her enslaved subjects and their intrusive allies, she summons a weapon that Ra held in reserve for just such an occasion. . . .

STARGATE™

RETALIATION

BILL MCCAY

BASED ON STORY AND
CHARACTERS CREATED BY
DEAN DEVLIN & ROLAND EMMERICH

A ROC BOOK

ROC
Published by the Penguin Group
Penguin Books USA Inc., 375 Hudson Street,
New York, New York 10014, U.S.A.
Penguin Books Ltd, 27 Wrights Lane,
London W8 5TZ, England
Penguin Books Australia Ltd, Ringwood,
Victoria, Australia
Penguin Books Canada Ltd, 10 Alcorn Avenue,
Toronto, Ontario, Canada M4V 3B2
Penguin Books (N.Z.) Ltd, 182-190 Wairau Road,
Auckland 10, New Zealand

Penguin Books Ltd, Registered Offices:
Harmondsworth, Middlesex, England

First published by Roc, an imprint of Dutton Signet,
a division of Penguin Books USA Inc.

First Printing, September, 1996
10 9 8 7 6 5 4 3 2

Printed in Canada

A wise author knows his limitations . . . and knows when to ask for help. I'd like to recognize several people who were instrumental in bringing about *STARGATE: Retaliation*.

Dean Devlin, the producer and originator of *STARGATE*, was most generous with his interest and suggestions in developing this story.

Michael P. Palladino, friend and fellow writer, not only shared his own military knowledge, but helped me tap the expertise of others: Lee Russell, Major Garrie Dornan, U.S. Army, and Lieutenant Chris Lewis, U.S. Marine Corps. The accuracy of military detail in this novel is due to their efforts. Mistakes are solely the fault of the author.

And then there is my most patient editor, Amy Stout, a voice of calm and good humor in the rising hysteria of finishing a tricky novel.

Thank you all—without you, this book would have never been the same.

CHAPTER 1
ARRIVALS AND DEPARTURES

Sergeant Eugene Skinner, USMC, ran a baleful eye over his honor guard detachment. In minutes, a general would come hurtling through the StarGate to inspect the expeditionary force on the planet Abydos. The first troops he'd see on this world would be Skinner's thirteen men.

The sergeant had been inspected by a lot of different people in some very weird places. But this was the first time he'd be on parade in a man-made cavern beneath a five-hundred-feet-high pyramid on an alien planet. Skinner intended that everything go well.

His Marines were not in dress blues but in desert camouflage BDU's, mottled tans and greens on a sand-colored background. Under the sergeant's unrelenting eye, the men had made sure that every item of kit and weaponry was in the only acceptable condition—perfect.

Sergeant Skinner did not like surprises, but he tried to prepare for them. That was why his men were already in formation well before General West's scheduled arrival at 1100 hours.

"Typical," the sergeant muttered as a low, nearly subsonic tone announced the beginning of a StarGate transition well before the general's official advent. "Trying to catch us looking bad."

"This general might be the one who looks bad," a corporal replied sotto voce. "Most people don't come out too great after a ride through the puke chute."

Skinner had to admit that the Marine slang for a trip through the StarGate was right on the mark. The million-light-year transition from portal to portal was a hellish rush, combining mind-warping geometry with the bruising punishment of a trip over Niagara Falls—without a barrel.

But no matter the general's condition when he emerged, he would find a picture-perfect reception party.

A glimmer of extradimensional energy gathered at the focus of the Abydos StarGate, congealing into a shining vortex of force that spewed from the torus of carved golden crystal to the accompaniment of a low, thrumming harmonic. Then the energy interface settled in the gleaming golden ring. It looked like soapy water stretched across a fifteen-feet bubble wand, or a reflection of rippling waters.

A silhouette darkened the iridescent energy field. Sergeant Skinner leapt in front of his men and shouted, "Ten-hut!"

The honor guard snapped to attention, presenting arms. Off to his left, Skinner heard the local commander, Colonel Jack O'Neil, bitching to his aide, "Where the hell is Jackson? He's supposed to be here—"

O'Neil's words were cut off at the appearance of the new arrival. The hulking shape erupting from the lens of energy didn't look like a general. It was only quasi-human, a tall hawk mask of golden crystal rising from its shoulders. The figure charged with a spear-like weapon leveled as four more masked figures appeared from the StarGate.

Skinner trained his rifle when he realized with horror that the guard was strictly ceremonial. To avoid the embarrassment of accidentally shooting a VIP, the M-16 rifles were empty of ammunition. Frantically clawing a full magazine from a web pouch, the sergeant shouted, "Lock and load! Fire at will!"

A dazzling blast flared from the intruder's lance. It caught Skinner and two of his men before they were even in firing position.

Prior to entrusting himself to the unearthly paths of the StarGate, Khonsu had forced himself through the requisite muscular and breathing exercises. Millennia of experience had taught the Horus guards how to minimize the effects of a translation through the inhuman geometries between gates.

Khonsu knew that every second would count when they arrived on Abydos. He and his companions had to be combat ready the instant of their arrival.

When he erupted through the Abydos side of the StarGate, Khonsu was every inch the avenging Horus guard. He found the sentinels on the other side standing rigidly before him, like targets. His blast-lance took out three men in the middle of the guards' skirmish line almost before the Earthlings had adjusted to his appearance. Even as he fired, Khonsu charged the line of warriors dressed in colors of dust and dung.

The Earthlings were torn, unable to believe a single attacker was engaging them. Their weapons wavered from Khonsu to the masked warriors materializing behind him, expecting a larger attack.

Now Khonsu was through their line, covering the entrance to the chamber. Shouting in their uncouth tongue, some of the warriors turned, bringing their weapons to bear. Others, the ones apparently operating the portal, leapt for weapons stowed uselessly too far from their positions. Khonsu ignored the furor, guarding the only entrance to the chamber.

His compatriots would handle the warders. His part was to keep reinforcements from arriving.

"No inspection-ready unit has ever passed combat." That old piece of barracks wisdom kept ringing in Jack O'Neil's mind as he struggled against the onset of invading warriors. A Horus guard hurtled past him as he yanked a Beretta 9mm pistol from his holster.

O'Neil forced himself not to turn after the lead man. There were other guards in the complex of passages that led to the StarGate. Let them deal with the single man while he and the surviving guards tackled the bulk of the invaders.

So far only four other Horuses had come through. But the StarGate was cycling again. O'Neil aimed his pistol at a shape that solidified into a heavy-set, jowly middle-aged man in the uniform of a U.S. Air Force general.

The colonel managed to ease the pressure on his trigger just before popping General West. The general staggered, nearly pitching on his face from the bruising transit.

But West's ungraceful entrance saved his life. A blast-bolt flashed where his head should have been, instead incinerating the top of his peaked cap.

"General!" O'Neil yelled. Reversing his pistol, he tossed it to his superior officer. "It's ready to go," he called. "I hope you remember how to use it!"

West's usual poker face stretched in a tight grin as he caught the weapon. He was a veteran of the shadowy world of special operations. Even as O'Neil dove for a dead Marine's rifle, West calmly put three bullets into the Horus guard who'd given him such a warm welcome.

"Not as much kick as my old Army Colt," the general commented, wheeling in search of new targets.

But the alien assault team was past them, having already vanished into the next chamber after leaving two of their number stark on the floor. M-16 in hand, O'Neil considered pursuing the survivors—for about a second. Then he shook his head. The corridors beyond had lots of fighting men, and they'd come running to the sound of the guns.

Now was not the time to leave the StarGate unguarded. "Reload," O'Neil told the surviving men in the room. Then he established the Marines and Army technicians to lay down a crossfire on anything else that appeared from the StarGate. "If you've got grenades, keep 'em ready," he ordered.

West nodded, then removed his still smoldering headgear. "No brass hats here," he said. "Just soldiers."

Khonsu held his blocking position for what seemed like forever. He forced himself not to turn back—that could be a fatal distraction. What was keeping the rest of his team? They should have dispatched all of the outlanders by now!

The Horus tensed as he detected the clatter of onrushing feet—more guards hastening to the sounds of fighting. A hand landed on Khonsu's shoulder. He turned to find his comrade Neb, the leader of this foray.

Behind his mask Khonsu's face showed his shock. The strangers had killed two of their number—and too many of the gate guards still survived!

With a brusque hand motion the leader gestured—*onward*! The three survivors rushed from the hall of the StarGate into a crypt-like chamber. Here they found another obstacle. The short-range matter transmitter they had expected to whisk them ahead of pursuit had been rendered useless, totally blocked with debris. With no signs of disheartenment, the leader pressed on into the larger colonnaded hall beyond.

Shouts echoed off the stone walls as some of the soldiers spotted him. The odd *brrrrrrp!* sounds of their armament blended with crashing counter blasts from the intruders' lances.

Neb raised his aim, firing at the ungainly lights strung in the hall.

The huge space was plunged into darkness as the enemy's cries rose in volume. But for Khonsu and the other Horus guards, the light intensifiers in their helmet-masks turned the blackness into a green-tinted image.

He saw a trio of warriors groping their way between the pillars, trying to reach him. Neb aimed—but their leader seized his arm. Khonsu understood. The glare of the blast would reveal their location to the enemies wandering in the dark, seeking some target for their weapons.

Sweeping his blast-lance at the ready across his chest, Khonsu advanced on the three interlopers. He swung his energy weapon like a quarterstaff, catching the lead warrior just under the left ear. The man went down as if the weight of the world had fallen upon him. The warrior on the felled one's right must have heard the scuffle. He called out in a sharp voice as he crouched, his weapon set to sweep the now suspicious blackness.

Khonsu thrust his blast-lance in a lunge that caught the man in the pit of the stomach. The soldier folded, triggering a burst into the floor. Flying rock chips stung Khonsu's legs as his eyes reflexively clenched shut against the agony of the intensified muzzle flare. He lashed out into the featureless red glare dancing before his eyes and felt his blast-lance strike something yielding.

"Forward!" The order came through his mask's communicator. Running strictly by rote, Khonsu threaded the route to the pyramid's entrance while still blinded. His sight returned barely in time to warn him of the single guard left at the adit.

A mistake, he thought. They seek to chase the mouse when their best move would be to seal off the mousehole.

The lone guard called into the darkness. Neb fired a blast-bolt straight into the warrior's chest. The man's torso exploded as his body fluids vaporized, and the hall filled with the smell of roasted meat.

Yells rose from behind as the air filled with the roar of the Earthlings' projectile guns. The three invaders darted out of the darkness and into the dim glow of a starship's emergency lighting.

Khonsu's briefing for this mission had covered several contingencies. One of these had been a foray into the disabled cruiser that had docked on the Abydos StarGate pyramid.

The war vessel *Ra's Eye* had come to Abydos in search of Ra, the ageless god-ruler of a vast interstellar empire. Instead it had found Ra's vessel destroyed the Abydos peasants in rebellion with the help of interlopers from Earth—the only world that, thousands of years before, had successfully thrown off Ra's domination.

Khonsu had been remorselessly drilled in the ship's deck layout. He was surprised to find improvised barricades set at the entrance to the StarGate pyramid and along the wide corridor that led to the main airlock. But Khonsu was even more shocked to find these barriers guarded by armed fellahin of Abydos.

Again, he'd been briefed on the warrior group the rebel fellahin had created, but it had sounded like fantasy. Slaves with weapons? Inconceivable!

Now he faced them. But the fellahin would-be warriors were even more disorganized than the Earthlings. At the first sight of their ancient overseers, the ex-slaves stood like night creatures caught in a bright light.

Khonsu's leader didn't give them a chance to recover. A slim hand shot out to an inconspicuous set of studs set into the crystalline wall. Fingers stabbed in the right combination, and the seemingly solid quartz surface reconstituted itself, forming an opening—an access hatch for maintenance technicians.

The leader vanished inside, followed by Neb. Khonsu waited until the first of the fellahin reached him. Seizing the luckless Abydan, he dragged him inside the service conduit. He'd broken the weakling's neck before the biomorphic quartz redeployed to its wall form. Stripping off the dead man's homespun cloak, Khonsu clambered up the stanchions to the next deck. He could hear the thudding of furious fists on the panel below.

No one saw them emerge through a hatch on the level above. Khonsu shrank his falcon mask back to its necklace configuration, slipped on the captured robe, and adjusted its hood to shade his features. He took the lead as the intruders headed for the nearest stairway.

A pair of guards were clattering upward as he arrived at the landing.

"Hawk-heads!" one cried in his Abydan peasant accent, thinking he spoke to a comrade. "They've broken into the ship. Keep an eye—"

That was as far as he got before Khonsu was upon them. He dropped his blast-lance. This was close work, best done by hand. Khonsu had no illusions as to why he'd been taken on this mission. He was Khonsu the killer, trained in the arts of silent death.

One fellah was down, his throat crushed. The other dodged Khonsu's blow, turning to flee. Khonsu caught him by the scruff of his cloak and hauled him back. The man was in midair as the killer seized him by the leg. The figure twisted convulsively as Khonsu brought him down across his left knee. The spine cracked, and Khonsu broke the neck for good measure as the body dropped. Quickly he stripped the dead Abydans and passed their robes to his companions.

Then came a stiff climb toward the zenith of the pyramid ship—to Launch Deck Four. Once this had been a hangar for part of the udajeet contingent carried by the battlecraft. But one of the antigravity gliders, crippled in the fighting with the Earthlings and their Abydan allies, had crashed into the open docking space, creating chaos inside—and jamming the deck's huge hangar doors in the open position.

While Neb and Khonsu kept watch, their leader produced a metal spool wound with an almost filament-thin thread. The Horus guard found a flame-blackened but still sound conduit near the open doors. The first few inches of thread unwound from the spool turned out to be a preformed loop. A gentle shake teased the loop open. Then the spool went through the loop to create a simple hitch around the heavy pipe. Khonsu and Neb each did the same, finding a suitable belay. They backed toward the open bay doors, paying out the monofilament cable until they stood right on the brink.

The invaders clapped handle-like devices to their spools of cable, then leapt backward. Khonsu felt his spool unreeling with an angry whir. His feet hit the sloping golden surface of the pyramid ship, and he tightened the brakes on his hand grip. The filament quivered under his weight but held. Khonsu knew better than to touch the thread that bore his weight. Under this tension the thin line would probably slice through fingers and bone like a razor.

He caught a glimpse in his peripheral vision of Neb kicking aloft. Releasing the spool's brakes, Khonsu leapt off, too. Again—and again.

In a quick series of huge rappelling bounds, infiltration team reached the base of the stranded spacecraft seconds before warriors came boiling out of the ship's square-arched entrance. Khonsu tossed away the now useless spool and twitched up the hood on his drab cloak. He wanted to make sure it covered his warrior's sidelock and the blue tattoo round his right eye. Others of the fellahin carried blast-lances. He and the other Horus guards blended into the milling crowd. The first step of their mission had been accomplished.

Now, on to the city of Nagada.

CHAPTER 2
STRATEGIES AND TACTICS

Colonel Jack O'Neil listened as the bedlam outside the hall of the StarGate began to die down. More guards arrived to bolster the defenses for the interstellar portal, until at last O'Neil felt free to leave with his aide, Lieutenant Charlton, and a shadow—General West. Armed with rifles and flashlights, the officers traced the path of the intruders until they reached the adit now blocked by the hulk of the starship *Ra's Eye*.

The entrance was blocked not just by the usual barricade, but by arguing troops, both American and Abydan. There was more here than just the transition from tunnel to spaceship. It represented a demarcation line. Within the pyramid the expedition from Earth held sway. But the derelict vessel had been taken by an ad hoc force composed mainly of Abydan militiamen. The Abydans had claimed *Ra's Eye* by right of conquest—and had pressed their claim by occupying the ship.

This corridor leading to the outside world had been garrisoned by armed militiamen and barricaded at each end—from possible attack from the StarGate, and from the Earther base camp that occupied the rocky plateau which supported the StarGate pyramid. The militia garrison stood as a tangible symbol of the tension between the Elders of Abydos and the U.S. government as represented by General W. O. West.

Right now that tension seemed to have reached nearly flashpoint dimensions. The sides could be easily told. O'Neil's men in desert BDU's confronted militiamen in brownish homespun robes. The primitive clothing clashed with the modern assault rifles in the militia members' hands, but that contrast was the same from the Montagnards of Vietnam to the mujahadeen of Afghanistan.

In this case, however, the weapons in some of the Abydans' hands made the modern assault rifles look primitive. The golden shafts of gleaming quartz looked like blunt spears. But O'Neil had seen demonstrations where those blast-lances blew holes through armor plate. He'd helped capture a few, which he'd sent via the StarGate back to Earth. The Abydans had many, many more, plundered from the inoperable spacecraft.

And now they were using the blast-lances to guard that vessel.

As O'Neil pushed to the front of his Marines, the young man in charge of the Abydans began to berate him.

"You let hawk-heads through to attack us," the

young officer accused. "Grabbed one of my men. Probably killed him."

"Where did they go?" O'Neil demanded.

He got a shrug for an answer. "They disappear into wall. I send out men to look—"

"You don't have enough men to search this whole ship," the colonel said flatly. The tip of the pyramidal bulk that made up the spacecraft *Ra's Eye* rose more than seven hundred feet into the air. Along its base, each of the four sides measured almost twelve hundred feet. Lieutenant Charlton had once calculated that the deck space aboard the vessel probably equaled half that of one of the World Trade towers.

"You not bring your people inside here!" The young Abydan's grasp of English slipped under stress.

O'Neil simply climbed the barricade, setting off down the corridor. He was quickly joined by Charlton and West.

"I will send to Skaara!" the furious young man yelled.

It was the only threat he could use. He knew his position couldn't hold against a determined assault from O'Neil's troops.

Jack O'Neil knew the militia leader when Skaara had been a simple shepherd. The colonel had befriended the young man when the original reconnaissance team had arrived on Abydos. Skaara had responded by organizing his friends into a group of boy commandos to rescue O'Neil and the other team members when they'd become the prisoners of Ra.

From that original resistance cell, Skaara's militia had grown to company size and beyond, attaining almost Frankensteinian proportions during and after the attack by the crew of *Ra's Eye*.

But the two commanders, Earther and Abydan, knew each other. O'Neil could imagine Skaara's reaction. "Call to Skaara on your radio," the colonel said coolly. "I bet he'll tell you to help us search."

O'Neil emerged to find a half-panicked mob of militiamen milling around in the midst of his camp and shook his head. He could only hope that the infiltrators were still aboard and not hidden in that churning mob.

Three intruders did not a major invasion make. But the very smallness of the force set off alarms in O'Neil's head. His background was covert work. And this fire drill had all the hallmarks of infiltrators being inserted. Maybe Hathor or whoever was heading up the opposition was looking for some intelligence—this threesome could be the Horus guard equivalent of recon Marines.

Or they could be up to some sort of deadly mischief. It seemed unlikely that three operatives—even high-tech ops—could jump-start the wrecked starcraft. If fixing the good ship *Ra's Eye* had been that easy, Hathor's crew could have done it themselves.

On the other hand, there were lots of sensitive systems left behind in the hulk—technological secrets that Ra's successors might prefer to deny Earth scientists. Selective sabotage or wholesale destruction—either strategy might be a possibility.

"Charlton, we're going to need additional security details. I want a perimeter established around the ship. No one to get in or out—"

O'Neil flicked a quick glance to West, but the general said nothing, leaving everything in O'Neil's hands—and if necessary, on his head.

"And let's get our own message to Skaara. We'll have to search that sucker deck by deck, and I'd rather do that with his approval—and presence, if possible."

Skaara put in an appearance well after the ship had been surrounded and sealed off. Several militia officers were still arguing about O'Neil's trespass aboard "their" ship when he arrived.

"I'm sorry, Colonel," the handsome young man apologized. "There's some trouble brewing in the city that needed my attention."

When he got the full story on the Horus guard incursion, he blistered his own people and opened the ship right up.

"The devils disappeared into the wall right here," a militiaman explained, pointing at an apparently blank wall of golden crystal.

"This stuff changes shape," O'Neil said to Skaara. "Remember when we were fighting our way to the command deck? Jackson found someone working on circuitry through a panel that had opened in the wall. Maybe there's the same sort of thing here."

Charlton didn't look happy. "That could mean the whole ship is honeycombed with secret passages. A lot of people will lose most of their night's sleep poking around in here, sir."

"We'll stick to the regular corridors first. But keep a strong guard on the exits. That includes lights and snipers on that open hangar deck near the top of this thing."

The first sweep had barely begun when the searchers found two dead, stripped Abydans in a stairwell.

"That makes sense," O'Neil said grimly. "It lets them blend in with the enemy—hide those tattoos around their eyes—"

"The eye of Ra, sir," Charlton hurriedly added, with a glance toward West. "Just like the name of the ship."

"And it means that everybody wearing a brown cloak aboard this tub may not be friendly." O'Neil turned to his aide. "Make sure nobody boards or leaves the ship with his hood up."

The searchers at last reached the ruined hangar deck, but the first sweep missed the monofilament lines. Charlton broke into frustrated swearing when he got the report. "We've been doing this all for nothing! The bastards were gone before we even arrived!"

"We can't be sure of that," O'Neil warned. "Though I can't imagine these guys hanging around to wait for our search parties. We'll continue the sweeps, on the odd chance. At least we'll be sure that they didn't leave any boobytraps behind."

"In the part of the ship we were able to reach," Charlton added sotto voce as he turned to pass on the appropriate orders.

Skaara came up from the checkpoints he'd arranged to keep the intruders from sneaking through the lines. "So, our efforts were too late," he said.

"And our descriptions don't give the best likeness," Charlton said. "Three men in brown homespun cloaks, with their hoods probably up. Doubtless they were still carrying their blast-lances."

"But there are more than enough of my own people who would meet that description," Skaara said.

"And you know where they were probably headed," O'Neil added.

"Nagada." Skaara's voice was tight. "They would have no trouble disappearing among all those in the city." He shook his head, his expression saying *I really need this*. "It's not enough to have people fighting in the marketplaces over food, and the disputes with Nakeer and his farmer folk. Now we must worry about spies."

He shook his head. "My people are halfway trained to fight, to mount guard. We know nothing of man hunting."

"You could at least check for strangers," O'Neil said.

Skaara gave a short, barking laugh. "You have not been able to look around inside our walls for a while, Colonel—other than trips to visit my father. Nagada is bursting at the seams. The streets are full of wandering beggars, people whose homes were destroyed in the fighting, farmers come to see the city. There are too many strangers passing among us. Three more won't stand out."

"You can narrow the description down a bit," O'Neil said. "Three males traveling together, all of military age, all with good builds—if I know my Horus guards."

"And probably with arrogance to match," Skaara agreed with a mirthless smile. "I'm afraid that's the only way they'll betray themselves."

O'Neil turned to Lieutenant Charlton. "Perhaps if we can lend some people with counterinsurgency or intelligence backgrounds," he said, waiting for West to speak up and kill the deal. "See who might be available. We'll try to give you some help, Skaara. But we'll have to improve our own security as well."

"If only that were the only help I needed!" Skaara burst out. He glanced at the strange officer and shut up. But when West began conferring with Charlton, the young man plunged on. "I wouldn't trouble you with this, Colonel. But I need advice, and the ones I might have turned to for their wisdom are gone."

O'Neil nodded. Skaara was referring to the alumni of the first Abydos expedition, Kawalsky and Feretti. The colonel himself often found himself wishing they were still around, instead of getting mysteriously transferred back to Earth. For one thing, they had good relations with the local militia. Hell, they'd helped Skaara train his initial force.

But their help had been unofficial—and it predated

the strained relations that now stood between Earthlings and Abydans.

O'Neil had expected the problems Skaara outlined in controlling a loose-knit militia force that kept growing. But he frowned when he heard Skaara mention a dangerous word for any military man—"politics."

"There's little enough I can suggest to help you, without getting Kasuf after you and West after me," the colonel said. "You might work at developing some esprit de corps among your people—a sense of shared purpose. Maybe Daniel Jackson could help you with that."

Which reminded O'Neil—where the hell was the sole Earth civilian on Abydos?

"The only purpose our people seem to share anymore is finding their next meal," Skaara said in disgust. "The other thing they're hungry for is guns. There are still poor ones going out to sift the sands where your people fought the Horus guards. They hope to find some sort of weapon to trade for food."

"I know," O'Neil said. "We've had patrols out, trying to discourage them."

"They're just sad," Skaara said. "We've had jackals breaking into our storehouses for weapons—"

"You have arsenals?" O'Neil said in surprise.

"Lieutenant Kawalsky explained about keeping our weapons safe and combat ready," Skaara said.

"Better to keep them off the streets and out of the wrong hands," the colonel agreed. "But you also have to protect the weapons. My advice is to post a twenty-four-hour guard—and use the most dependable soldiers you have."

Skaara sighed. "If I use those men to guard our guns, who will be left to guard the streets?"

It was nearly noon as Daniel Jackson strolled the company streets of the terrestrial base camp. He was intentionally late for General West's arrival. Daniel didn't like the man, having had run-ins with him before. And although he wanted to talk to the general, he wasn't about to stand hanging around through a military inspection. A dedicated civilian, Daniel had no interest in "playing soldier," as he put it.

Daniel had walked from the city of Nagada, a dusty trip across the desert. The hood on his robe of native homespun was up to protect his fair skin from the double suns of Abydos. He'd just finished the cool drink he'd cadged in the mess tent, glanced at his watch, and figured it was time to put in an appearance.

Although Daniel noticed a little more activity than usual in the streets, no one had told him the cause. So when he reached the open square around the pyramid and the downed spaceship that covered it, he started past the Marine guards with a casual wave.

"Halt!" The order came in both English and somewhat mangled Abydan.

I don't have time for whatever soldier boy happy horseshit they're up to, Daniel thought, taking another step.

The harsh *snick!* of bullets being chambered warned

Daniel of his error. He stopped, glancing around to find at least four rifles being aimed at him.

"What the hell is going on?" he demanded.

"We got a special on body bags," a hard-faced Marine noncom responded. "One to every customer who breaches that perimeter. Free."

"Yeah, they're dying to get 'em," another Marine added.

"Look, I'm in a hurry." Daniel quickly moved his hands, nearly got shot, and throttled back to slow motion as he slid down his hood to reveal his face and Earthman's blond hair. "I'm supposed to be meeting General West," he said, not mentioning his tardiness.

"Oh, it's *him*," one of his Marine captors muttered in disgust.

The noncom's face didn't change. "Send for the Eltee," he ordered, and one of his men set off.

At least, Daniel noticed, they weren't pointing their rifles at him anymore.

Jack O'Neil's aide, a young lieutenant named Charlton, came to collect Daniel. As they moved off toward the pyramid, the offended guest demanded, "So what the hell is going on here?"

"Didn't anyone tell you?" Charlton stared in disbelief. "We had a raid through the StarGate just as we were expecting General West. A bunch of Horus guards came through. They nearly nailed the general, and did kill several Marines and Abydan militiamen. They could be still around the camp, wearing captured local desert gear." He fingered the sleeve of Daniel's robe. "Any locals with their hoods up are immediately suspect."

Daniel, who'd just been about to raise his hood again, stopped. "Oh," he said.

"It's been a hell of a mess," Charlton went on. "Searching for these guys has completely screwed up our schedule. We're only about to start the inspection now."

"Damn!" Daniel exclaimed. Whether it was for the incursion, the deaths, or being trapped in the inspection after all, even he couldn't say.

As the search for the infiltrators went on at lower gear, General West emerged again from the downed starcraft to see just what the Earthmen had been doing on the planet Abydos. The terrestrial base camp had been established on a rocky outcrop some miles from the city of Nagada and its quartzite mines, with hexagonal earthworks surrounding the pyramid that housed the Abydos StarGate. To West, the locale looked like the butt end of beyond, a godforsaken plateau surrounded by reddish-yellow sand dunes.

West's spirits weren't lifted when he saw Lieutenant Charlton approaching with the lone Earthling in residence on Abydos, Daniel Jackson. The Egyptologist's wayward genius might have deciphered the cryptic inscriptions that allowed West's research team to unlock the ten-thousand-year-old artifact Jackson had named the StarGate. But ever since he'd wangled a place on the reconnaissance through the portal, Jackson had become a loose cannon.

He'd gone native, marrying Sha'uri, daughter of a local chieftain. The two of them, with the aid of Sha'uri's brother Skaara, had played important parts in destroying the half-human, half-alien god-king Ra. But then they'd nearly wrecked West's attempts to mine the strange golden quartz found on Abydos—the mineral that fueled all of Ra's enigmatic technology.

"General." The civilian slouched up, apparently dressed in a bathrobe, to shake West's hand. After O'Neil's military courtesies, the contrast couldn't have been greater.

West suffered the familiarity. "Sorry you were delayed, Doctor. But you're right in time for the start of our inspection."

Jackson's eyes glazed in palpable boredom.

West was very interested to see how the expeditionary force had handled the latest attack from the former overlords of Abydos. The past week had been spent repairing the damage of invasion from the alien starship. Tents had been replaced to house a much smaller force. New strongpoints had been created, minefields laid. But there were still slagged areas where energy weapons had melted solid rock. Wreckage from crashed udajeets, the enemy's antigravity fliers, was still being examined and removed. And, of course, the hulk of the immobilized starcraft loomed over the whole base like an unspoken threat.

When the vessel had landed, it had enlarged the area of the Abydos pyramid by acres—and obliterated a quarter of the former base camp. West tried not to think of the tents, equipment—and men—who had disappeared under the craft's bulk.

The general's concern for the expeditionary force, heightened by the sneak attack that had almost killed him, abated somewhat as he conducted his inspection. Morale among the mixed-service garrison was high—not surprising, under O'Neil's command.

West found the camp defenses tight, the equipment spotless. Techs were even working to repair some of the vehicles destroyed when Hathor's ship had confronted advancing troops.

"Commendable," he told O'Neil. "You're doing very well, Colonel."

"With what I've got," O'Neil finished for him. "I know why you don't want to send replacements. But did you have to take away the best of my old Abydos hands? I could really use Feretti and Kawalsky—that's not a slight on Charlton here." The young lieutenant stood straighter. "It's just that members of the original team have better connection with the locals. With them transferred back to Earth, we've had to depend more on Dr. Jackson."

"That's a valid security concern," West replied. "But believe me, those men are doing more good where they are right now. If I can't give you men, I will send more equipment. After this morning I see more of the dangers you're dealing with."

If he'd followed his own wishes, West would have recalled the troops from Abydos and buried the StarGate, closing a dangerous doorway of opportunity for an attack on Earth. But he couldn't do that without depriving his country—and his world—of the technological benefits of Abydos quartz. So he allowed the danger, both military and personal.

The general had earned his reputation—and his stars—by being an expediter, by making things happen. That was not a way to make friends. The fact was, there were lots of people hiding in the bushes with baseball bats, waiting for a crack at West.

And this debacle on Abydos might just have given West's enemies their opportunity. Brigade-sized assets blasted down to a heavy battalion—and for what? A "space program" with only one known destination, vulnerable to counterattack from at least one other planet—probably others.

West had to admit that he'd severely miscalculated the situation on Abydos. To develop the mines at Nagada, worked by Abydan muscle power, he'd brought in a company with experience both in the Third World and in intelligence circles. But the United Mining Cartel had made a mess of things. They'd nearly pushed the Abydans to rebellion—under the unlikely leadership of Daniel Jackson.

The general had even been pushed to replace Jack O'Neil as commander on Abydos—UMC had complained that O'Neil was too partial to the natives. But O'Neil's replacement, General Francis Keogh, had been about to start a shooting war when the spaceship *Ra's Eye* had appeared—commanded by yet another ancient Egyptian deity.

Between his overeagerness to get the wonder crystal and his underestimation of the enemy, West had opened the door for disastrous losses on Abydos. Hawk-masked Horus guards had ventured through the StarGate to attack Earth itself.

Luckily, the alien incursion had been contained within the former missile silo where Earth's StarGate was now located. More troubling was the problem of explaining away the losses in the Abydos fiasco—how hundreds of soldiers could die in the midst of peacetime.

But the fighting had left a new treasure on Abydos—a damaged spacecraft whose weaponry could destroy tanks the way a human swatted flies. If West could bring home a starship, even a damaged one, it might make up for his earlier miscalculations.

"Have you made any progress deciphering information aboard the wrecked craft?" the general asked.

"We've got something about the size of a large office building," Jackson replied. "And judging from the inscriptions, about half the doors are marked 'Danger—Do not enter."

The young lieutenant serving as O'Neil's aide spoke up a bit more diplomatically. "Sir, Ra's empire seems to be a paperless culture. But we found several crystal slabs about four by five inches and a quarter of an inch thick, covered with hieroglyphics."

"They were hard to miss, glowing in the dark," Jackson added.

"They seem to be miniature computers," Charlton went on. "Dr. Jackson and the Abydans have begun translating."

"To begin with, we've gotten into some records about who was aboard," Jackson explained. "You know about the Horus guards? They represented several . . . factions is the word, I guess." He shrugged. "The leaders are all names out of Egyptian mythology. Sebek—the crocodile-headed god. Apis, the bull god. Ram-headed Khnum."

"And the commander, who I understand spoke to you?"

"The cat-headed goddess of good sex and deadly vengeance," Jackson said. "Hathor."

"A rather odd combination," West commented.

"Half of the stories about Hathor make her terribly fierce," Jackson replied. "There's a legend that Ra asked her to deal with some rebellious mortals, and she almost exterminated the human race. That seems to be rooted in fact—according to the secret archives in Nagada, Hathor was dispatched to put down a rebellion on a colony called Ombos, and covered that world in blood."

"Charming," West said.

"On the other hand, you have tales like her involvement in the great court case between hawk-headed Horus and his uncle Set."

"And what kind of head did Set have?" West said skeptically.

"Nobody's been able to identify it from the pictures," Jackson said. "Some scholars have identified it a gazelle's head. Others think it's the pig—unclean flesh, and all that."

"That's a pretty wide range there," Jack O'Neil said.

Jackson shrugged. "That's why a lot of people in the field just call it the typhonic beast. We don't know what it is. Set is also covered all over in red hair—that's an evil sign. As Egyptian culture went through the millennia, Set went from a brave warrior god defending Ra to the personification of evil, fighting Ra."

He waved a hand. "Anyway, Set killed Horus' father and stole the crown of Egypt. Ra was supposed to judge the case, but got offended by one of the other gods and refused to go on. Hathor got Ra in a good mood and the trial back on track by, well, flashing him."

West shook his head. "*This* is what you spend your time translating?"

"Actually, I spend my time trying to bring literacy back to this world—Ra tried to destroy all scribes and history. And I teach the younger people English, so they can deal with you and your people. They need all the help they can get. Things are tough here on Abydos—"

"We'll come to that," West said decisively, cutting Jackson off. "It's your call, O'Neil. How best can you protect our people from a pagan nympho-killer and those boy scouts with blast-lances?"

"Maybe you should remember, General. Those boy scouts have pulled our asses—and your chestnuts—out of the fire several times now." Jackson glared.

O'Neil spoke up, eager to furnish his wish list. "If you can't give me men, I'll take vehicles. We need to expand the perimeter here. I want long-range patrols. For all his annoying editorial opinions, Dr. Jackson has pointed out how little we still know about this world."

The general nodded.

"I could use more Humvees," O'Neil went on. "And a couple of helicopters." He glanced at West, matching his poker face. "General Keogh's chopper contingent was completely destroyed. We already have foot patrols in the nearer desert. If we extend long-range patrols out there, I'd like to have the ability to back them up."

"Is there some reason for patrolling so vigorously?"

O'Neil pointed westward. "As the general knows, we established a sizable cemetery out that way." Even his voice became expressionless. "Certain of the locals have disturbed the remains."

West stopped and whirled on his junior officer. "Cannibalism?"

"No, sir," Lt. Charlton spoke up. "Grave robbing. They thought we buried personal effects with our dead."

The general's frown deepened. Such practices

suggested that many in Nagada must be in dire straits. He decided on a change of plan.

"Dr. Jackson, do you think it would be possible to speak with the Council of Elders?" he asked abruptly. "I'd like to put an offer to them personally."

"Are you kidding?" Jackson said. "They'd love to have a chance to go face-to-face with you."

A radioed warning from Skaara ensured that the Humvee caravan from the base camp got Nagada's version of the red-carpet treatment. The Elders of the city stood lined up to greet the general in the huge gateway. Kasuf stood in the lead, eyes sharp as knives in his impassive, gray-bearded face.

General West and the rest of his delegation of Earthmen were marched through town to the hall of the Elders. There they sat down to a feast, cutting slices off some fricasseed beast that would haunt the general's nightmares for weeks to come.

Finally they got down to business.

"I have two concerns," West began. "One is the declining quantity of quartz ore now coming through the StarGate. The other is the need to get qualified technical people aboard that disabled starship. Please ask Kasuf how we can improve the first and accomplish the second."

From all reports, this Kasuf—Jackson's father-in-law—had distinguished himself as a tough negotiator. *Fine,* West thought. *Let the bargaining begin.*

Jackson passed along West's words, and Kasuf

responded in Abydan. But it was obvious as he went on that he was showing more and more irritation. As Kasuf finished, he produced a handful of silver coins and threw them on the floor.

West blinked for a moment when he recognized the coins as Susan B. Anthony dollars. Then he remembered that the UMC had been using the coins to pay the Nagadan miners.

"What did he say?" the general demanded of Daniel Jackson.

"He said that the decline in the tonnage of quartz going through the StarGate is because there are a lot of people leaving the city of Nagada. And, ironically enough, that's due to the flood of Susan B. Anthony dollars you've sent here."

The muscles in West's poker face set so hard, they hurt. "Explain," he said.

"In a couple of months you've taken Abydos from a slave, barter economy to a coinage-based free market. Speculation has raised its head—and the biggest market is in food. People are buying up grain, hoarding it—driving up the price. So the city folk are leaving the city for the farming enclaves where the food is."

"But these people here are the government of the planet! Can't they regulate the labor force—"

"That has an unpleasant ring for people who are just up from slavery," Jackson replied. After a brief discussion with Kasuf, he returned to the general. "Things aren't as monolithic as they seem," he said. "There are two tribes on Abydos—the miners and the farmers. Each has its own Council of Elders, and the farmers have their own chief—a guy named Nakeer."

"Nakeer." Kasuf nodded and repeated the name, then added more in Abydan.

"Since times are tough in Nagada, a lot of miners are deciding to become farmers," Jackson translated. "They blame the economic dislocations on the intervention from Earth."

"But we helped them win freedom, we've given them the benefits of modern medicine—" West said in annoyance.

"Which translates as freedom to starve, while our modern medicine just serves to baffle them. Stick a needle in your arm and you won't get sick? I'm afraid there haven't been any miraculous cures. That only happens in the movies. The Abydan in the streets doesn't see us as wonder workers anymore."

"Wait till they see what we've been doing with that quartz back in the labs," West muttered. He stiffened, glancing from the military officer with him to Jackson. "Forget I said that."

The general frowned. "We need to get researchers aboard that ship," he said. "Since our money isn't any good to the people here, what can we offer?"

Jackson transmitted the question. Then it was Kasuf's turn to frown. He began to talk rapidly, forcefully, leaning forward from the pile of cushions where he half reclined.

Whatever he's saying, it's very important to him, West thought. *I hope this won't turn out to be the deal breaker.*

"As you heard, Kasuf wants a lot of things for his people. But they really break down into two things. Health care and education. Kasuf wants his people healthy, especially the children. And since he sees ever more machines coming through the StarGate, he wants his young people trained for the future. That means knowing how to use our technology, how to fix it, and further down the road, how to make it."

"I'm willing to guarantee that," West said promptly.

Jackson translated, and Kasuf and his colleagues exchanged dubious looks.

Are they annoyed because they set too low a price? West wondered. *Or is this just suspicion that I gave in too easily? Maybe I should have haggled a bit more.*

One of the other Elders spoke up. He didn't sound friendly. "Old Tatjenen here thanks you for your quick agreement. But he says words are cheap. For some reason, the Abydans don't trust you. In fact, the Elders of Nagada have a hard time accepting the word of anyone from Earth." Daniel Jackson's voice was cutting.

"*You're* from Earth," West pointed out.

"And they know I've been straight with them," Jackson shot back. "So has the colonel here."

"You filled the locals' heads with doubts about UMC," West continued.

"Only after they started screwing over the people here," Jackson replied. "And I'd say those UMC guys justified everybody's doubts after they maneuvered you and Keogh into almost starting a war for them." He glanced at West. "So you'll have to excuse Kasuf and the others for being a little dubious about your proposals."

"All right, here's something a little more concrete," West said, nettled. "Since we took over the mining operation, we've been providing health care for the workers. And I know Colonel O'Neil has been sending his medical personnel into the city. I'll expand that by offering a complete immunization project for the city's children—"

Jackson cut him off with a quick interchange in Abydan between himself and the Elders. The old men were looking at West like a collection of hungry eagles.

"That's much better than the promises UMC made—and never kept," Jackson said. "But I think you'll have to sweeten the pot considerably more."

West took a deep breath. "All right. Besides classes in machine operation, I'm willing to give Kasuf and his people all the equipment presently invested in the mine—when they're qualified to operate it. That's a bit more than the steel picks and shovels our engineers provided to replace those copper mattocks they were using."

Jackson passed on the offer, to voluble discussion among the Elders. West noticed that Jackson was participating, even arguing. In the end, the translator shrugged. "A week after you start the inoculations, they'll allow a small group in—perhaps a dozen people or so. We'll also provide help with translating, which you'll have to pay for."

After some haggling, they at least reached a reasonable ballpark figure. It was exorbitant compared to the wages for a miner, but West was willing to pay.

"Incidentally," Jackson said, "only part of that figure goes to a stipend for the actual translators. The rest is going to expand our English classes."

"Money well spent," West said.

"Your people will be there on sufferance," Jackson warned. "They're still debating the rest of your deal. This is just a show of good faith on their part."

The general nodded. "Understood." He glanced at his watch. "If you would please thank them for their attention, I'll stop taking up their time."

West stood for a formal farewell, with fulsome hopes that this time harmony would prevail.

As West left, he was a little surprised when Jackson accompanied him to the Humvee convoy for the ride back to the base camp. "General, I don't mean to knock your proposition, but what you're offering is just a Band-Aid for the problems here."

"It's all I can give," West replied. "Even with secret appropriations, I don't have bottomless pockets. We've got a Congress that wants to cut all spending."

To give the Egyptologist some credit, he argued eloquently for his adopted people all the way to the StarGate.

"Understand, Jackson, I don't want to cause

dislocations in the society here," West finally said. "I want things stable, so we'll receive dependable shipments of the golden quartz. From our side, we'll give all the tools and training the people of Abydos can absorb. But if that causes troubles, your Abydan friends will have to find their own answers."

He turned to the technician in charge of the alien installation. "Warm up your magic donut there, Corporal. I've got to be back in Washington by this evening."

CHAPTER 3
DOMESTIC DISTURBANCES

The sun was setting by the time Daniel Jackson got back from the base camp. Though the twisting streets of Nagada were in shadow, a stifling heat seemed to radiate from the adobe brick walls of the buildings around him.

A wasted day, Daniel though moodily. The problem was, most of his days seemed wasted—spent in meetings with the Elders, or translating for the Earthling *du jour.* His hieroglyphics literacy courses had gone to Sha'uri and some of his brighter students. All he had time for was the advanced English class. On rare occasions he managed to snatch a few minutes for pure research.

Abydan culture was a treasure trove for an Egyptologist, ancient ways of life and thought perfectly preserved like an insect in amber. Even more fascinating, if somewhat gruesome, were the ways of Ra's empire. From the hidden histories and folk tales came tales of striking personalities—people who had been worshipped as gods. Some of the tales were nightmares, recollecting Ra's cruelties or Hathor's massacre. Some were garbled tales of great constructions raised, of battles between gods.

Daniel found them all fascinating—when he could wedge a little space into his schedule. Unfortunately, his schedule generally seemed devoted to meetings to change the very culture he wanted to study.

Like today, when I played glorified tour guide to General Close-to-the-vest West. Oh, he'd been there as Kasuf's representative, to speak his piece for Nagada and Abydos. West had upped the ante a little, but not too much. Daniel feared there wouldn't be enough to cushion the painful transition Abydos would have to make. The day had been a double waste—he'd been taken from things he could have done well to be virtually ineffective, telling West things he didn't want to hear.

Daniel was abruptly reminded of his student days, when the department head would shepherd well-heeled types through museum workshops to generate the wherewithal for another dig. That's what he'd been doing today—playing *administrator*, the one job he'd always hated.

He rounded a bend in the road and stopped short. Squatting against a wall, head lolling, was a man with a chipped pottery bowl in front of him. His eyes were closed, and insects crawled on his face.

Some sixth sense warned the man of Daniel's presence. "Please, lord, spare a coin . . ."

Daniel hurried on. There never used to be beggars in Nagada. Families took care of their own. Or, he reflected with a chill, Horus guards disposed of indigents.

Everywhere he looked, the old, pre-revolutionary society seemed to be breaking down. The malaise showed in the repairs made after the udajeet strafing attacks. The new buildings and patched walls were done in a slapdash manner. Why craft and carry bricks with pride after seeing the Earthlings' machines move tons of dirt and sand?

Daniel felt a stab of relief as he finally reached his home. Within the mud-brick walls the rooms were cool—and dark.

"Sha'uri?" Daniel called, although it was obvious his wife wasn't home.

He fumbled around, finding an oil lamp and lighting it from a banked fire. Well, this was just perfect. Here he was, home after a hard day of pissing the time away, and the lady of the house was nowhere to be found.

Daniel ventured into the kitchen area and poked around in the larder. Frankly, it looked pretty bare. And he wasn't quite sure what to do with the stuff on hand.

The problem was, Daniel hadn't gotten the hang of Abydan cuisine. Back on Earth, his notions of home cooking had revolved around Spaghetti-O's and microwave meals.

He was flopped on a pile of pillows, trying to read by the flickering flame on the lamp when a tired-looking Sha'uri finally came in.

"There's nothing to eat—at least, nothing I could make," he said, rising to his feet. "So, what's up? You're kind of late."

"Father and the Council came to a decision about the offer from the general," Sha'uri announced. "Unless you were able to get better terms."

"He doesn't care what happens here as long as he gets his gold quartz," Daniel said bitterly. He glanced at his wife. "I'm surprised the Council took so long to decide on the deal."

"Oh, the agreement came quickly enough," Sha'uri said. "They were asking me which people we could spare from our literacy classes to work with the scientists from Earth. The job requires people who can both read hieroglyphics and speak English. And, of course, we don't want to strip your English class—"

"Wait a minute!" Daniel interrupted as her words finally penetrated. "I'm in charge of those classes. Don't you think I should have been consulted?"

"We wanted to begin—what is the phrase? start the ball rolling?—as soon as possible," Sha'uri said.

Daniel knew she was nervous. She didn't usually stumble over idioms like that.

"Father arranged a good rate of pay for the translators, as you may remember," Sha'uri went on. "The Council thought the quicker we were ready, the better."

"That's the sooner the better," Daniel said. "I still want to look over the roster."

"Do that," Sha'uri replied in annoyance. "You complain about overseeing the tasks of others till you have no time to work yourself. But when someone tries to relieve you of that labor, you insist on playing the overseer anyway. You can't—" She snapped her fingers. "What is the word?"

"Delegate," Daniel interjected. Then he wished he hadn't opened his mouth.

"Always correcting!" Sha'uri flared. "Always you act like an overseer!"

Coming from a person just recently up from slavery, her choice of words was deliberately provocative. Daniel had seen the overseers at work in the mines of Nagada. Ra's brutal Horus guards had carried a blast-lance in one hand and a leather lash in the other.

He held up a hand. "Just because I want to make sure things are done right—"

"You don't think I could sort through for the best translators?" Sha'uri demanded. "Must I be your student forever?"

Daniel sighed. More and more of late, their evenings had been marred by arguments. Usually they were over trivial things, but it meant going to bed angry with each other.

It seemed that the honeymoon was definitely over.

"Sha'uri, I'm tired. I spent the day doing a job I'm not good at, and perhaps missing a job where I *could* have been useful. If I take what I'm doing too seriously at times, it's because I've never handled so much responsibility."

He rubbed a hand over his face. It felt gritty. "All I want is some rest, some food—"

Uh-oh. Bad choice of subject change.

"Oh, yes, you talk all the time of how we're partners—until you come home and expect me to have a meal all ready for you. My father and mother were better partners. They worked together in the mines—and when he had to, Father could come up with something to eat for Mother, Skaara, and myself."

"I can cook—sort of. But this isn't the kind of food I'm used to from back home."

"Your splendid planet Earth, where everything comes in little boxes and people have wonderful lives that make us look like savages." Sha'uri had worked up a good head of steam by now. She went to another section of the kitchen and dug out a pair of packages. Daniel recognized them from the Marine camp—Meals, Ready to Eat.

"If Earth is so wonderful, why don't you go back?" Sha'uri demanded.

Daniel became exasperated. Hadn't he explained it often enough? "The StarGate on Earth is guarded. If I went for a visit, I might not be able to come back."

"And why should that worry you?"

Sha'uri's bitter words brought Daniel up short. "Hey, my life is here now. You're my wife—"

"Am I? I've talked with some of Colonel O'Neil's Marines. We didn't marry under the forms of your world. If you're so committed to me, why do you keep cadging those ugly little cloaks you put on before we make love?"

Daniel flushed. It was bad enough, dealing with the military joshing as he begged for condoms. Now to be criticized for his precautions—

"Sha'uri, I told you, that's to protect you. These are crazy times. Neither of us wants to be saddled down with a baby."

When he saw the tears trickling down Sha'uri's face, he wished he'd made his point more gently. "We've talked about this. You don't really want a baby right now." He gulped. "Do you?"

"Yes—no! You don't understand what it's like!" Sha'uri's voice was hoarse as she spoke through her tears. "In the days before, under Ra, no one knew how long they'd live. Children were the only way to reach toward the future. Of course, Ra took a crueler view. The Horus guards used to say, 'Breed early, breed often—make more workers for Ra.' "

She stared at Daniel with red-rimmed eyes. "Things may have changed, but the old ways remain. Some of us—young ones, like Skaara—we see that new times need new customs. But it's easier to free ourselves of Ra than to change the ways of thinking—especially for the older folk. My father keeps expecting grandchildren—the sooner, the better. He hints, and asks, and pokes about . . ."

"Then we'll have to tell him to wait," Daniel said.

Sha'uri's eyes filled with renewed tears. "There is another answer we could give," she faltered. "Maybe I can't free my mind from the old ways, either."

Daniel tried to be logical, pointing out the inconvenience, the problems, a pregnancy would cause. His fledgling academy would lose Sha'uri as a teacher and translator. She responded that Abydan women worked in the mines almost to birthing time. Surely she'd be able to do the same in a sit-down job.

Then Daniel played the health-care card. He'd prefer to wait until Earth doctors and medicines were available.

"But they'll be coming now, under this agreement with the general," Sha'uri said.

In the end, there was only one argument left to him, one he didn't wish to use. Daniel Jackson was scared green of fatherhood. "I'm committed to you," he insisted to Sha'uri. "I love you, I want us to be together. We should be enjoying this time. To bring in a kid—I think it's too soon."

The discussion went downhill from there. Daniel ended in full retreat, disguised as storming out the door.

Should have taken the MRE with me, he thought, striding through the dark streets. His stomach was roiling with tension. But when it finally settled down, hunger pangs took over.

Daniel set a course for the building that housed the Council of Elders. With luck, he might be able to horn into a meal there—eat at government expense. Maybe he could take Kasuf aside, ask him to cool it with Sha'uri—

The little square in front of the adobe hall was full of people. Some were shouting, others had their fists raised. Daniel had been on Abydos long enough now to recognize accents. By their speech, these were members of farmer clans from outside Nagada.

"We came many miles to bring our petition!" one farmer cried. "Why will the Elders of Nagada not hear us? We cannot spend another day waiting to catch their ear. Let us come to them now!"

Another man complained more sharply. "These Elders grow fat on the tools and coins they get from the Urt-men!"

The linguist in Daniel wondered where the guy had appropriated the English word "Earthmen." Obviously, it was a case of street phonetics, a term reproduced by word of mouth. Pidgin English had come to Abydos.

So, apparently, had protests by the have-nots against those perceived as the "haves."

In a way, Daniel was reminded of his college days. There was the same mixture of a few vocal types fronting a large crowd waiting to see what would happen. But this wasn't campus politics. These were people in deadly earnest, coming before their government for a hearing, and, hopefully, justice. By Abydan tradition, they had the right to petition the Elders.

They'd picked a lousy day for it, though. Kasuf and his confreres had been closeted the whole day, listening to General West's offer, negotiating with him, debating the proposal, then deciding how to implement scarce resources to meet their end of the bargain. By now they were tired old men who wanted rest, not wrangling.

As far as the farmers were concerned, there were secret deals afoot to make the Nagadans richer—and the farming clans poorer.

The vocal minority led the crowd in a rush for the doors, intending to put their case forcefully.

Then the doors opened and militiamen marched out. The Abydan militia organized by Sha'uri's brother Skaara was not a spit-and-polish outfit. His citizen soldiers wore their street clothes, robes of brownish homespun. Usually the only clues of military organization were proficiency in maneuvers—Skaara drilled them mercilessly—and the weapons they carried.

The unit deploying to cut off the mob was armed with M-16 rifles recovered from the battlefields outside Nagada. These militiamen also wore another item of military salvage—the new Kevlar helmets issued to American troops. In the torchlit square, the coal-scuttle helmets gave them the appearance of cloaked Nazis moving into battle.

Confrontation quickly turned to bloody riot control. The protest leaders tried to push through, and were met with rifle butts. Apparently, the militiamen were under orders not to fire. No shots rang out, but there were plenty of broken heads and bloody faces.

The militia troopers ruthlessly drove the angry farmers about halfway across the square. There, the resistance of the hustled protesters began to stiffen.

Surprisingly, the militia riot squad broke contact, stepping back. The farmers were preparing a charge when a single rifle shot resounded across the square.

The sound came from above. Daniel and the protesters looked up to find a line of militiamen strung across the roof of the Elders' hall. They leaned across the waist-high parapet, aiming their rifles down at the crowd. The unspoken threat was enough. When the militia officer on the ground told the farmers to disperse, the crowd began melting away.

The least committed went first. They'd have to be back at their farms before sunup to begin a new day in the fields. More and more of the protesters drew away, until all that remained were the real fire-eaters—and those too banged up to move quickly.

All that was left was the mopping up. The helmeted riot-control line moved forward again, chivvying the last of the protesters away. At least they were more sparing with their gun butts.

Daniel stared, so spellbound by the unpleasant spectacle that he didn't notice the militiaman advancing on him until it was nearly too late.

"Get moving, scum!" The hard-eyed trooper reared back with his rifle. Instinctively Daniel moved to grapple with him. A flurry of movement from the corner of his eye gave an instant's warning. Daniel twisted as another militiaman charged in, ready to smash his face with the butt of his M-16.

The guy's face seemed vaguely familiar under the Fritz helmet. His features slackened in shock when he apparently recognized Daniel. Stepping between the struggling pair, he waved back his snarling comrade.

"He ain't one of the troublemakers," he said. "Look at the yellow hair. That's the chief's brother-in-law!"

The first militiaman let down his gun, giving Daniel the disgusted look reserved for innocents who interpose themselves in police actions anywhere.

Daniel found himself a little breathless as he asked the other to give him a safe-conduct across the square to the Elders' hall.

The rope and wood bridge under Skaara's feet swung slightly in the breeze. He stood equidistant between the watchtowers that flanked the main gates of Nagada. The height gave him a vantage point to observe inside the city as well as beyond its walls. He lowered the binoculars he'd aimed toward the central square. "They're leaving," he said. "We've won."

Baki, the young warrior who stood beside him, called down to the group of messengers crouched by the gate, ready to run. "They're breaking up, but keep ready. We may still have to call out more men."

"I don't think so," Skaara said. "The fight seems to be knocked out of them."

In Baki's hand, a field radio crackled to life, reporting the retreat of the disruptive elements. Skaara sighed. "And you told me I was crazy to train a troop to control crowds."

"I just didn't think you could convince any of our men not to shoot first," Baki responded. "A volley or two into that crowd would have dispersed them sooner, with a lot less effort."

"At too high a cost," Skaara said.

"We're not *that* low on ammunition," his lieutenant objected.

"That's not the price that worries me." Skaara's face was grim as he surveyed the square again. His line of men had almost cleared it completely. "Crack a man's head, and he gets up and perhaps fears you. Kill him, and you spark a feud with all his relatives."

"That makes sense," Baki admitted. "But why are we up here, commanding through runners and radios? Are you afraid of blame in case things went wrong? After all, your father is in that hall—"

"That's why I *couldn't* be there," Skaara cut him off. "Those people were coming to complain to Kasuf—to protest against him. How would they react if Kasuf's son came forth to drive them away?"

Baki gave him an eloquent shrug. "That's politics, not war."

"Wrong," Skaara said. "Politics *is* war—merely carried on at a slower speed. Mark my words, Baki. We're fighting a war right now."

He could feel the uncomfortable glance from his subordinate, even though Baki said nothing.

Good old Baki. He was a survivor from the very beginnings of the militia. They'd begun herding *mastadges* together. Baki had been one of the boy commandos who'd defied Ra and fought to save the captured Earthmen. Half of those young rebels had died from the blasts of the Horus guards and their udajeets. Baki had been promoted to command his own troop in the expanded militia. Skaara trusted him as his chief aide.

Yet Baki didn't understand the battle that faced them.

Skaara had formed the militia for two reasons. First and foremost, he'd wanted to protect his home and family. Both had proven so terribly vulnerable when Ra's wrath had fallen on Nagada.

He'd also had a dream of leading brave forces through the StarGate to bring the revolution of Abydos to other worlds in Ra's former domain.

That dream had been put off as Skaara had organized a larger militia to defend against the avarice of the mining company that had come from Earth. It had been a shock for Skaara to learn that all allies were not necessarily friends. The ones who had originally come with Colonel O'Neil—Lieutenant Kawalsky, the little one, Feretti, Daniel, who had married his sister—they had proven themselves. Feretti and Kawalsky had helped him train his fledgling recruits. Even the great O'Neil had given him advice.

But they had also nearly gone to war against him. Only the arrival of a battlecraft from Ra's empire had averted that conflict.

Still more problems had come with victory. New volunteers swelled the ranks of the militia, some of them joining on the battlefield as they picked up guns. There was status to be enjoyed from being a soldier. Some looked for power. Others wanted to settle old scores. Too many men, both in Nagada and the farming lands, wanted guns for their own uses.

The influx of manpower had been too much for Skaara's trained cadres. Some units were now commanded by men who had never shared Skaara's dream. Even among those who could be trusted—Baki, the troops in the square—the hope of expanding freedom had been postponed.

How ironic, Skaara thought. *My dream helped build a potent weapon. But that weapon may shatter in my hand to kill the dream that birthed it.*

CHAPTER 4
NEW KID ON THE PLANET

Daniel Jackson stood with his hood up in the broiling sun. In a few minutes he'd be taking part in one of the biggest meetings ever held on Abydos. His hand crept into his robe to touch a bar of heat-resistant chocolate. He'd found it left beside his clothes that morning—and the only place it could have come from was Sha'uri's MRE from that awful night. She was already off to work, preparing for the scientists from Earth.

But at least he had a peace offering as he joined the welcoming committee for Abydos' first summit conference. Sha'uri knew he was a chocoholic.

In the distance Daniel could just make out a mastadge caravan toiling its way over the dunes. A warning had come just moments before from the watchtowers of Nagada. So Kasuf and other town notables of Nagada stood to greet the arrival of Elders from the farming communities.

This was the one good result of the free-for-all in the market square four days ago. After Skaara's militiamen had dispersed the protestors, the Elders of Nagada had decided to talk with some of their opposite numbers from the farmer tribe. Messengers had gone out to the nearby farming enclaves with invitations for a joint deliberation on the farmers' complaints.

By good luck, Kasuf's counterpart among the farmers, an Elder named Nakeer, had been not too far away. As chief Elder of the farmer tribe, Nakeer spent his time traveling around the farm communes, somewhat like an old-fashioned circuit judge.

Hearing of Kasuf's call, Nakeer had summoned all the nearby Elders and set off for Nagada. Judging from local politics, Nakeer would probably have his positions ready and his people lined up by the time they arrived.

The mastadge cavalcade didn't seem to be in any great hurry. Watching the leisurely progress of the great beasts with palanquins on their back, Daniel had lots of time to notice details.

The farmers' mastadges appeared pretty much the same as the big galumphing beasts Skaara and his friends used to herd. Their humpbacked bodies looked like spindle-legged crosses between musk oxen and bison. Then nature had added a face more like what you'd expect to see on a brontosaurus—and tacked on a beard.

To ride these elephant-sized beasts required a combination saddle and seat—with a sun shade on top. The outriders on the caravan had shades like moth-eaten army blankets. The VIPs in the middle of the group had silks and tassels to keep the sun off. As usual, rank had its privileges.

What really caught Daniel's attention were the weapons some of the caravaners were waving. Those guys were toting M-16 rifles!

Standing beside him, Kasuf spotted the weapons, too. He stiffened in his ornate robes. Before Nakeer had even arrived, the farmers' Elder was making a point.

The outriders parted, and the Elders they guarded rode through the gates. Their leader pulled up his mastadge before Kasuf and his entourage.

"Welcome to Nagada, Nakeer of the farmer clans," Kasuf intoned.

"And greetings to our mining brothers of Nagada." The rider was a villainous-looking character with a black beard marked on one side with a white blaze. Nakeer seemed younger than Kasuf, but his face was seamed from years of riding beneath the desert suns.

"We have arranged a feast of salutation," Kasuf said as the leaders of the farming clans dismounted. Maidens of the city advanced, carrying gourds of water.

"How refreshing," Nakeer said as he sipped the liquid. "But I would also like to cleanse the dust of my journey before settling to eat. Perhaps you would accompany me, Kasuf, while the others go ahead."

Attended by Kasuf and Daniel, Nakeer turned away from the arranged welcome. "There is a hall of bathing nearby," Kasuf said.

"Forgive the subterfuge, Kasuf," Nakeer said as they stepped within. "I wished to speak with you—away from the ears of that multitude."

The farmers' leader stared as Daniel slipped back his hood, revealing his blond hair. "And this must be one of the Urt-men," he said.

"Earthmen," Daniel corrected. "Earth*man* in the singular."

"Singular or plural, you've caused many changes on this world." Nakeer's voice was almost accusing.

"They helped us escape from slavery—and destroy Ra," Kasuf protested.

"And in doing so, they broke the bonds that had held our tribes together since our people were brought to Abydos," Nakeer said. "Always before, our people knew their roles. Now my peple desert their fields. They come to Nagada, where they hear the streets are paved with these."

He produced a Susan B. Anthony dollar from inside his robes and held it out. "These are ill things. They make my people mad. In the days of Ra, we provided supplies for Nagada because of the fear of the Horus guards. If discrepancies were found between harvest and what was sent, a settlement suffered. Even so, we usually managed to hold aside a little of the best for ourselves."

Nakeer scowled, looking like the villain in a Foreign Legion movie. "Then the strangers came through the StarGate, offering these coins. Instead of supplying Nagada, the nearby farmers began selling all their crops and buying from the outlying communities. Then traders from Nagada came traveling, also bearing these coins. They bought up more crops. What we would have bartered or been forced to provide, we sold. There are towns where people are starving because they sold all their food—even their private supplies."

Pinning Kasuf with his eyes, Nakeer went on. "Yet with all this abundance of foodstuffs sold, our communities have received a flood of wanderers from Nagada. These folks say they're starving and have traveled to where food is to be found. Where are our crops going, Kasuf of Nagada?"

"Your harvests have not been appearing in the Council granaries, that I know," Kasuf said. "These traders you speak of—they're trying to exploit the coinage our Earth friends brought to us. They come to your communes to seek cheap food to sell dearly in Nagada. They store the grain to keep your payments low and our prices high."

He shrugged. "I argue with my fellow Elders, but for different reasons we cannot come to an agreement on what to do."

Nakeer nodded grimly. "I have the same problems with my fellows. The Elders whose towns are getting fat from this trade won't vote to regulate it. And I have no desire to impose a settlement by destroying those towns."

"The same holds true in Nagada," Kasuf admitted. "I believe that our new lives of freedom call for new ways—like doing business with these coins. Yet I fear that the new ways will cause disagreements among the people and result in fighting."

"We've been able to keep the peace in our places," Nakeer said. "But not all those leaving the city have joined us in the fields. Some skulk in the dead lands and seize what they want. Caravans have been attacked in the desert for the food they carry."

He turned to Daniel. "And some of those raiders were using the weapons of your people."

"We can't take the blame for that," Daniel objected. There's a battlefield full of lost weapons, which anyone could pick up."

"But most of those weapons have gone to Nagada," Nakeer said. "Skaara son of Kasuf has organized his own little army—"

"To fight for all of us who live on Abydos!" Kasuf flared. "Just as we battled against Ra and Hathor when they oppressed us. You yourself admit that the farmers were able to hold back something for themselves. But every *khar* of crystal we dug up was earned with our blood. We were the target of the udajeets—our people died fighting the Horus guards."

"A fine speech," Nakeer retorted. "But there were many farmer folk conscripted to work in the mines. They fought and died, too. And I will *not* have them die so that Nagada will dictate the future with guns and the aid of the Urt—*Earth*men. We fought so that we would no longer be slaves of Ra. Nor will we become slaves of Nagada."

Kasuf frowned. "I have no need of slaves. What is it you want, Nakeer?"

"My folk need the new weapons. And we need to be able to speak with the strangers from the gate." Nakeer's voice was flat, outlining his bargaining position.

Kasuf's face grew intent. "Skaara has talked about how his new recruits need training. If they were formed into guard contingents for your caravans—"

"He must also recruit from my people," Nakeer said. "We must also learn the Earthmen tongue—rather than picking up some few tattered words here and there."

"Since I run the English classes, I think I can speak for that," Daniel said. "Send us your best and brightest—men *and* women. My best student is my wife."

Nakeer looked from the Earthman to his father-in-law. A slow smile came to his villainous-looking face. "These are things that we can agree on. And I think the others will agree, too."

Maybe they never got out of the Bronze Age here, Daniel thought. *But they still know that politics is the art of the possible.*

He could hardly wait to see the next round of wheeling and dealing.

Barbara Shore released a long-pent-up breath as she stepped out of the lens of energy that marked the StarGate's farther terminus. It seemed as though the realization of traversing all that distance hit her all at once—or maybe it was the aftereffect of that wild, bumpy ride. Her legs abruptly didn't seem to want to support the rest of her shapely form.

She tottered, and the young Marine lieutenant awaiting her stretched out an anxious hand. But Barbara evaded him, aiming for the strapping Marine gunnery sergeant at the lieutenant's side.

"Sorry, darlin'," Barbara said in a broad Texas drawl, "but if I gotta fall into somebody's arms, I'm gonna pick the handsomest guy in the room."

Muffled laughter from the rest of the guard detail was cut off by a lethal look from the red-faced young officer. The poor gunny was red-faced, too, almost standing at attention as he supported the female astrophysicist. Barbara just grinned and snuggled as she got her balance back. The noncom's response was one she'd encountered often enough. Even extremely competent men—athletes, scholars . . . and a few Marines—somehow had their gears unmesh when they got an arm around her.

Barbara extricated herself from the man's hold and took a couple of experimental steps. "Looks like I can make it by myself now, Gunny. But it was fun while it lasted."

She patted the noncom's behind, then turned to the young officer. "Where to, Loot? Do I dump my stuff at my quarters first, or does that wait until Colonel O'Neil gives me the final okay?"

"I've detailed a man to move your baggage, Dr. Shore," the lieutenant said after clearing his throat only once. "The colonel is eager to see you."

"If you say so, sport," Barbara replied as they set off down stone hallways still festooned with cables for temporary lighting. In the distance she heard the echoing racket of a gasoline generator.

You're nervous, she told herself as they walked down a colonnaded corridor in what seemed to be a larger empty space. You always mouth off when you're nervous, and that's all you've done since you arrived in this crazy place.

Six months ago, if someone had told her that she'd actually step through the StarGate and land on an alien world, Barbara would have dismissed the idea as sheer fantasy—not even science fiction. In those dark days the StarGate had been an enigmatic portal that had steadily resisted all their efforts to open. Then cute, somewhat flaky Dr. Daniel Jackson had come along and produced the key.

The StarGate had actually worked! They'd sent a robot probe through what looked like a rippling pond of light and received information from another planet! Colonel O'Neil and his boss, General West, had promptly wrapped the project in top secrecy and fired all the civilian workers. Barbara had spent months exiled from the missile silo that housed the StarGate. Then one day the general's shadowy minions had contacted her, and here Barbara was on the other side of the interstellar portal.

It felt about as real as going to Oz.

But the young lieutenant had promised that she'd be going to see O'Neil, and that was all too real.

Barbara was torn. One side of her wanted to kick the military man's ass for leaving her more unsatisfied than any male ever had. The other side was willing to kiss that same fundament if she could keep playing with the StarGate.

They reached the end of a hewn-stone passageway, and Barbara could see light at the end of the tunnel. But the next stage of her trip took her through a golden-walled hall at least a block long. No, it wasn't gold, Barbara realized; it was that same glassy,golden-opalescent material that made up the StarGate.

She could see corridors branching off from the one she was following. Barriers had been arranged across them, and young men in brownish outfits obviously stood guard. Equally obviously, they were not like the Marines at the StarGate. When they saw Barbara, they muttered among themselves in a language that sounded vaguely like Arabic but wasn't.

Barbara stumbled out of step with her guide as the realization struck her like a blow. They hadn't just found a planet out here. They'd found people!

Then they were outside, and the heat of the two suns overhead settled over her like a dry but very heavy blanket. Barbara was wearing a sky blue jump-suit. She liked the functionality of the garment. Besides, with a little tailoring it emphasized the lilt of her butt when she walked. But they had hardly gone a few steps before she was aware of sweat staining her armpits and back.

"This is worse than a summer in the Panhandle," she groused. "You could have given a gal some warning about what the weather was like. Half of my wardrobe is going to be useless."

"Oh, wait till you see the nights," the young lieutenant told her. "Then it just about hits freezing."

They made their way through the organized bedlam of a military camp. Barbara noticed that the uniformed personnel seemed to be digging themselves out of the results of a sandstorm. At last they came to a larger than usual tent. The lieutenant gestured her in.

Colonel Jack O'Neil sat behind a simple camp table. He gestured to the only other empty seat in the tent—a folding chair. "It's very nice to see you again, Doctor."

"Hell," Barbara drawled, determined not to give an inch. "Here I thought I was the first woman through the StarGate. But it looks as though you brought your secretary ahead of me."

O'Neil didn't rise to the provocation. He simply introduced the two women. "Dr. Barbara Shore, meet Sha'uri, who is, of course, not my secretary. Sha'uri lives here on Abydos, and will be serving as the chief interpreter for your team." He paused for a second, the only time Barbara had ever seen the man hesitate. "She was appointed to that post by her husband—Dr. Daniel Jackson."

"Really, now?" Barbara said, shaking hands. "You know, I had my eye on that little blond-haired honey once. But he seemed to have more of a thing for hieroglyphics than women."

Careful, now, Barbara warned herself. You're taking out your bad attitude on this woman when you should be saving it for O'Neil.

"So, Colonel," she said, turning back to her main target, "I'm heading a team, am I? And what are we supposed to be doing? West's people weren't exactly forthcoming when they contacted me."

"I'm told you didn't seem to be involved in any other research," O'Neil replied.

"Funny how hard it is to get a job during funding cuts and the last place you worked was a hush-hush government project," Barbara said. "And it's so much easier when you're not allowed to talk about anything you did while you were under wraps. Not that I would. I could just imagine the reaction if I told an interviewer that the last thing I saw on my previous job was a glorified version of one of those robot mail carts disappearing in one hell of a light show. The only position that would qualify me for was a spot in the rubber ward."

"This will be a somewhat more responsible position," O'Neil assured her dryly.

"Fine—but I don't screw over as easily as the old StarGate team leader," Barbara said. "She was asking what, if anything, I'd heard about the project."

O'Neil's eyes were suddenly tracking her like a pair of radar-operated guns. "You spoke with Catherine Langford?"

Barbara shrugged. "Just a little hi-how-ya-doing?—enough to know that she hadn't been contacted by West. In my book, that stinks, Colonel. The woman spent her life trying to figure out the riddle of the Star-Gate. She hasn't got much time left—and you intend to keep her in the dark."

Barbara glanced over to see how Sha'uri was taking all this. She could see the Abydan girl didn't understand everything that was being said, but from the looks of things, she had a healthy suspicion of General West. That was a good sign. Hmmm. She was actually rather pretty, in a delicate way—like a fine-hewn Egyptian statue.

O'Neil actually seemed jolted. He took a moment before he answered her. "Formidable as Ms. Langford's organizational qualities are, they're not what's needed on this project," he finally said.

"She couldn't come out and play anyway," Barbara said. "She's broken a hip and is afraid she's going to get stuck in a rest home. But she did something odd, Colonel. She sent me a present for Daniel Jackson—as though she expected me to see him."

Barbara reached into the pocket of her jumpsuit and produced a gold chain and bronze pendant. The heavy medallion had been incised thousands of years ago with a symbol that fused a bird's body with a gigantic eye—the Eye of Ra.

Dumping it on the desk, she said, "Now that I've delivered it, can you give me one reason to stay?"

"You saw that pyramid built over this world's StarGate." O'Neil was obviously choosing his words carefully.

"Yeah," she replied. "A bit more gaudy than sheathing the place in limestone, like they did back home. Reminded me of Vegas."

O'Neil continued, refusing to respond to her jibes. "You no doubt noticed that this 'sheathing,' as you call it, is quite thick."

"I've seen streets that didn't extend as far," Barbara admitted.

"The artifact was not there when my initial reconnaissance team came to Abydos," O'Neil continued.

"Wait a second," Barbara interrupted, her voice sharpening. "You're not telling me that whole pyramid—"

"Oh, the pyramid was there," O'Neil said. "But not this so-called sheathing. The stone construction is actually a docking station. But the rest—the section made of quartz material—is a starship. It's not operational now, unfortunately. Your job—" the edges of his lips almost rose in a smile—"should you choose to accept it, is to examine the systems on board. See how they work. We've found several functional submicrocomputers on the ship. You'll be able to get information from them. Sha'uri and her assistants will translate for you. Of special interest are the power plant and engines."

O'Neil leaned back in his chair, studying Barbara intently. "The StarGate is a fascinating artifact, but if we disassembled it to see how it worked, we might end up destroying it. This spaceship offers a complete but nonfunctional stardrive. If you could determine the operating principles—"

"NASA will be going a lot farther than Mars in the next few years." Barbara gripped the edges of her chair to stop the room from spinning. "An honest-to-Pete starship. Why did—what—?"

"In this case, Doctor, the only relevant question is, 'How does it work?' " The colonel glanced at his watch. "The rest of your team should be arriving within the hour. You've already met my aide, Lieutenant Charlton. He'll serve as your liaison." For a second O'Neil looked almost human. "I understand you've been handed a lot to assimilate. Lieutenant Charlton will show you to your quarters, and Sha'uri will brief you on the local conditions. Good luck, Doctor. I'm expecting you to hit the ground running."

His eyes turned remote again. "And now, if you'll excuse me—"

Barbara found herself back in the charge of the young lieutenant. He conducted her and Sha'uri to another tent, this one in the shadow of the glassy-golden pyramid—the starship, Barbara corrected herself.

"I'm still arranging accommodations for the rest of your team, Doctor," Charlton said. "Would you prefer to be briefed—?"

"Actually, I think I'd rather prefer to get *de*-briefed," Barbara said, tugging at her sticky jumpsuit. She glanced apologetically at the young man. "Look,

Lieutenant. You've got things to do, and when the others arrive, we'll both have people to see. What do you say you come and collect me about five minutes before the troops come through?"

"Yes, ma'am." At least the young snot didn't salute.

Barbara stepped through the tent flap, beckoning Sha'uri inside. Her bags were parked neatly on the tent's single cot. "The first thing I want to do is get out of this suit and into something more suitable for the weather. I'm sweating like a pig."

She unzipped the front of her suit and shrugged it off before she noticed Sha'uri's expression. "I'm not embarrassing you, am I, darlin'?"

"N-no," Sha'uri said, looking embarrassed. "It's just that you're so—"

" 'Direct' is the word I think you're looking for," Barbara said, rummaging in her luggage. "Would it break any local taboos if I wore these?" she asked, holding out a pair of shorts and a T-shirt.

"Just that?" Sha'uri said, looking very young.

"I can see that you tend to wear a bit more," Barbara said, examining the homespun dress and shawl. "But I'm damned if I'm going to roast if I don't have to. Are you ashamed of your bodies around here?"

"Ashamed? No." Sha'uri gestured upward with her hand. "It's just that the suns—"

"Oh, right," Barbara said. "Desert people don't really go in for sunbathing."

"Bathing? In the sun?" Sha'uri's face showed bafflement.

"I guess that's a bit of English Daniel didn't teach you," Barbara said.

"An idiom," Sha'uri enunciated carefully.

Barbara grinned. "Yeah, I'm just full of idioms. We don't actually bathe in the sun. We lie out in the sun's rays—to get a tan. But I guess under those two babies up there, you could get a hell of a burn—or heat stroke. That's why you keep that pretty skin of yours wrapped up. Still having trouble following me?"

"Your words—they sound different—"

"That's because I come from a different part of the country than Daniel. I've got a Texas accent, darlin'."

" 'Darlin',' " Sha'uri echoed. "Not 'darling'?"

"Where I come from, they drop some of the final Gs" Barbara said. "And *darlin'* probably doesn't mean as much as when Daniel says it to you."

Sha'uri's expression was unreadable, but she blushed.

"So how did you manage to hook that old boy? He always seemed like such a shy one."

"If you had tried to 'hook' him, you'd probably have scared him to death," Sha'uri said with a smile.

Barbara laughed out loud. She was beginning to like Sha'uri. "How did you two get together?"

"I first saw him at the mines outside our city of Nagada," Sha'uri said. As she continued with her story of gods, wars, and rescues, Barbara's eyebrows rose. "I see there's a lot the good colonel didn't bother to tell me," she said. "So Ra kept your people illiterate?

Daniel wound up teaching you hieroglyphics as well as English?"

"That's right," Sha'uri answered.

"So why isn't Daniel running the show on the translations?"

Before Sha'uri could answer, Barbara went on. "No offense, Sha'uri, but even star pupils aren't as good as the teacher. We'll need an expert in ancient Egyptian—especially if we're going to decipher hieroglyphics that describe high-tech processes." Barbara recalled how Daniel had blasted through the translation of the proto-hieroglyphics on the stone that had covered the StarGate. "I wish your husband was working with us."

Sha'uri gave her an unhappy smile. "So do I, Barbara. So do I."

The young Abydan woman was explaining the tense division of property between Earthlings and Abydans after the seizure of the starship when Charlton returned.

"West would have promised us the stars above to let you poke around inside *Ra's Eye*," Sha'uri was saying when they heard a male cough outside the tent. "I hope he means—ah, hello, Lieutenant."

"Ladies," the young officer greeted them. He turned to Barbara, a spark of interest in his eyes as he took in her tight shorts and T-shirt. "The rest of the technical team should be exiting the StarGate shortly."

"Fine, Loot," Barbara said as she headed for the tent flap. Charlton had to hustle to act like a gentleman and twitch it aside for her.

"Before we go back into the pyramid, I want to make a stop at the medical tent," Barbara said as she slipped on a pair of sunglasses.

Charlton looked alarmed. "You're not feeling ill, are you, Doctor?"

She shook her head. "I want to see if I can steal one of their lab coats," she said. "They're loose and white, so they'll help with this intense desert sunshine. And," she added, grinning as she brushed a hand along her bare thigh, "they'll help me look a little more professional when I have to greet the troops."

The smallest lab coat available swirled voluminously around Barbara's shapely figure—apparently in government issue, "small" translated as "medium large."

But Barbara simply buttoned a few buttons and rolled up the sleeves, and had a reasonable facsimile of a caftan as she, Sha'uri, and Charlton set off for the pyramid.

"Make a note—we're going to need coats like this for everybody," she told the lieutenant. "And hats. I don't want anybody suffering sunstroke because they didn't have a hat."

"Fifteen hats," Charlton muttered, jotting down a note.

"So we have fifteen people on the team?" Barbara said. "Does that include me?"

"Yes, Doctor, including yourself," the lieutenant replied. "But not including the Abydan interpreters."

Sha'uri had raised the shawl she was wearing over her head to avoid the beating suns.

"Quite right." Barbara smiled at the young woman. "They know how to take care of themselves. Oh, and sunglasses," she suddenly said. "We have to make sure my people have sunglasses."

Her own eyewear had to come off when she entered the crippled starship. The relentless glare outside made the directionless light aboard *Ra's Eye* seem particularly dim.

"It was worse when we first fought our way aboard," Sha'uri said. "The lights were hardly working at all, then they went totally dead. Since then we've wound up with this dim sort of glow. From what we've gotten out of the computer slates, this is emergency lighting."

Barbara glanced at the young woman, impressed. "So you were able, with Daniel's help, to make some repairs?"

Sha'uri shook her head. "Our best guess is that some of the circuits repaired themselves. There are references in some of the files we've accessed—"

Barbara walked on, frowning in thought. Circuits that repaired themselves? Stardrive could be the least of the things they uncovered aboard this tub.

They moved out of the ship and into the original pyramid. The metal temporary lights tacked onto stone walls and pillars seemed harsh, an ugly intrusion—lacking the seamlessness of the ship's high tech, or the clean lines of the low-tech stonework.

A deep throbbing tone seemed to reverberate through the passages. "That's the StarGate warming up," Charlton said. "We'd better hurry, ladies."

Barbara was not about to miss that show. They reached the hall of the StarGate just as the energy backwash billowed out of the energized torus, an auroral vortex of light seemingly turned liquid.

The field stabilized into a rippling lens of light like a pool of water somehow standing perpendicular to the pull of gravity. Then the surface of the pool became disturbed, as if somebody were diving in. A silhouette appeared in the shimmering field, turning into a human form in silvery bas-relief, then finally becoming a person as the star traveler stepped all the way through to Abydos.

"Well, *that* was intense," said the bearded young man staggering drunkenly as he tried to overcome the vertigo of his trip. With a beret cocked at a jaunty angle on his head, he looked like a road-company Che Guevara.

"Storey!" Barbara burst out, running to hug him. She had spent several months cooped up with Special Operator Technician Mitch Storey, and appreciated him both for his sense of humor and his expertise in electronics and controls.

He grinned at her. "If I'd known I would get this kind of a welcome, I'd have volunteered to go first all over again."

A new figure formed in the shimmering StarGate lens, resolving into a face and body that Barbara didn't know. The man managed a shaky smile as he saw Barbara's arms around Storey. "Isn't there anyone to catch me?"

"Dr. Barbara Shore, meet Pete Auchinloss. Or should I say Professor Peter—"

"I know who Professor Auchinloss is," Barbara said. "One of the hottest shots in the world of mainframe computing."

More men and women came through, a baker's dozen of experts from technicians to designers of exotic weaponry.

"Wait a second," Barbara said, counting. "Haven't we got one more?"

"Your translation expert," Charlton said.

"Yeah, he was a little nervous at committing himself to the StarGate," Storey said with a grin. "Hold on, here he comes."

A bulky figure appeared in silhouette against the radiance of the StarGate. It resolved itself into a tall, stocky man with heavy features and an Oliver North haircut. Barbara instantly recognized pompous Dr. Gary Meyers, on loan from Harvard to the original StarGate project. Barbara always figured Harvard had given Meyers to the government to get rid of a pain in the ass around campus.

But for once the professor's face wasn't set in its usual expression of complacent condescension. Meyers gulped, took a couple of shambling steps, then vomited all over the floor.

"Thanks, Gary," Barbara said as she jumped aside. "Nice to see you, too."

CHAPTER 5
FINDS AND BARGAINS

The room was dark and stuffy as Gerekh sat on a low stool behind an empty counter. Most merchants of Nagada conducted business beneath awnings in the marketplaces. The bargains Gerekh made, however, could not be carried on in the open.

Gerekh was mildly surprised as his bulky doorkeeper brought three customers in. They stood blinking in the difference between burning sunlight and the shadows inside. Almost unbidden, the merchant's hand slid to the butt of the handgun he kept under the counter.

Then he recognized his visitors—a family group, led by his old friend Ipy. Not so long ago Gerekh and Ipy had labored together in the mines of Nagada, wresting bits of golden crystal from the surrounding rock. They'd slaved for Ra, then worked for the Earthmen. But after the great battle that left equipment strewn across the desert, both men had figured there was an easier way to make a living.

They'd started from the same place, and Ipy

considered them to be the same—independent businessmen. Gerekh, however, considered Ipy to be a fool. At the start of their prospecting, when there was the most money to be made, Ipy had turned his finds in to the Elders and the Earthmen, earning a paltry bounty.

But Gerekh had found other buyers, who paid in stacks of the shining silver coins the strangers had brought to Abydos. He'd invested his riches in the caravan trade, making further profits, then moved into a consortium of traders buying food from the farmer clans. His business was booming. Not only did the food trade make his wealth grow, it allowed him to save his silver and deal with the remaining weapons prospectors in kind—salvaged guns for food.

Ipy had changed since the days in the mines, and not for the better. Always lean, he was now almost skeletal, his skin almost black from the sun. The prospector's wife looked half starved as well. The best-fed member of the family was their twelve-year-old son, who merely looked pinched and famished.

Eyes gleaming, Ipy carried a long bundle wrapped in the tattered remains of a cloak. "Everyone said there was nothing more to be found where Hathor blasted the boxes that moved—the ay-pee-sees," Ipy said proudly. "But everyone is sometimes wrong, so I looked there, thinking, 'If I find anything, I'll bring it to my good friend Gerekh—' "

Gerekh cut off the flow of self-congratulation and flattery. "So what did you find?"

"These!" Ipy let his bundle down on the counter with a metallic clatter. He unfolded the threadbare cloth to reveal an M249 light machine gun, complete with bipod, and an M-16 rifle, its butt charred and scorched.

With a frown Gerekh pushed the machine gun aside. "This one will have few buyers, if any. It eats up bullets and who other than the Earthmen can afford to feed it?"

"I have people to feed, too," said the desperate Ipy.

"We shall see what can be done," Gerekh replied, examining the other weapon. "It's fouled with sand—the barrel is full of it." At least he'd taught the scavengers to leave their finds alone. Some idiots like Ipy had managed to destroy valuable weapons by attempting to clean them up for a better sale.

Reaching under his counter, Gerekh brought out a loaf of day-old bread, a small sack of grain, a smaller sack of flour, some beans. Perhaps enough to keep a family of three going for a few days. Ipy and his wife exchanged tense glances.

"And for the useless gun . . ." Gerekh added a couple of handfuls of beans and some overripe fruit. Inwardly he rebuked himself for showing favor to an old friend.

Ipy scooped up the pitiful supplies—another lesson Gerekh had taught his scavengers. Unlike other merchants, he didn't haggle.

Putting up a hand to forestall the speech of thanks

tumbling from Ipy's lips, Gerekh said, "Always a pleasure to do business with an old friend."

"And we will be back to do business again next week!" Ipy assured him. Gerekh repressed a wince at the thought of the family subsisting for so long on such scanty fare.

"Perhaps luck will smile on you," he said to the poor, deluded scavenger. "If you find a weapon of the Horus guards, come to me immediately. I could be very generous."

Indeed, for a working blast-lance he might offer enough to feed them well for two or three weeks.

In spite of the fact that he was the teacher, Daniel Jackson had a strange back-to-school feeling whenever he initially faced a class. He'd awakened before sunrise from the final exam nightmare—a ludicrous dream where he was forcibly taken back to college to make up an examination in a subject he'd never heard of before.

Daniel put the nightmare down to the dinner he'd cooked the night before as an attempt at domestic harmony. The mess of beans and onions had been made palatable only by a heavy lacing of tabasco sauce bummed from the Marine base. That would be enough to give anyone bad dreams, he supposed.

For the last couple of days, the first wave of new students had trickled in from far-flung communities of farmers. There'd been quite a scramble to secure student accommodations, since a sizable reality gap had set in between the planned numbers and the actual arriving students.

Today's classroom reflected part of the improvisation in the program. It was an outdoors setting, protected from the sun by a large awning. The rows of tables and chairs had come from the ruins of UMC's translation school, as did the portable blackboard. There were even some textbooks rescued from the defunct mining operation's school.

Daniel took his place by the blackboard as the classroom filled. Nakeer had apparently taken Daniel's words to heart—the students offered a mix of sexes and ages. There even appeared to be a couple of Elders on hand to learn the new language—or keep an eye on their compatriots.

The usual hubbub of an arriving class died down, and Daniel took a deep breath. "Welcome. Today we begin the study of the English language—one of many tongues on the world I come from—"

His rehearsed speech sputtered to a stop as a young woman dashed under the awning. She was tall for an Abydan, and moved with an unconscious grace that was a delight to see. Wide, dark eyes gazed in consternation around the room, seeking an empty seat. The girl—somehow she seemed girlish to Daniel—had a light olive complexion and a stunningly beautiful face, even while biting her full lower lip. The aquiline features approached the sculptor's ideal, but were animated with so much life—she had the expression of a beautiful statue come to life and realizing its nudity.

"I yam saw-ray, Dan-yer," the young woman said. Her musical voice almost canceled out the problems of her accent. Switching to a rich peasant strain of Abydan, she apologized again. "I didn't mean to be late, but all those streets . . ." She made a helpless gesture.

"Well, you know where to come now." Daniel lifted an interrogatory eyebrow.

The girl supplied her name: "Faizah."

"There's an empty seat right here, Faizah. Why don't you settle yourself, and we'll start?" Daniel pointed at a space in the first row. Like poetry in motion, she took her place.

Just as well she's in front, Daniel thought. *Half the male students will be gawking in her direction anyway.*

He decided to jettison the rest of his welcoming speech and get right down to work. "Let's see how many of us understood what Faizah first said as she arrived . . ."

Whistling tunelessly to himself, Gerekh wrapped a wad of rag around the end of a long, thin wooden rod. Then he rammed the wadding down the sand-fouled barrel of the M-16 Ipy had salvaged.

Gerekh had become fairly adept at stripping and cleaning lost weapons. He'd paid generously for expert tutelage from an early volunteer in the militia, part of the first wave that had been trained by Skaara and the outworld warriors.

Pursing his lips, he peered down the rifle barrel, a small oil lamp providing dim illumination. Perhaps the level of cleanliness wouldn't have passed muster for a Marine, but it was more than sufficient for purposes of sale.

Gerekh hastily swept away his cleaning apparatus as his doorman announced a visitor. The newcomer had a harsh, sun-seamed visage, and the squint of a man who habitually taxes his eyes for a glimpse beyond the next dune. A caravan leader, most certainly.

"I am Menna," the man said abruptly. "My mastadges travel the high desert to the black lands of the distant farmers. I am told that you sell—"

His voice broke off as he saw the rifle being reassembled under Gerekh's deft fingers. "Yes. You deal in the sort of merchandise I desire."

The traveling merchant was a fierce haggler. But in the end he had to part with silver coins for the rifle and two thirty-round magazines of ammunition. The amount would have kept Ipy and his family in luxury for more than a month.

Gerekh drew out the other weapon he'd received, the light machine gun. He hadn't cleaned it, having only removed the bipod from the weapon's muzzle.

"Another of these death sticks?" Menna said.

"This one is not so useful," Gerekh warned. "It spits out bullets too quickly—*brrrrrrp!*" He imitated the sound of an automatic weapon. "None but the Urtmen can afford to keep it fed. I don't think it pays for me to clean it and put it right. But seen from a distance, in the hands of a man on mastadge-back, it would seem that a caravan had twice as many weapons—even if it was empty."

Menna frowned. "Buying the weapon that works has dug deeply into my silver."

A new round of haggling ensued. By its end Gerekh had agreed to part with the dummy weapon not for silver, but for a portion of the caravan's bounty when it returned to Nagada.

Gerekh bowed graciously and offered the caravan leader some advice for free. "Among Skaara's militia is a young warrior named Sek. For a modest fee he will show you how to operate the weapon."

Sek was a useful contact with the warriors, sometimes sending ammunition to Gerekh. The weapons merchant smiled. Sek could also be depended upon to kick back some of his training fee.

In the former command deck of the starship *Ra's Eye,* Barbara Shore sighed as she leaned her elbows on her desk—a piece of wood sitting on two sawhorses. A week into the job, and what did she have to show for it? She riffled through the thick sheaf of papers decorating her In box. A line of hieroglyphics was followed by a line of isolated English words—then a running translation from the pen of Dr. Gary Meyers.

"What is this crap?" Barbara demanded. "I send Gary Harvard a file from one of those computer slates—we think it's about how circuits regenerate aboard this oversize suppository. His translations are all about Ra's magic, with some sexual allusions."

Looking up from a similar makeshift desk, Sha'uri nodded in embarrassed agreement. "I saw some of it when he was at the copying machine. When I questioned his translation, he looked like an Elder who'd made a misstep in the mastadge field. " 'Young woman,' " she said, deepening her voice and jutting her chin to mimic the good doctor, " 'I have several degrees in this field. This passage is transliterated according to the standard, generally accepted meanings of the symbols in question.' "

"In other words, he translated that file into the priestly hoo-raw the hieroglyphics came to mean in later centuries," Barbara said in disgust. She looked at her head local translator. "Can you take over that file? We'll try to stick Herr Professor Meyers with something a little less demandin'."

"How about this?" Sha'uri produced a pile of photographs, each taken of a new "page" that had appeared on the face of one of the slate computers. "Mitch Storey says it seems to deal with operating toilets in zero-G," she said, reading a note clipped to the top photo. "I'm beginning to wonder what kind of translator *I* am. I know what a toilet is: I know zero is a number and G is a letter. Are we marking the decks in some new way that no one told me about?"

"Zero G means no gravity. I suppose that file covers emergency situations when the artificial grav—" Barbara cut herself off when she took in the expression on

Sha'uri's face. She wasn't giving Barbara a blank look. Instead, Sha'uri was registering a desperate attempt to comprehend. But there wasn't a shared vocabulary or knowledge pool.

We're trying to get these folks to translate post-Einsteinian physics when they've never even heard of Newton's laws, Barbara thought with a chill.

"Okay. Gravity is the attraction between two bodies—whoa. Now *I* sound like I'm making sexual allusions. Have you ever wondered why things fall down? One of our great thinkers suggested that there is a force that draws things together. A large object, like a planet, tends to draw smaller objects to it. We call this attraction the force of gravity."

Sha'uri nodded. "But if there was no gravity, no reason for things to fall . . ." Comprehension flashed across her features. "I could see why people might be worried about toilets."

'So would you mind passing those pictures to Gary?" Barbara asked.

Sha'uri's expression dimmed. "If I must."

Barbara's eyes narrowed. "So what else has Gruesome Gary been up to? Now give."

Sha'uri hesitated for a second, then said, "Remember what you said about all of us being Daniel's students? I've had to complain to Daniel about that sometimes. But with Dr. Meyers—we're not merely students but rather dull ones. He's asked me to route all translations through him—so he can correct them!"

"Did he, now?" Barbara purred. "And what did you do?"

"I said he'd have to discuss it with you."

"Just the right answer!" Barbara nodded in approval. "Good ole Gary can't complain that you ruined his little power play. And he's too fond of his skin to come to me."

"His skin?" Sha'uri gulped.

"Just an idiom, darlin', " Barbara assured the young woman. "Although Dr. Meyers might not be sure of that." She looked searchingly at Sha'uri. "Is that all?"

The young Abydan woman looked uncomfortable. "It's bad enough that Dr. Meyers looks down on us. But for the female translators—"

"He's not playing touchy-feely, is he? I'll break his arms."

Sha'uri shook her head. "It's just that he seems to feel a certain—gravity. If he tells me once more what a lucky man Daniel is—!"

"I suppose he thinks he's turning on the old charm." Barbara made a face. "It's too bad we can't distract him with a little sex. It might make him a little more human."

She glanced apologetically at Sha'uri. "Sorry about that. Sometimes I get a little too blunt. It's the problem of comin' from a free-and-easy planet."

"Ah," said Sha'uri. "I suppose so."

Half-trained soldiers on undemanding guard duty—a dangerous combination, Sek thought as he leaned against a large pottery vessel that contained three M-16 rifles. Several more of the sealed urns served as storage for other militia weapons salvaged from the battlefield—pistols, grenades . . . ammunition.

The men on their knees in the pool of light from the room's single lamp had stood unflinchingly before the Horus guards of Ra himself. They'd fought and risked their lives bravely enough.

But without an enemy to confront . . . they grew bored. That's why these brave militiamen passed their time with a friendly game of knucklebones.

Sek could understand their motivations. When Hathor had attacked, he'd followed Skaara's militia onto the battlefield, found a gun, and joined the fighting.

But when his ardor cooled, he'd collected several guns and sold them.

Skaara worked hard to make his militia a good thing for all of Abydos. Sek saw where it could also be a good thing for himself.

The gambling game ended with a series of imprecations that would have earned the swearers immediate death from the members of Ra's pantheon—not merely for blasphemy, but anatomically impossible blasphemy.

The most creative and heartfelt swearing came from young Aha. As Sek had hoped, the new man in the company had lost—and lost heavily.

"You know, pup, a man of this company has to be

good for his losses—we pay in silver," one of the old hands said.

"Silver?" the young soldier repeated in dismay, coming out of his gambling fever to realize the depth of his losses. He'd need weeks of back-breaking work in the mines to earn the amount his comrades demanded.

"And we'll expect it tomorrow," another militiaman added.

Dismay went to despair on Aha's face.

Sek stepped in. "Hold on, you sons of mastadges! I'm sure Aha will make good." He took the grateful youngster aside among the stored weapons.

"Thank you, Sek," Aha said nervously. "I don't have the kind of money the others are demanding. Unless," he said hopefully, "the Council of Elders decides on this plan to pay the militia from their earnings from the mine."

Sek shook his head. "From what I hear, pup, they'll only be paying us in food. Good enough, but it won't satisfy our comrades." He held up a hand. "And don't look to me. I don't have that sort of coin. Though I know a fellow who does."

"He'd lend me that much silver?" Aha said in disbelief.

"No, but he's a buying man, is old Gerekh. He deals in weapons—ammunition. And here we are, in the middle of urn after urn of bullets. A handful or two from each jar, some stones in the bottom—"

He raised his eyebrows expressively. "You may

even find a few stones in the bottom already. There was a time when that pack in there had no silver to bet, either."

Sek said no more, leaving Aha to come to his own conclusions. But he had high hopes that Gerekh would be paying him the usual finder's fee.

After all, it had worked with the rest of the company. . . .

"I guess some people just have this knack for languages." Daniel Jackson was so enthusiastic, he was eating his own cooking without complaint. "When I saw the progress Faizah was making with English, I wanted to put her immediately into the advanced class."

"She's really that good?" Sha'uri said dubiously.

"Better," Daniel assured her. "But Faizah asked for a place in the hieroglyphics class instead—she did outstandingly there, too." He smiled complacently. "You've got to see her work. It's as though she instinctively knew how to put the symbols together."

Sha'uri rolled her eyes. In the past couple of weeks, she'd grown to expect a running commentary on Daniel's star pupil. There'd been no report for several days, so she figured her husband was just about due.

"What has the paragon accomplished now?" she asked.

"Your vocabulary keeps expanding," Daniel complimented.

Sha'uri shrugged. "I pick up the oddest things working with Barbara Shore. Which reminds me. What is testosterone poisoning?"

Daniel's latest mouthful nearly came out his nose. "Where did you hear that?"

"Barbara mentioned it about Dr. Meyers. She didn't make it *sound* as though he were seriously ill."

"He's not," Daniel laughed. "That's just a phrase some Earthwomen use when a man is acting like a fool."

"A jerk," Sha'uri said.

"Uh—right." Daniel blinked. Sha'uri was certainly picking up a lot of slang from the feisty physicist.

"So, what has the fabulous Faizah done now?"

Daniel's smug smile returned. "For the past week she's been handling a triple course load—the original English class, hieroglyphics . . . and my advanced English class."

Sha'uri's eyebrows rose. She didn't know that she could have handled that much work. "And what's the verdict?"

"Today we decided to try an additional project. Starting tomorrow, Faizah will be working part-time on your translation project."

Now it was Sha'uri's turn to blink. She ought to feel glad that her husband would be spending less time with a beautiful girl who also had a superlative mind.

But she wasn't sure she wanted to be responsible for the Fabulous Faizah.

"Daniel," she asked, changing the subject. "Why do you never call me darling?"

CHAPTER 6
DISCORD RISING

The long single file of mastadges covered ground with their peculiar ambling gait. Most of the hairy, skinny-legged beasts bore packs on their backs—the caravan's cargo of food. But there were outriders and caravaners as well. In the lead, caravan master Menna leaned forward in his travel-worn howdah, scanning the dunes around them.

The farming enclaves where they had traded were far behind them now. The caravan was in the high desert, where of late, too many human lice were to be found—raiders in search of food.

Menna shifted the rifle he carried braced against his hip. He hoped that the working weapon and the dummy his son carried at the rear of the caravan would be enough to keep any would-be reavers at bay. If not, he had two magazines worth of ammunition—sixty shots.

In his mind Menna ran over the demonstration the warrior Sek had given him, dry-firing the M-16. He wished he could actually have fired the weapon for practice, but every bullet was worth its weight in silver. He'd just have to be content—

Menna stiffened in his seat. His eyes, roving the dunes as usual, had caught a glint of metal ahead—an unsheathed blade, he thought.

"Bata," he called to his son, "bring up the other weapon. The rest of you sons of mastadges line up on either side of us. Look ready for a fight."

The outriders formed a rough skirmish line, fingering the clubs and knives they carried in case of trouble. With luck they'd show the skulkers in the dunes that they weren't to be trifled with. Whoever made that glint would disappear, waiting for easier prey.

Menna went to engage his weapon. "Ra's ass!" he swore when instead he released the magazine.

He snatched for the other magazine, seating it quickly but not chambering a round, when a flare of pure energy lanced from one of the dunes. The bolt caught Menna in the chest, superheating the fluids in his chest cavity.

The caravan leader literally exploded.

Menna's son Beta watched in horror as the caravan's defensive line disintegrated. Men and mastadges plunged away from the horrible form that moments before had been their boss.

Other forms appeared out of the dunes—the raiders charging in to reap the rewards of their ambush.

Bata threw his useless weapon away, urging his

mastadge toward his father's mount, which stood frozen, honking in terror at the smell of burnt meat.

The M-16 lay across the palanquin. Bata snatched up the weapon, aiming it to spray across a knot of men rushing towards him. Their leader was brandishing a particularly nasty-looking blade.

As he futilely jerked the trigger, the blast-lance in the dunes fired again.

Bata's mount reared on its spindly legs. A lifeless form toppled from the howdah, the rifle still gripped in its hands.

Pa'aken had watched the caravan trickle its way from dune to dune, following its progress with the distance watchers the Urt-men had brought to Abydos. He'd salvaged the binoculars from a dead Army officer in the killing fields outside Nagada. But he'd been too late getting to the battlefield to secure one of the wonder weapons.

By the time Pa'aken had arrived, warriors of the Urt-men had returned to the field, separating the wounded from the dead and discouraging those enterprising souls who were trying to loot the burnt-out personnel carriers.

Pa'aken had just tucked the glasses into his robe when he'd been evicted. He still felt a bit put out. Imagine attending the greatest battle in the history of Nagada, and having only binoculars to show for it!

That might change today, he thought greedily,

surveying the oncoming file of burdened beasts. *They've got two guns over there.*

Normally, his band would never think of attacking a caravan so heavily armed. But he had an extra blade up his sleeve this time . . .

Crouched beside Pa'aken, Hay ran his knife across a whetstone. The monotonous *scrape-scrape-scrape* began to get on Pa'aken's nerves. Besides, sound carried out here in the high desert—something city men never seemed to realize.

"Will you stop that?" he finally demanded in a tight hiss.

"As you wish, lord," Hay replied sarcastically, using the term of address usually reserved for a Horus guard. He held the blade in the sunlight, examining it critically. "Looks sharp enough—"

Pa'aken snatched his fellow thief's arm. "What kind of idiot shines light across a blade in an ambush?" he rasped.

One glance through the binoculars showed that Hay had given them away. The caravan master was bringing his men into a defensive line. This might be too difficult a proposition. . . .

A blast-bolt lashed out. That did for the caravan master. Pa'aken rose to his feet. The choice was out of his hands. "Up! Now! Take them!"

Members of the raider band erupted from the sands, rushing to take the disorganized line. Pa'aken clutched his staff as he charged down the dune. He'd always been good with the long stick, and it was useful against a mounted foe.

Hay was in the lead, waving that damned knife of his.

A figure on mastadge-back aimed a rifle at them, and the blast-lance flared again. Then there was no time for fancy shooting. They were mixed in with the enemy, fighting hand-to-hand.

Metal flashed in Pa'aken's face as he twisted aside. He could feel the slash of pain across his cheek, then the slow ooze of blood. Even as he moved, his staff battered the arm wielding the knife. In quick succession the rider lost his weapon, his seat, and his life as Pa'aken knocked him to the ground and bludgeoned him to death.

Clapping a hand to his bleeding face, the bandit leader quickly surveyed the field. The caravaners were finished. Most of them were stark on the sands, except for the few that were riding for their lives.

A couple of his men were bruised or bloody. And Hay's knife glinted in the sun not far from his outstretched hand where he lay, brained by an outrider's cudgel.

Exactly what he deserved, Pa'aken thought. He bent to retrieve the caravan master's rifle, shaking sand from the barrel. He'd have to search carefully. Somewhere there might be more bullets.

As Pa'aken arose, he saw another figure coming toward them over the sand. The newcomer moved with his hood up, his cowled shape seeming to shimmer in the heat haze from the sands. The weapon he carried was as tall as Pa'aken's staff, but it gleamed gold in the burning sunshine.

"Was my contribution worthy of its reward?" the late arrival asked in a quiet voice.

Pa'aken gazed at the blast-lance with naked greed. But the stranger had proven himself too formidable even to allow the hope of stealing that weapon.

With a snarled order Pa'aken ended his men's pillaging of the pack animals.

"As we agreed," he said to his powerful new ally. "You get first pick of the loot, Khonsu."

Lieutenant Charlton was not a happy camper as he reported to Jack O'Neil. "Some of our people on long-range reconnaissance found another caravan wasted."

The colonel frowned. Desert raiding was becoming serious enough to have an impact on the Nagadan economy—and his own force's supplies.

But Charlton had worse news to impart. "Six locals killed and just left out for the local wildlife. Even so, the recon boys could tell that two of the dead had been toasted by a blast-lance."

"Won-der-ful." O'Neil bit off each syllable. Raiders with Ra's technology represented a new low in the high desert war zone that had developed in the last couple of weeks. Regular patrols by the militia and O'Neil's forces had kept the areas around the base camp, the city, and the mine relatively safe. Inside Nagada was another story. Despite Skaara's best efforts, the place was turning into Dodge City. Scavenged Earthly ordnance was being used in faction fights all over the town.

"What do we have next?" he groaned. "Drive-by shootings on mastadge-back?"

"I couldn't say, sir," Charlton said almost primly. "But Skaara is here to see you."

O'Neil was inwardly amused at the lieutenant's faint unhappiness. Charlton wanted to tack on a proper military rank to the leader of the Abydan militia. But Skaara had resisted the urge to name himself generalissimo, or even acting colonel. He believed in leading without ranks. O'Neil only hoped his young friend could make that notion stick.

Nonetheless, Skaara gave the colonel his usual crisp salute as he entered the office. His face went pale as O'Neil passed on the long-range reconnaissance report. "If the sand scum have gotten weapons like that, we have troubles indeed."

He sighed. "And here I thought I had good news to report. My people caught a caravan trying to smuggle two blast-lances out of Nagada."

"Where were they going?" Charlton wanted to know.

"The farmers." Skaara made the term sound like a curse.

"I thought you were bringing some of Nakeer's people into the militia," O'Neil said. The deal between the two head Elders had been one of the few bright spots in the present political scene.

"Oh, some of the farmers are good fellows," Skaara

admitted. "But even if I could trust Nakeer—which is not necessarily a sure thing—his people have as many factions as mine. I know there have been farmers in town, offering lavish amounts of food for any guns—pardon, *weapons*—they can get their hands on."

He gave the Marines a sour smile. "Certain merchants have been very annoyed—the farmers have been driving prices up."

"Where did the blast-lances come from?" O'Neil wanted to know.

"Probably they came from some of the shot-down udajeets out on the battlefield," Skaara said. "At least they're not militia items. I checked our stocks, both here at the ship and in the arsenals."

He looked as if he'd taken a large bite of rotten fruit. "But rifles and grenades were missing. Urns of ammunition turned out to be mainly filled with stones. My people have been selling to the farmers and the factions in town—Ra damn them, some of them probably *belong* to the factions."

"We'd heard about fighting in town," O'Neil said diplomatically.

"And what they're fighting over is weapons," Skaara burst out. "The only good thing is that sometimes the fighting uncovers a faction's cache. We had an explosion in a ruined building after a firefight. The place burned down. We found several bodies, grenade spoons—and what might be the remains of another blast-lance."

He looked helplessly at his former mentor. "But we

can't search every mastadge going out of the city for contraband—or burn down every house where weapons may be hidden."

"It's what you may have to do," O'Neil said unhappily.

"The Elders would never agree to such a course."

Translated, that meant Skaara couldn't go against his father, or the deal with Nakeer.

"Then you'll have to do your best to protect the weapons you're responsible for," O'Neil said. "Close the arsenals. Put the rifles and ammunition in the hands of those you really trust. The blast-lances here are reasonably safe—they can't be smuggled through our camp. In town, you may want to gather your blast-lances at your headquarters."

O'Neil stepped to a footlocker, rummaged for a moment, and produced a large padlock and key. "Put this on the door. Then put people you absolutely trust outside that door."

"What's been getting into Gary Meyers?" Barbara Shore asked as she paged through the latest set of translations on her desk. A flood of material had hit the translators after Pete Auchinloss had managed to pry it from what passed for mainframe computers aboard *Ra's Eye*. Even Gary Meyers had been pressed into service. "This stuff looks . . . coherent!"

"Maybe it's more a case of what Gary's been getting into," Mitch Storey smart-mouthed.

"Do tell," Barbara said. "Maybe we can get some more of it for the rest of the staff."

The bearded technician shook his head, his lips twitching. "It's dumb gossip. I shouldn't have said anything."

Barbara said nothing, just training a pair of piercing brown eyes on him.

"All right. The new girl on the project, Faizah. I hear Meyers is all over her."

"Is that a trace of male ego I detect, darlin'?" Barbara inquired sweetly.

"*Bruised* male ego," Mitch admitted. "Hey, I checked her out. There was a major babe alert when Faizah came on board. But either Meyers has latched on to her professionally—or she's hooked up with him personally. I hear she wraps him right around her little finger."

"Good," Barbara said. "Gary needed someone to take the starch out of his shorts."

Storey looked a little alarmed. "But if she's sleeping with him—"

"They've managed to make beautiful translations together," Barbara finished for him. "This stuff is clear, concise, and best of all, it make sense to me as a scientist. We'll try her on the next batch from Auchinloss alone. And if she works out the way I think she will—we have a new star translator!"

Sha'uri stepped quietly down the stairwell, away from the command deck. She hated herself for standing there, eavesdropping on the conversation between the two Earthers, especially since she and Barbara Shore had become friends. But although she hadn't understood all the slang, two things seemed perfectly clear. Her husband's people seemed frighteningly casual in their approach to sex and relationships. And Faizah seemed to be exploiting that casual attitude to further her interests.

The uncomfortable question arose—had she done it before?

Had she done it with Daniel?

"Are you nuts?" Daniel Jackson hooted with laughter, "Faizah and Gary Meyers?"

Slowly his laughter faded as he tried to understand what was bugging Sha'uri. Because something definitely was.

"What's wrong with Dr. Meyers?" Sha'uri asked. "I've heard you say that he is respected in your field—more than you were."

"The guy's a stiff!" Daniel burst out. "Faizah could do much better."

She could? Sha'uri thought. *With whom?*

Daniel stared at his wife as he chewed a piece of bread. *She can't be jealous of Faizah on the job.* He tried to edge around the subject. "I think I did the right thing, putting her on the project. From what I hear, Faizah has helped clear up a bunch of those technological hieroglyphics."

"Yes. Dr. Meyers speaks very highly of her, too."

Daniel swallowed a little too hard. Why was Sha'uri

giving him the old skunk-eye? "What does that mean?"

"Just that it's interesting how many men think Faizah is quite remarkable. Especially men from good old sleep-with-anyone-you-feel-like Earth!"

"Barbara Shore certainly isn't a man. And she thinks that Faizah is an exceptional translator," Daniel said reasonably.

Perhaps he'd have done better not invoking a woman who'd admittedly pursued him back on Earth.

The discussion that followed was not at all reasonable.

But it was quite heated.

Faizah looked at her teacher with wide eyes. "But why shouldn't I be friendly with Gary?" she asked in astonishment.

"It just gives people the wrong idea," Daniel said in an uncomfortable voice. "You work under him—"

He bit off that sentence while he was still ahead. Hoo-boy!

Faizah's face radiated puzzlement. "But I call you Daniel, and I learn under you."

Daniel was very glad that Sha'uri hadn't heard that comment.

He retreated to the proprieties of teaching. "I shouldn't have phrased the sentence that way," he said stiffly. "Although there's an accepted sense of working under someone's direction, there's a double meaning—"

A sort of naughty comprehension came over Faizah's mobile features. "Oh, yes, we have that, too. We call it 'agreeable work'!"

Looking into her laughing eyes, Daniel had to admit that farmers often had a more barnyard simplicity about procreative matters.

"But who would object—oh. It's Sha'uri, isn't it?"

Again, Daniel had to credit his star pupil's quick mind.

"Things don't seem to be getting any better between you, do they?" she said.

"Just bigger and better arguments," Daniel admitted.

It seemed that the more difficult it became to talk to Sha'uri, the more understanding Faizah became. At first Daniel had just spoken in generalities, trying for a second opinion from a woman of the same age and culture. But oddly, their conversations had grown more specific—and downright personal—while also broadening into discussions of policy and politics.

"I've been thinking about why Sha'uri feels troubled." Faizah spoke in that odd combination of innocence and forthrightness that reminded Daniel of the midnight talk fests of his university days.

"She's one of the people who had the most to lose when the world changed," Faizah said. "Think about it. She was one of a very privileged few on this world. Her father was the virtual ruler of Nagada, in the absence of Ra or the Horus guards."

The girl shook her head. "I guess there's a little bit of Ra in all of us. When people have power, they want to keep it. I saw that when I met Gary. He had to be the boss. Maybe it's the same thing here. Kasuf still runs Nagada, with your help. Skaara leads warriors. And Sha'uri . . . found you."

"I—ah, think you're oversimplifying," Daniel said, his voice constricted. He'd always considered his marriage a piece of almost Hollywood luck—the end-of-the-movie scene where the hero weds the chieftain's daughter.

But what had Sha'uri gotten out of the bargain?

Faizah was still talking. "It must be hard, I suppose, to face what Abydos has become if you're still connected to the old ways of things. Like children. Old fogies—"she smiled at the idiom—"tell me I ought to be married and pregnant by now. It's one of the reasons I was glad to leave home. I can't tell you how glad I am to be here, making a future for my possible children rather than making children for a possible future."

She was very serious now. "I mean, I've got the rest of my life for kids. With the work we have to do now for Abydos—opting out now would be just about the same thing as—as treason."

"That's a pretty strong statement, young lady," Daniel said. "We've talked a bit about how things work on my world and how they work here. But what you're talking about now sounds very much like what we Earth folk call politics."

" 'Politics.' " Faizah repeated the word as if she were tasting it. "If that means how I think this world should be—well, you might not like it."

"As long as the program doesn't start with 'Round up all the Earthmen and kill 'em,' I think I can take it." Daniel smiled.

"I belong to a group called Freedom," Faizah said. "Some of the more extreme members might like your idea."

Daniel's smile faded. "I'd heard that some of this faction stuff was getting out of hand."

"But—but—!" Faizah stumbled over her words. "We thank you for what you've done. Without the Earthmen we'd still be a slave planet. But we're not so grateful that we'll follow every order—or even suggestion—that comes through the StarGate."

Thinking of the bitter struggle with the United Mining Cartel, Daniel had to admit the young woman was right.

"We can't stay with the old tribal ways," Faizah went on. "That would leave me back home, planting fields—and being planted with babies. Learning to write is good. Everyone on Abydos should have that, if only to read the hidden histories. Once we all know where we came from, we can decide on a destiny for this world."

"And what do you think that should be?" Daniel asked.

Faizah shrugged enchantingly. "I'll be honest—I don't know. But I *feel* that maybe the people on Earth had the right idea when they buried their StarGate."

She raised a hand toward his shocked expression. "I don't mean for thousands of years—maybe for a century or so." Faizah smiled. "So the people who live on Abydos can just get to work building their world—undisturbed."

Daniel found himself smiling at his student's audacity. *I wonder how General West would react to that,* he wondered. *His cold, drafty door into the unknown being slammed shut—from the other side!*

Then Daniel suddenly found Faizah's plan less funny. How would West react to a movement that would cut off his only supply of Ra's wonder quartz?

CHAPTER 7
COUNTRY MATTERS

"Well, sir, the motor pool has just put its seal of approval on the last shipment of Humvees to come through the gate," Lieutenant Charlton reported to Jack O'Neil.

"No embarrassments like overinflated tires to explode in the heat here?" the colonel inquired.

"Sir, I doubt the motor pool will ever live that one down." Charlton smiled. Some people were still being called "desert cherries" because they had thought they were under attack.

"The news couldn't have come at a better time," O'Neil announced, holding up a piece of paper. "We've just gotten a note from Daniel Jackson, who's the closest thing we have to an Abydan Department of State. All the parties—Kasuf, Skaara, *and* Nakeer—have agreed to extended mechanized patrols."

"Everybody agreed?" Charlton said, impressed.

"They're all having enough of a problem maintaining order where the population is heavy," O'Neil said. "None of them can spare people for the high desert.

Besides, Humvees can travel farther and faster than any mastadge—and carry more firepower."

His face hardened as he spoke to his aide. "I want to put maximum destruction on the sand lice preying on the caravans," he said. "But I also want something else. We still haven't found a trace of those Horus guards who came though the StarGate—except, perhaps, for all hell breaking loose off in the desert. If there's anything to be found out there, I want it found."

Charlton responded with an enthusiastic salute. "Not a problem, sir."

"I don't know how I let you talk me into this," Daniel Jackson miserably called to Faizah as he clung to the howdah of his riding mastadge. He'd traveled on the backs of the odd beasts for short distances. It was sort of like riding a giant, animated dust mop with a weird gait. Prolonged traveling, however, brought aches and pains to his thighs and butt.

But there was worse. Since the death of his parents in a horrible plane crash, Daniel had suffered from hodophobia, a psychosomatic disorder also called "the traveling allergy." Even considering a journey set his nose running. He'd had a miserable, drippy adjustment to Abydos—since just the thought of being on a strange planet had been enough to set off his allergy.

This cross-country mastadge jaunt was bringing out his hodophobia in full force. Daniel's nose was running like a faucet. His handkerchief had been soaked hours ago, and it had picked up a fine film of grit stirred up by the caravan's progress. Whenever he wiped his nose, he also felt as though he was sand-papering it.

And now, to add insult to injury, the mastadge's galumphing, stilt-legged progress was beginning to give him motion sickness.

Sure—barf all over the place—that should really impress Faizah, he thought. How *had* he let her talk him into a field trip, of all things?

Faizah couldn't believe that he'd never been to a farming enclave. With typical efficiency she had made arrangements for a quick tour. She'd wished she could show him her own hometown, but that was just too far away. Instead, they'd set off for the farm area nearest Nagada. That had been the better part of two days ago, and Daniel was nearly at the end of his rope.

Astride her own mastadge, Faizah looked as fresh as when she'd mounted the hairy beast two mornings ago. "Oh, come on, Daniel. We're almost there. See how the mastadges are acting."

Indeed, both their mounts had raised their bearded, stumpy heads, expanding their nostrils and bleating like air horns.

"They smell water," Faizah explained.

The caravan crested the next dune—and the desert abruptly stopped. It was as though some titan had drawn a line. On one side was lifeless sand. On the other side was a riot of green, growing things amid the glint of irrigation ditches.

The abrupt transition struck Daniel almost like a blow. Even his nose turned off.

At an order from the caravan leader, the file of beasts veered off to parallel the fields. Apparently, mastadges couldn't be trusted among the crops. Daniel jounced along, watching the farmer folk at work. Some would pause in their labors to wave to the strangers. Feeling like a tourist, Daniel waved back.

It seemed that every square inch of arable land was intensively tilled. At last, however, they came to a stony height that overlooked a river. It was crowned with the town of Ezer.

Daniel stared. The walls enclosed a space as large as Nagada. He said as much to Faizah, asking, "How many people live here?"

"Not many," she replied. "Most of the space is now used for granaries." She cocked an eye at him. "Ezer was originally built by the miners. It was the Nagada of its time. There are empty mine pits off to the west."

She gave him a *don't you know anything?* look. "Farm clans take over locations when the diggings run out. Nothing could grow here until the golden quartz was gone."

The caravan climbed a well-defined trail to the town gates. Coming closer, they could see that most of the buildings were in near-ruinous condition cannibalized to provide repairs for the farmers' homes and granaries. The walls were well maintained, however. They were needed to provide protection from dust storms—and nowadays, from human predators.

Guards met them at the gate. Most carried staffs, and he saw the hilts of knives on others. But a few carried rifles.

There was a brief ceremony of welcome. The local Elder's daughter, a pleasant, homely girl, presented Daniel with a gourd of water. Then came a guided tour of the town. Daniel was surprised to find a Humvee in the central square. A medical team was examining children and treating ills.

"I didn't realize you guys made house calls," Daniel said as he was introduced.

The Navy corpsman just shrugged. "The colonel sends us far and wide."

Daniel looked hungrily at the big four-wheel-drive vehicle. It could probably make the trip back to Nagada in a quarter of the time it had taken to get here. But his hopes of a lift were cruelly dashed when the corpsman mentioned his next destination—an enclave even farther away.

There really wasn't all that much to see in the town. Somewhat to the local Elder's embarrassment, the granaries were all but empty. Ezer had cashed in early on the flood of Susan B. Anthony dollars coming from Nagada. But the people seemed to live well, and the children appeared a bit less pinched than their counterparts in the big city.

Faizah took Daniel to the gates again, and they looked down at the croplands and the river below.

"Ezer is the collection point for crops up and down the river," she said. "The food is barged here, then stored for the Nagada caravans."

"Just like ancient Egypt back home," Daniel said. "Even to building the town on infertile land."

The farmer's daughter gave him a scandalized look. "Who'd waste good soil by building a house on it?"

Faizah offered to take Daniel down into the fields. The local Elder let them go. A field was a field, after all.

Daniel wouldn't have minded a little welcoming feast and a chance to wash the desert grit off himself. But he followed Faizah down the dusty trail. Soon they disappeared into green shoots of head-high grain.

Faizah sighed, kicking off her sandals and digging her feet into the soft, dark earth. "I've missed this," she admitted with an embarrassed smile.

They wandered along through the profusion of growing things until Daniel began to worry that they would get lost.

Faizah laughed at the idea. "It can't happen," she assured him. "Just follow the irrigation ditches, and they'll either lead you to the river, or to the edge of the fields."

They must have been heading close to the river, because the irrigation ditches were becoming larger and larger, until at last they stood on the banks of a respectable canal.

Faizah looked back and forth through the green fields. They hadn't seen anybody in more than a mile. "This is something else I've missed," she said, a sparkle in her eye.

She shrugged, and the shawl fell from her shoulders. Ever the gentleman, Daniel went to pick it up. His hand had just landed on the garment when Faizah's robe slithered to her ankles.

Daniel jumped back so quickly, he almost went crashing through a couple of rows of grain. "Fa—Faizah," he stammered. He tried his best not to stare as the golden girl stepped forward, extending a toe into the water to test its temperature. From the rear her body was a symphony of tautness and softness, planes and curves.

Another theory proven, Daniel thought numbly. *Ancient Egyptians didn't use bathing suits.*

"Mmmmmm, just right," she said, glancing mischievously over her shoulder.

Daniel suddenly realized that the loudest sound in the area was his breathing.

With a smooth, sinuous move Faizah dove into the water.

She disappeared beneath the surface, then burst up, doing a lazy backstroke. She grinned like a naughty child at the quick revelation of her body beneath the water.

Daniel's breath caught in his throat.

Impishly, she dove under the water again, giving him a flash of a delectable rear end. Faizah reappeared at the edge of the canal, directly at his feet. Her short black hair, now wet, clung close to her head like a seal's or otter's pelt. She was treading water at chest level. Her dark nipples seemed just to float on the surface, standing out against the olive skin gleaming with wetness.

"It's much more comfortable in the water," she said. "You seem to be sweating up there."

"Ah," Daniel said brilliantly. His tongue seemed slightly too large for his mouth, which was odd, since his skin suddenly felt a couple of sizes too small. He could feel every sand grain he'd picked up on the trek through the desert. Maybe it was a case of sudden sunburn. Daniel felt warm, very warm.

The skinny-dipper splashing in the water gave him a mock pout. "Come on," she invited. "You'll like it once you get in."

Faizah smiled up at him, a young, healthy animal in her element. Her lips seemed a little fuller as they curved in an unspoken promise. *Play your cards right, stud. . . .*

Daniel struggled with a welter of irrelevant thoughts. *Sha'uri.* Every farmer's daughter joke he'd ever heard flitted through his head. *Right, I "get in" with her, and a moment later, Farmer Geb turns up with his pitchfork.*

At last he managed to get his mind in gear with his mouth. "Uh, thanks for the invitation, Faizah. But I don't think so. We have an idiom for trouble in

English—to get in hot water. I think that's what I'd be doing." His voice was still hoarse as he spoke.

"Okay." Faizah gave an entrancing shrug, then struck out in a side stroke. She disappeared under the water again, then climbed out of the canal, giving herself a good shake.

Daniel quickly scooped up her robe and stood holding it.

"Ah, that was *so* good!" his student said with her innocent smile. "You don't know what you missed!"

"Probably not," Daniel agreed, handing over her shawl.

Faizah's hair had completely dried by the time they climbed back up to the town. She spent the night with the local Elder's slightly homely daughter.

A caravan bound in for Nagada was leaving the next morning. Daniel, Faizah, and their mastadges joined the group. Soon Daniel was lurching along across the dunes as if the green fields (and Faizah's pass) were just so many dreams.

The reality was grit, sneezing, and the threat that he'd spend the rest of his life walking bow-legged. Then, to make things complete, a huge cloud of dust rose off in the direction they were headed.

Perfect, Daniel thought. *A sandstorm is just what we need.*

His mastadge shied, disrupting the single-file progress, and soon Daniel realized why as a sound came to his less sensitive ears. A low mutter came from over the dunes in the distance. Most of the Abydans had never heard that noise before. But Daniel recognized them as diesel engines—*large* diesel engines.

That sand wasn't being blown—it was being thrown in the wake of a heavy patrol.

Daniel's suspicions were justified a moment later as an Apache helicopter cruised by in the distance.

Three of Skaara's militiamen accompanied the caravan. They'd gathered dubiously, their M-16s aimed against the possible threat. But they had seen gunships before and relaxed.

Unfortunately, most of the caravan had scattered, apparently thinking Ra himself had come back in one of his udajeets.

As they waited for the line to reform, Daniel and Faizah discussed the passing soldiers. "O'Neil moves quickly," Daniel said. "He's barely gotten the okay for patrols like this, and already he has people out here."

True to her politics, Faizah wasn't pleased with what she saw as foreign interference.

"Somebody has to do something about the desert raiders," Daniel said.

"Those somebodies should be Abydans," Faizah replied. "We shouldn't have to depend on Colonel O'Neil." She gazed off after the dust cloud, now disappearing off toward the horizon. "Besides, I don't think it will do much good. Those machines are too noisy. Any competent raider would hear them coming and just hug the sand until they went away."

The mastadges were back together again, and the caravan master gestured for them to move off. For Daniel, the miles passed in the usual tedious agony. He was blowing his nose so hard, at first he missed the sounds of the gunshots.

His first clue of trouble was something that went *wheek!* past his ear and shattered one of the poles supporting the sunshade on his howdah. The woolen awning flopped down, blinding him. From behind came a blast of a grenade.

"Wha—?" He pushed the shade off his head and discovered a scene of pure chaos. One of the Abydan militiamen had been knocked off his mastadge, either by a lucky shot or the aim of the greatest native marksman on the planet.

One of the others had emptied his entire magazine into a sand dune. He was now having problems reloading. The last rifleman was sending shots toward a howling mass of raiders who'd apparently materialized out of the sand.

Bitterly, Daniel remembered Faizah's assessment of the patrol. It looked as though she was right. Maybe O'Neil's people would hear the sounds of distant gunfire over their engine noise. But even if they came back, it would probably be too late.

Daniel skidded off his mastadge, going for the rifle lying half under the dead militiaman. Maybe it was a hopeless gesture, but he had to try to defend Faizah.

He was just pulling the dead man aside when the gunfire suddenly surged in intensity. Daniel glanced around to discover that new players had suddenly surged out of the sand. A dozen riflemen in the chocolate-chip cammies of American soldiers were firing with deadly effect into the raiders.

Most of the bad guys either went down or ran away at the surprise intervention. A few ran on into the caravan, trusting that the soldiers wouldn't fire at friends. One raider, hefting a club with what looked like a railroad spike sticking out of it, headed straight for Daniel Jackson.

Actually, Daniel couldn't be sure that he'd been picked as a target. Maybe he was just an obstacle on the guy's route to the riderless mastadge he'd left. Either way, it looked as if he might be leaving his brains smeared over the desert sands.

A mastadge suddenly burst from the churning mass of the caravan. Faizah crouched low over the ungainly beast's prehensile neck, urging her mount to greater speed.

The charging raider saw her and turned with a two-handed grip on his club.

Daniel fumbled the M-16 out of the sand. *Please, don't let it be jammed,* he prayed.

There was no time to shoot. Faizah was on the guy. At the last second she pivoted her mount slightly. The raider's club stroke missed. The mastadge hit him with its shoulder. The guy went down.

Then came a gruesome *crunch!* as the mastadge's rear leg trampled the guy.

Daniel rose shakily from his knees, the rifle held loosely in his hand. He watched as Faizah reined in her panicky mount. The girl's usually mobile face was frozen and hard, a grim mask in the harsh sunlight.

Odd. He'd seen that face somewhere before.

CHAPTER 8
THE RADICALIZATION OF DANIEL JACKSON

Daniel looked up, still a little dazed. An Apache gunship—probably the one that had flown by before—came sweeping down out of the sky, strafing the dunes where the caravan raiders had run for their lives.

One of the riflemen who'd broken the raiders' attack—probably the sergeant who commanded the squad—approached the caravan. He held out empty hands and shouted in pidgin Abydan that he was a friend.

Leaving the others to deal with the skittish mastadges, Daniel stepped out to greet the soldier. "Not just a friend," he called, "but just in time."

The noncom's face went from astonishment at being answered in English to recognition and concern. "Dr. Jackson! Are you okay?"

"One of the militiamen guarding the caravan is dead. I don't know about any other casualties." He resolutely didn't look at the raider Faizah had trampled. "At least on our side."

Astonishingly, no one else had gotten shot. Sergeant Ingraham, the commander of the ambush party, wasn't surprised. "The locals don't have the ammunition for target practice," he said. "And even if their barrels aren't fouled with sand, enough grit gets in to screw up the rifling grooves. The damn things just don't shoot straight."

"I thought I heard a grenade behind us," Daniel said.

Ingraham shrugged. "That was supposed to goose you forward into their arms," he said. "But they didn't want to damage the merchandise."

The sergeant explained that his men had been dropped off by the mechanized patrol Daniel had spotted earlier. "We'd gotten reports of bandits operating in this area, so we really had our eyes out. These clowns figured they'd break their teeth on us, so they hunkered down. But the chopper spotted them, and we put on a big parade past them while my squad marched into position. I'm sorry we wound up using your caravan to draw them out."

By now the rest of the heavy patrol had chugged into view. Daniel had a brief discussion with the officer in charge and secured a lift on a Humvee back to Nagada. The officer was already getting on the radio requesting that a message about Daniel's return be forwarded to Kasuf.

Daniel stewed for the whole bumpy ride. After the adrenaline of the fight wore off, he felt vaguely sick. It had been a case of kill or be killed, and he'd been willing to shoot any of the raiders. But Faizah, having to trample that guy—he noticed that she was uncharacteristically quiet as they jounced across the dunes. Daniel began to get angry. They had been damned lucky that those Marines had turned up when they did.

But they shouldn't have to depend on O'Neil's people. Faizah was right about one thing. Abydans should be working to solve this problem.

And he was going to make sure the process started in Nagada.

When they arrived at the city gates, Daniel saw a delegation drawn up, awaiting him. Sha'uri, Kasuf, and a gaggle of the city's Elders were on hand. It looked like a combination of "Hail the Conquering Hero" and "The Prodigal's Return."

Suddenly, Daniel was glad that Faizah had convinced the driver to drop her at the base camp first. Daniel had serious business at hand, and it wouldn't help if people thought he'd been off junketing with his pretty protegée.

Taking a deep breath, he stepped out of the vehicle.

Kasuf stepped forward. "Husband of my daughter," he greeted Daniel. "Son. We were so worried when we heard your caravan had been attacked—"

Daniel cut off the rest of the speech. "We've got bigger worries than that." He spoke in Abydan, letting his anger take command. "The attack on me was just a symptom. We need to deal with the whole disease."

He looked from Kasuf's shocked face to the other

surprised councilors, all standing around in their fancy robes of office.

"We freed a world, but now that world needs *governing*. What does your council stand for, other than your own interests? It barely governs Nagada. You haggle over deals with the farm clans, deciding who will be important where. But nothing is getting *done*! Every day a little bit more of Nagada falls to pieces, while out in the desert our people rend one another like wild animals."

Kasuf was pale with anger. "It is a fine thing to talk about governing, but I don't have the omnipotent power of a Ra. I can't stretch out my hand and cleanse the desert of thieves, nor can I make food where there is none. The farm clans are the ones with the food, and they play their own games. We all know how well a man can eat if he sells a rifle or a grenade—yes, or even a blast-lance! The nearer enclaves fear us; those farther away accuse us of cheating them. I respect you, Daniel, but this is a knot that will not untie easily."

Daniel pointed at himself. "It took a bullet flying past my ear to open my eyes. It was a narrow escape, but I don't care for myself. If we keep on going as we have, hoping for a slow resolution, the animals out there will end up killing all of us!"

He'd never been so brutally hard on Kasuf. Even when he had showed the Abydan that the gods he worshiped were merely men in masks, it hadn't been a personal attack. And it hadn't been an assault in front of his fellow Elders.

For a second as Daniel stormed off, he was ashamed of himself. Then he hardened his heart. Things had to change on this planet. From now on, there could be no business as usual.

Daniel busied himself for a while with the affairs of his academy, but in the end he knew he'd have to go home.

Here comes round two, he thought.

Sha'uri had a good-size fire going, but even as she stood beside it, she had her arms wrapped around her body as if to ward off a chill.

"Welcome, Professor Jackson," she said bitterly. "Have you been working on another interesting lecture?"

"I said something that needed saying," Daniel responded.

Her hands came down and clenched into fists. "You spoke to my father as I've never seen you speak to your stupidest pupil! And what was his crime? We were all worried about you! He was being thankful for your narrow escape."

"That's the problem!" Daniel burst out. "We have feasts to welcome people to the city, little ceremonies to greet them after returning. And we're not getting any work done."

"Those things you sneer at are very important work." Sha'uri glared at him. "They're the traditions that hold this place together while we try to move forward. Not that you helped that cause today! Father didn't mention it in front of all those people, but there are enough factions here in Nagada setting up their private armies and arsenals. They're just as ready to kill those who oppose them as those 'animals' you met in the desert. And you ought to know that!"

"So why does Kasuf shy away from mentioning them?" Daniel demanded.

"Because some of his most dangerous enemies were standing in the crowd today!" Sha'uri responded. "You've never much paid attention to how the Elders worked in council. So perhaps it may be news for you that some of the people buying up the food in this town—and running the marketplace for guns—are respected Elders."

"Then Kasuf should expose them," Daniel said.

"You forget where this all comes from," Sha'uri said in frustration. "The council was a mutual-aid society in the slave days. Council members aren't supposed to rat on one another. If a member seems to threaten the others, he ends up isolated."

"Great! The closest thing you have to a government operates like a gang of thieves!"

She stepped face-to-face with him. "Someone with an interest in language could probably make a wonderful lecture on how you switch from 'we' to 'you' in this discussion. Yes, 'we' don't have elections the way 'you' do on 'your' planet—for the last two hundred years, if I remember rightly. Since time out of mind, 'we' were slaves. 'Our' government was in the hands of a mighty but cruel god—and we could do little for ourselves. Abydos has a lot to learn—but maybe you have a lot to decide, Earthman."

Daniel could feel a hot flush creeping onto his face. "I made my decision when I decided to stay here. I want all of us to have a future. And I finally realized today that Abydos won't have a future if we stick with the Elders."

"So who chooses this future? The militia? There are enough people there who want to run things. Or the new merchants who only want to amass your Earth coins and use them to buy a tee-vee? The beggars in the streets? They'd like a tee-vee, too, but they don't want to work for it. What about the ones who think that those silver coins are Set's own invention—they ruined our nice, simple lives? There are a lot of them about, you know. It was so much easier having someone to tell them what to do—even if it was a Horus guard. They're still slaves—and there are plenty of would-be masters."

"So what's your problem?" Daniel demanded, stung. "Your family doesn't like the competition?"

Sha'uri's lips twisted as if she'd just tasted something bitter. "I'm sick to death with those little pinpricks of yours about the 'soft life' we had. If it was so good, why do you think we rose against Ra? We were slaves, and had to work just as hard as any of the other slaves on Abydos! If my father sat at the head of the welcome feasts, that merely meant he was the first target for any of Ra's people who came here."

She leaned into him, her finger digging into his

chest. "Do you remember your first night here? Our first night? We saw you as a strange figure, a golden man wearing the Eye of Ra. When Father noticed your interest in me, he . . . asked me to give myself to you." Sha'uri's voice quivered a little. "And I went, be-because I thought you were kind."

Her tone hardened. "But any of Ra's people, any who wore the golden masks, could have *demanded* me."

Daniel gaped. "Your father pimped you—?"

His whole head rocked from the force of her open-handed blow.

"You still don't understand!" she cried. "My father—all of us!—walked the edge of a knife serving Ra. And when Ra's anger fell on Nagada, it fell on my father first and most heavily."

Sha'uri was shouting now. "That was our 'easy life'—being a target while trying to protect the people. And if you ask me, what my father did was much harder than tearing everything down, like that gang behind Faizah wants to do."

"This has nothing to do with Faizah!" Daniel shouted back.

"Oh, no. You disrupt your classes and our translation schedule to go off with that bimbo—"

"You've been talking too much with Barbara Shore again," Daniel tried to interrupt.

Sha'uri paid no attention. "Just because she decided you should see a farm. She almost got you killed—"

"She saved my life!" Daniel protested.

"She's not the first one!" Sha'uri yelled louder. "Jack

O'Neil has saved your life! Skaara has saved your life! Kawalsky has probably saved your life! And dammit, *I've* saved your life, Daniel!" she shouted into his face. "But now a bullet has passed your ear, and none of that counts anymore."

"I'm fighting the same battle we fought then," Daniel said, storming off. "It's too bad you have other battles in mind." He turned back at the door. "I can be reached at my office." Then he left.

Sha'uri stood looking into the fire for a long while. Then she packed up a few items and headed for the market square. The Marines usually had a medical unit stationed there—part of its outreach program. She should be able to get a lift to the base on their Humvee.

I just hope Barbara Shore doesn't mind an unexpected guest, she thought as she left.

Untended, the fire quickly burned out and died.

Sitting in his office in yesterday's travel-stained robes, Daniel Jackson sipped a cup of herb tea and stared unseeing at the messages on his desk.

One, typewritten on crisp paper, was the weekly request from Barbara Shore to help translate the mountain of mystery files her people were getting out of the starship's computers.

The translation project—where Sha'uri and Faizah were working.

Fat chance of him turning up over *there* very soon.

The other notes were scrawled on scraps of paper

or on chalkboards, some in Abydan hieroglyphics. They mainly had to do with running the school. Somehow, he couldn't summon up much interest in them right now.

Daniel rested his face in his hands. Bad move. It reminded him he needed a shave.

He could probably get a quick wash at one of the halls of bathing. They'd even shave him there. The question was, where could he get hold of a toothbrush? Most of the Marines he had been halfway friendly with were gone. He'd annoyed most of the rest, thanks to his never-ending quest for condoms—

Well, he wouldn't need those anymore, it seemed.

If only Kawalsky were still around! The big guy was pretty decent, when he wasn't so busy being The Lieutenant. What did the enlisted men call him? Ell-tee?

One thing was certain. There was no way on Abydos he could talk to Jack O'Neil.

"Jackson"—he seemed to hear the colonel's voice—"do you just intend to make a career out of being a dork?"

"You can call me anything you want, Colonel, as long as you get me a toothbrush." Abruptly, Daniel realized this wasn't an imagined conversation. O'Neil's voice had come from the door, and he'd answered out loud.

A little shamefaced, Daniel turned to the door.

Colonel Jack O'Neil hadn't spiffed up for this personal call. He was wearing what Daniel considered the colonel's standard undress uniform—a tight black

T-shirt over a baggy pair of chocolate-chip fatigue pants. O'Neil's trademark black beret was rolled up and neatly stowed in a pocket.

He was still shaking his head over Daniel's brilliant response.

"As usual, out in the Twilight Zone," the Marine commander said. "I probably should be glad you didn't answer me in ancient Assyrian or something." His eyes narrowed. "If you're really serious about that toothbrush, you can go home and get your own. Your wife moved in with Barbara Shore last night. That's one of the things I want to talk to you about." He paused. "Personally and unofficially, of course."

"How else?" Daniel asked with an ironic smile.

"I found out about your wife this morning, when Dr. Shore informed me she'd be staying." O'Neil's jaw muscles tightened for a moment. "She thought it would be a simple matter of moving in a better cot and fixing up an extra helping in the mess tent. It's not as easy as all that, unfortunately. I'll have to explain why I've got a foreign national camping out in the middle of a high-security establishment. When Dr. Shore told me what had happened, we both agreed that you had to be a dork to the nth power."

"That sounds like a physicist," Daniel agreed.

"She called you a lot of other things, too," O'Neil assured him. "For myself, I was reminded of a current bit of military slang. You ever hear the phrase 'Foxtrot Bravo?' "

Daniel shrugged. "Can't say that I have."

"It's from the phonetic alphabet. We use it for clear identification of letters in radio transmissions," O'Neil explained with commendable patience. "A is Alpha, B is Bravo, C is Charlie, and so on. In Vietnam, Victor Charlie was the VC, Vietcong."

"And Foxtrot Bravo?" Daniel asked.

"It stands for fucking bastard—which is what you're being," O'Neil told him baldly. "You had quite an eventful time yesterday. First, one of my long-range patrols picks you up out playing the sheik with, and I quote the unofficial report, 'a prime piece of ass.' "

O'Neil's eyes seemed to be focused above his head. So why did Daniel feel like something the colonel wanted to scrape off his boot soles?

"I was going to admonish the officer in question until I discovered that Sha'uri had been engaged yesterday in her translating duties aboard the ship *Ra's Eye*. So the woman in question could have been a piece of ass—I wouldn't know. Although from the description, she sounds like the new addition to the translating staff, who seems to have some interesting political connections."

O'Neil made a brushing gesture with his hand. "Be that as it may. You returned to Nagada, where no sooner did you enter the city than you began publicly to berate and embarrass Kasuf, your father-in-law and, as far as I can figure out, the one decent political figure on this planet."

Now O'Neil's eyes met Daniel's. "By the way, your

wife didn't tell me about that. My staff comes complete with an intelligence section—and it would have been hard for them to miss your performance. Thanks to you, it's estimated that Kasuf's position vis-à-vis the Council of Elders has been seriously damaged. But that wasn't enough. You still managed an argument with your wife that succeeded in driving you both out of your own house."

O'Neil gave him a drill sergeant's stare. "I'm surprised you didn't manage to cap it all off with a drunken brawl somewhere," he said gently.

Daniel tried to meet O'Neil's scrutiny with a cool, disinterested stare, but his face felt tight and hot. Still, he tried to brazen it out. "Well, when you're on a roll . . ."

The colonel shook his head in wonder. "We'll have to invent a new term for you. Delta Foxtrot Bravo. *Dumb* fucking bastard."

His tone showed that any amusement he'd taken from this exchange was now gone. "My intel people say you're getting more into politics, Doctor—maybe over your head. I can't say, 'Don't do that.' You're a free agent. But I hope you're going in with your eyes open. The situation in Nagada—all over Abydos—is far more volatile than any college-campus 'isms' you may have experienced. Think about it. Your actions have already gotten people hurt. You may do worse."

"Why is everyone getting on my case?" Daniel exploded. "I finally had my nose rubbed in how wrong things have gotten around here. I'm trying to save the world."

"In my old job, I met dozens of guys, all of them trying to save the world," O'Neil told him coldly. "Some were decent men. A few were sincere. But the majority were so intent on saving the world, they didn't care who got hurt in the process. I had my orders. I killed them all."

"You were an assassin?" Daniel's voice sounded stupid in his own ears.

"Special ops. Spook work." For an instant Jack O'Neil's face was as remote as that of the late, unlamented, not-quite-human Ra.

Then a littlc feeling showed in his eyes. "That's why I'm very careful about politics, Jackson. I've been out on the sharp end."

CHAPTER 9
THE LIMITATIONS OF DIPLOMACY

Long after Jack O'Neil strode out of his office, Daniel Jackson sat at his desk, dissecting the conversation—and himself.

By the time he was finished, he had to admit that O'Neil's description was all too fitting. Delta Foxtrot Bravo, indeed! People who want to save the world shouldn't alienate two of their major allies in the fight. Nor was it a good idea to have O'Neil thinking he was a loose cannon.

First things first. He called in one of his students and sent him with a message to Kasuf, asking for a private meeting as soon as possible. If that came through, he'd have to go home, clean up, and change his grubby clothes.

Daniel's heart sank at the prospect of returning to an empty house. He wouldn't be able to stay there. Too much history and emotion was tied up in that little adobe hole in the wall. The happiest times of his life had been spent in there. Unfortunately, there were also some of his worst times. He hadn't fallen this low since he—and his theories—had been laughed off the stage by his fellow Egyptologists.

The StarGate had come through to rescue him that time. Now—damn it, he had a world to save. Once he'd guaranteed a future, he could rebuild a life with Sha'uri.

One thing was certain. He had to keep his distance with Faizah. In politics, appearances were just as important as reality.

And Daniel Jackson intended to get into politics in a big way.

Shaved, showered, teeth brushed, and dressed in a new robe, Daniel felt like a new man.

The question is, he thought worriedly, *can I convince Kasuf that this is the new Daniel Jackson?*

Kasuf had sent a message setting the meeting at his own house. On the way in, Daniel bumped into Skaara and received an unreadable look.

Perfect. Another ally squandered.

Kasuf sat stiffly on a pile of cushions, his eyes almost wary as Daniel entered. Every other time Daniel had been in this comfortably shabby room, there had been trays of sweetmeats around.

Today there wasn't a crumb to be found.

Daniel's stomach gave a hollow groan. Herb tea did not a breakfast make.

But Daniel had decided on the proper approach. There were enough precedents in Egyptian funerary painting—and in every old Jon Hall movie. Daniel sank to his knees and bowed low enough to konk his forehead on the floor. "Kasuf, Father of my wife—" Funny how that title seemed to hit him in the heart.

"I want to apologize for my foolishness yesterday. Perhaps the bullet that almost missed filled me with too much passion. I let my tongue run away with itself."

"It seems that is not the only thing that has run away on you," Kasuf said coldly.

Daniel rose up on his haunches, looking Kasuf right in the eye. "Sha'uri and I have had our troubles before this," he admitted. "My behavior yesterday did not help our problems. I love your daughter and hope to have a future with her. To make that happen we must have a future for this whole world. There are many points of view about where Abydos should go. The best thing might be to allow the people to air their differences—before they begin fighting."

Kasuf nodded. "What do you suggest?"

"In my own world, my country was founded in revolution. But the revolutionaries found they needed to invent a new way to govern themselves. They gathered leaders from all over the country in a grand convention to draft a blueprint for government—what we call our Constitution."

He looked at Kasuf, who seemed interested. "You could call together all the Elders on Abydos—farmers and miners—to discuss our problems. Perhaps," Daniel added, thinking of Faizah's group, "you could even invite representatives from the people. The job would be to hammer out a government that will protect the rights and freedom of everyone. I'll get you copies of my land's Constitution. It's been used as a model by many countries on Earth."

"You ask much of me," Kasuf said. "There will be difficulty—people will say I'm reaching for power, or trying to foist an Earth government on them."

Then the older man gave Daniel a slight smile. "But your idea holds out a goal for everyone to work toward. Get me copies of your people's Constitution. Let us start."

Thus, in addition to running a school and teaching, Daniel Jackson became a de facto constitutional lawyer. He translated the document into Abydan, and discussed the fine points with Kasuf and other Elders. It wasn't a perfect cultural fit. Kasuf himself was scandalized that it had taken Daniel's "perfect" government eighty years to abolish slavery.

But it gave the Abydans a basis for discussion on how to run their affairs. Even Jack O'Neil grudgingly admitted that was a good idea—even though Daniel was driving him crazy with requests for books on the Constitution and similar charters to come through the StarGate.

"I wish West would relax his sphincters and let some experts on law over here," Daniel complained one day. "It's hard enough translating this stuff without acting as an advocate for it. But I guess that's the military for you—they can blow stuff up or dig it up, but they're not really interested in building up."

"Right," O'Neil agreed sarcastically. "Like the way our occupation government helped Japan set up its constitution." He frowned. "I'll see if I can help round up any local talent on my staff."

"Oh—Army officers who don't do things the Marine way," Daniel joked.

"Hey, you're the one asking for help."

"We all need it." Daniel had turned deadly serious. "The situation is getting worse in Nagada—and everywhere else. It's like watching a pressure cooker build up steam. If we don't manage to vent things off . . ."

He looked at the colonel. "West hasn't said anything on what we're doing, has he?"

"No." O'Neil was surprised. "Why should he?"

"I was just thinking . . . a power vacuum here might just suit his needs right down to the ground."

"I think you're a little paranoid on the subject of the general, Jackson."

"Why?" Daniel demanded. "Isn't destabilizing regimes something that hush-hush types do?"

"First of all," O'Neil said from harsh experience, "you need a regime that's halfway stable to begin with. I can't see any advantage to the mining operation in having starving people shooting one another. So I'd say no, West isn't pulling any strings here." The colonel managed a wintry grin. "If he were, we'd be having political assassinations by now."

It took Daniel a moment to realize that O'Neil was grimly joking.

The colonel wasn't smiling as he went on. "But that doesn't mean West doesn't have contingency plans set up in case things get out of control. I think he'd be happy to see a peaceful, productive democracy take root here."

O'Neil tapped Daniel's shoulder with a heavy finger. "With the emphasis on *productive*. He's depending on regular shipments of that gold crystal they dig up in the mines. If he thought that supply line was threatened—well, let's just hope this constitutional convention of yours works."

For the first time since the initial, heady days of freedom, hope walked the streets of Nagada. Young Aha could actually feel it in the air as he marched his contingent of militiamen to the hall of the Elders.

Personally, he was sick of the petty corruption, the feeling that everything was sliding out of control. He'd joined the militia to defend Abydos, not to steal from armories and lean on businessmen. The Elders had tried to arrange food allotments for militia members on full duty. But week by week Aha had watched supplies dwindle as prices rose. Even as he'd risen to command a squad, he'd seen the growth of scams as his soldiers struggled to feed themselves.

Aha glanced back at the squad marching behind him. They were fundamentally good men, he knew.

But they were hungry—not just for food but for *leadership.*

And now, it seemed, they might be getting some.

Kasuf had managed to blandish, bully, or blackmail every Elder on Abydos to come to Nagada and discuss the planet's problems. But it was an open secret that the Elders would be working to create a real government to take care of those problems. Committees would be formed to listen to the viewpoints of every interested citizen.

Oh, there were always the few who viewed any change since the overthrow of slavery as a dreaded Urt-man conspiracy. But in the last few days before the Convention, as it was coming to be called, faction violence had fallen in the town.

Some of the delegates from the more remote areas were still en route. Their caravans were protected by special details of militia. The Earthman Marines were giving logistical support. And it didn't hurt that their huge tanks and patrols had eliminated the raider bands close to the city.

Today marked the second set of meetings—Aha heard people using the Earth word "conferences" between Kasuf and Nakeer. The pre–Convention connection between the two tribal leaders was the cause of much of the euphoria in town. If the chief Elders finally decided to get things done . . . .

Aha's command reached the market square before the hall of the Elders. There he found another contingent of militia, this one recruited from the farming communities. The two groups would form the security detail for the front of the building and serve as an honor guard for the tribal leaders meeting inside. All the guard posts in the area would be manned by mixed bands from the major factions.

Aha grinned as he recognized his opposite number in command of the other squad, a big, stolid farmer named Perre.

"What kept you city boys?" Perre inquired with pointed good nature. "You get lost in all these streets?"

"Nah," Aha joshed back. "We just don't get up with the crack of dawn like farmers. What do you do, getting up that early? Get naughty with the mastadges?"

The kidding had been an important social lubricant between the different tribal units thrust into working together. Miners screwed rocks, farmers had to be told to wipe mastadge shit off their sandals.

Aha and his men didn't mind the humor. In fact, he'd been a bit surprised at Perre's inventiveness in the subject of good-natured abuse.

Despite the farmboy's pointed reference to the time, both contingents were early. Aha let his men fall out and talk with the members of the other unit.

Soon enough, though, the men fell into formation and marched through the changing of the guard.

Once their people were on post and ready, Aha and Perre fell into conversation again.

"So," the farmer asked, "you think we'll see any . . . Earthmen today?"

He'd grown very careful pronouncing the foreign word, having quickly learned that "Urt-man" was the hick's term for the strangers who had come through the StarGate.

"We'll probably see Daniel turning up," Aha replied. "He's usually around Kasuf."

"Ah, him," Perre said dismissively. "He's just like one of us, anyway."

Aha broke into a crack of laughter. "Ha! How nice of you to notice. Most of you shitkickers came here thinking that Urt-men were nine feet tall and covered with hair all over, like mastadges."

Score one for the city boys.

"Nah, the Earthmen look like people. There's just some of them I'd like to look at more than others." Perre had a glint in his eye as he leaned toward Aha. "That hot little brunette we saw yesterday with the Earthman warrior. What did they call her? Babrazhor?"

"These Earth types have two names," Aha said. "Don't ask me why. But I know the one you mean. She's called Barbara. And she's supposed to be pretty hot stuff—pretty free with her hands, if you know what I mean."

The two men snapped to attention as a procession arrived at the square. Nakeer was staying at Kasuf's house, but the two leaders were holding their meetings in the official place of government.

Kasuf wore the formal red robes of the miners. Nakeer wore the green traditionally associated with his tribe. To Aha's eyes, the color seemed especially brilliant against the drab dun walls of Nagada.

Aha and Perre both saluted as the leaders left their honor guards and entered the building. The door guards snapped to action, pulling the portals open.

The big shots entered, the honor guard marched off, and life returned to business as usual.

Perre resumed their earlier conversation. After all, a good-looking woman was always pleasant to talk about. "Come on, city boy. Tell me more about this Barbara."

Aha happily passed along the barracks gossip on the flamboyant Dr. Shore. "You were lucky to see her in that blue outfit. Usually when she comes to town, she wears this baggy white thing that's almost like a tent." He lowered his voice. "Once, though, I saw her leave it open . . ."

"Get out!" exclaimed a scandalized Perre.

"Well, she had clothes under it—sort of. Some kind of white thing that covered her up to the neck—but it was tight across the breasts. And you could see her legs—up to here!"

Aha used his hand to indicate the thigh height of the doctor's shorts. Considering that they saw their women either robed or nude, it made for an exotic story. Perre begged for more.

"Most of the Earthers speak only a couple of our words," Aha went on. "But Barbara can sure curse and swear! For her feast of welcome she wore one of our robes and sandals. She stubbed her toe coming in here and muttered something that made Kasuf jump!"

Perre laughed appreciatively. "I wouldn't mind if she made *me* jump," he said. "Looks to me like it would be agreeable work."

"Sure," Aha scoffed. "I bet she'd be eager to play cow-mastadge to your bull."

"Give me a chance to find out about that hairy all over story," Perre said with a coarse laugh.

"Dream on, soldier."

"Anything's possible," Perre argued. "That Daniel yellow-hair wound up with Kasuf's daughter, didn't he? It's only fair that a worthy Abydan win an Earth-woman." He grinned. "Hey, I feel worthy."

"Then who am I to stand in the way of such an admirable quest?" Aha laid it on thick. "Go forth! And if you fail, I shall try—for the honor of Abydos!"

"I like that," Perre said. " 'For the honor of Abydos.' "

Their chuckling was abruptly cut off by the sound of gunfire—from within the hall.

Aha whipped around, ordering his second in command to hold the front of the building while detailing a section to accompany him inside. Perre was doing the same.

The mixed group burst inside, rifles at the ready. Aha's hands were sweaty on his weapon as he led the way to the feasting room, where the two leaders had intended to breakfast and discuss strategy.

Nakeer lay facedown on a pile of pillows, blood and brains soaking into the rich fabrics. Kasuf sat up amid a sort of throne of pillows. Aha's heart leapt, thinking his leader might be all right. Then he saw the wet stain across the chest of Kasuf's red robe.

The clatter of a door latch tore the attention of the two squad leaders from the still figures to the far end of the large room. A cowled figure in drab Abydan homespun leapt through the doorway into the darkness beyond. As he did, however, the escaping man's hood fell down . . . to reveal a shock of brilliant yellow hair.

Aha swore by several highly indecorous parts of Ra's anatomy.

"Urt-man bastard!" Perre roared. "He's killed Nakeer!"

Automatic fire from both men's rifles tore the heavy wooden portal as it swung shut.

With the hood of his robe up, Daniel Jackson hurried along through the streets of Nagada, tugged along by the clutch of a firm, warm hand. His mind was full of misgivings. The careful campaign to keep his relations with Faizah formal and public had crashed and burned this morning. She'd appeared in his office, literally rousted him out of his makeshift bed, and hauled him off to this unfamiliar quarter of the city.

Daniel's attempts to stop their headlong rush had gained him an incoherent, fragmentary story. If he understood the breathless tale, Faizah had overheard some compatriots of the Freedom party planning to disrupt the Convention.

"It's the extremists," she panted. "They say you're behind it all—we'll wind up with an Earth government."

"They'll have a chance to make their comments, like anyone else," Daniel said stupidly as they darted down a narrow, crooked alleyway.

"Our moderates have already signed up for that." Faizah's reply was overshadowed by the rattle of gunfire in the distance. "But these ones—I'm afraid they'll try to stop things before they even begin!"

Daniel grew more worried. Something was up. The gunfire was a dead giveaway. Maybe he shouldn't be stumbling into this situation weaponless, with only a girl to back him up. A company of Skaara's militiamen would be handy.

The headquarters of the Freedom faction lay in a ruinous adobe dump that made Daniel and Sha'uri's hole in the wall look palatial by comparison.

A trio of young men sat on threadbare pillows, eating dried fruit and bread as they conversed tensely. If they were into mayhem, they seemed only in the planning stages. Daniel noticed no weapons or guards present. Seeing the food, however, reminded him that he'd been shanghaied without even a taste of breakfast.

The tallest of the three conferees leapt up when Faizah burst through the door, yanked Daniel in, then latched the portal closed.

"Faizah!" the young fellow exclaimed, brushing spilled pillow stuffing off the rear of his robe. "What are you doing here?"

The guy looked like a younger, bearded, less nourished version of Gary Meyers. His eyes got wider as Daniel let down his hood, revealing his blond hair.

"And what in Ra's name are you doing here—with *him*?" the horrified leader of Freedom demanded.

"Djutmose, I had to bring him." Faizah was almost sobbing.

"Look, Djutmose," Daniel said, "I've worked too hard planning things for you to crash in and start wrecking it all."

He leaned in hard, thrusting his face nose to nose with the young man.

Djutmose recoiled as if Daniel were radioactive. "Crash in?" he gobbled. "Wreck it all?" With a visible effort he pulled himself together. "Earthman, I want no part of your plans."

"It's not for me, it's for Abydos," Daniel said. "Can you guarantee you won't go near Kasuf and Nakeer?"

"Why should I want to do that?" Djutmose stared at him, obviously afraid. "Especially after what you did to them!"

Daniel finally realized they seemed to be engaged in two different conversations. "Ammit eat you!" he swore in Abydan, "what are you talking about?"

A pale-faced Djutmose pointed to one of his companions. "Kasara just came in with the news."

Kasara ducked as if he expected to be shot.

Djutmose spoke in very gentle tones, the way one would talk to a raging psychopath. "Nakeer and Kasuf have both been killed. And you're being hunted as the murderer!"

CHAPTER 10
REVELATIONS

The guard station was a minor one—just two men stationed in a small side street off the market square. That didn't stop Skaara from turning up for inspection. He intended to keep every security person on his toes for the Convention. Too much was riding on the meetings to allow some fool even to disturb, much less disrupt the deliberations.

The pair of slouching guards—one miner, one farmer—snapped erect when he came down the street. Skaara stopped with them for a moment. "Keep your eyes open," he said. "I don't want a sandfly getting in—"

Gunfire erupted. It seemed to come from the direction of the council hall. Both guards took a step toward the disturbance, their rifles leveled.

"No!" Skaara snapped. "Stay here. No one comes in or out through this street. Wait for orders. I'll check this out."

He hadn't brought a rifle because, like everything in his improvised army, they were in short supply. But he had tucked one of the smaller weapons—a pistol—into his belt.

Skaara waited until he reached the square before he broke into a run. A crowd was gathering—he'd have to use the honor guard at the door to break them up. But his sentries were bunched in the doorway as some of the council servants tried to push their way out.

"It's the Urt-man!" a cook screamed, her voice hysterical. "He's killed Kasuf and Nakeer!"

A low moan shook through the assemblage. Some crowded closer, hoping for a show. Others began to break away, to pass the news.

Skaara cursed. He'd have to send out runners to all the guard posts. If word of this got out, with the city in its present mood, it would be like setting a torch to tinder.

He pushed his way to the entrance and took command. "Where are the squad leaders?" he demanded.

One of the second-line commanders answered. "Aha and Perre went in at the first shooting."

Skaara frowned. He hadn't heard that. "Guard the door," he ordered. No one goes in or out until I say otherwise. That includes them." He directed a bullying glare at the bawling servants. "And send a runner to the other guard posts. I don't want wild rumors circulating."

"It's the truth!" the cook yelled. "I came in after the warriors! There was blood all over!"

He whirled on the woman. "Shut up!" he snapped.

Then Skaara pushed inside. A few of the servants

pointed the way to the feasting chamber, as if he'd never been there before. He pushed open the main door—and found himself looking down a rifle barrel.

"Sir!" The warrior, a farmer recruit named Perre, raised his weapon. "Aha took most of the men to chase the assassin. I figured I'd do more good here, on guard."

The damned cook had been right with most of her screaming. Nakeer was indeed dead, his head blasted with several bullets. There was indeed blood around, most of it leaking from his father. But Kasuf was still alive, although his face was gray.

"Father." Skaara reached out to Kasuf, only to realize that while his father's eyes were open, they were unseeing.

A couple of the more level-headed servants were striving to stanch his wound. Skaara couldn't tell if their fussing was actually doing any good.

Steeling himself, he turned to other problems. "What's this I hear about an Earthman making the attack?" he demanded.

Perre shrugged. "I saw the yellow-hair running away. He left this behind."

The squad leader held up a pistol, nearly the twin to the one Skaara carried.

A chill invaded Skaara's spine. Sha'uri had used a weapon like that, both in the fighting against Ra and in the disabled starcraft.

He pushed the thought away. "Which way did Aha give chase?"

Perre pointed at a side exit, the door chewed up by rifle bullets. That must have been the gunfire that attracted him.

First things first. Leaving Perre on guard, Skaara returned to the front door. The secondary squad leaders were getting nervous as the crowd got larger. The more their numbers grew, the uglier the group's mood became.

"Let us in there!" a fat farmer shouted. From the green he was wearing, he was probably one of the farm clan Elders. "We want to see for ourselves."

Skaara pushed into the rank of militiamen screening the door. In a loud, clear voice he said, "If this mob tries to push its way in, I want that man shot first!" He pointed at the fat bellower.

"Do you know who I am?" the Elder blustered. But the color was leaving his reddish face.

"Right now you're a troublemaker—and a target," Skaara told him. "There's nothing very pleasant to see inside. Nakeer has been killed, but Kasuf lives. The one who attacked them is being pursued."

The crowd had remained silent, stunned, for that much. Now a madness of questions burst forth.

The only one Skaara dealt with was the cry from the targeted Elder. "Is it true that the Urt-man did it?"

Skaara shook his head. "I don't know who fired the shots," he said. "And I won't until the assassin is caught."

He pushed off into the crowd. People plucked at him, hoping for more details or explanations. Skaara had time to give neither. He pushed ruthlessly for the open space at the end of the square, with an important destination in mind.

Displaced from the market square by the political hoorah going on there, Dr. Terrance Destin sat under an awning, his Humvee filled with medical supplies, waiting for patients. The inoculation business was slow today. Maybe there was a parade or something.

Destin heard gunshots in the distance, but paid them little heed. He'd served in the Gulf, where the locals celebrated everything from military victories to weddings by emptying a magazine into the air. Maybe he ought to get set up to treat victims of Stray Bullet Syndrome . . .

A young guy—a kid, really—came racing down the street. With his youth and the dreadlocks streaming back from his face, Destin would have taken him for some sort of gangbanger back home. On beautiful Abydos, however, the kid could turn out to be a company officer in the home guard they'd erected for themselves.

In a swirl of robes the kid skidded to a stop when he spotted Destin's Humvee. "You're a medic?" he said in surprisingly passable English. This must be one of Daniel Jackson's graduate students.

The young doctor nodded, glad he didn't have to use his fractured Abydan phrases like "where does it hurt?"

"You've got to come with me."

Looking more closely, Destin realized the kid was under a lot of stress. The morning heat had yet to come, and he already had a sheen of sweat on his face.

"Look, I can't leave this." Destin nodded toward the Humvee. The locals had started getting very light-fingered as hunger raised its ugly head. Destin didn't want to be known as the founder of the Abydos drug trade.

The kid produced a Beretta 9mm pistol from his belt and pointed it at Destin's nose. "Bring the Humvee. You come. Now," he demanded, losing his English.

Directing the Navy doctor through the streets at gunpoint, Skaara could feel the sweat dripping between his shoulder blades. They *had* to be in time!

The closer they came to the market square and the council building, the more the streets were clogged with onlookers. A nasty buzz ran through the Abydans when they saw the Earthman. Destin went pale.

Skaara waved his pistol and shouted. The people recognized their militia leader and grudgingly parted.

They'd almost reached the hall when Skaara heard the distant explosion of a hand grenade. It came from the *opposite* direction of the assassin's escape path.

Skaara grew cold. The outbreak he feared was already beginning. There was so, so much to do.

But he had to handle this first. He ordered the doctor to get his medical bag and marched him past the guards and into the feasting chamber.

From the look on Destin's face, he recognized the departed Nakeer and the wounded Kasuf.

"This is bad," the doctor muttered.

"Can you help my father?" Skaara tightly demanded.

Destin gave him a grim smile. "Hey, kid, I learned my trade in a shoot-and-stab emergency room. I'll get your dad patched up so we can get him to some *real* help."

The doctor knelt beside Kasuf, ordering the kitchen people in broken Abydan to start boiling water.

Skaara turned back toward the door. He'd just have to hope. . . .

In the hall of the StarGate, located in the midst of the Marine base camp, Sergeant Ernest Brubaker was getting a little bored of the scenery. There were only so many times you could watch the expression on a truck driver's face as they came out of the rippling lens and discovered themselves in a kill zone.

Since those Horus guys had come through the gate, security around the StarGate had been enhanced by a couple of orders of magnitude. The technicians had been moved into improved positions, and so had the gate guards. The area in front of the gate, which meant the ramp leading directly up to the glittering golden torus, was enclosed in four rings of claymore mines.

With one squeeze on a handle, the innocent-looking little plastic boxes could spew a hail of ball bearings through an arc of sixty degrees. Being on the receiving end would be like taking the mother of all shotgun blasts. At first it had been interesting to see which drivers had encountered claymores in the past. They would generally blanch when they realized what they were facing. Then those in the know would gingerly drive their way out of the death trap.

There had been lots of complaints from the Earth side of the StarGate that Colonel O'Neil was slowing the flow of quartz crystal to a crawl, but the Old Man was adamant. No transgressors were coming through the StarGate ever again.

So, when the sound-and-light show in the big gold donut started up again, Brubaker just stifled a yawn. But the silhouette that finally appeared in the rippling gossamer energy field was no truck. It was people—a hell of a lot of people, taller than normal humans because they were wearing oversized hawk-masks.

"Incoming!" Brubaker yelled, hitting the idiot button that started an *ah-OOO-gah!* blat of sirens through the pyramid complex, as well as warning the officer of the guard.

Brubaker's other hand darted to the switch that triggered the first wave of claymores. The crash of the curved plastic explosive charges detonated in counterpoint to the three-round bursts from the riflemen of Brubaker's guard detachment.

The invaders hesitated, irresolute, right in the middle of the kill zone. Claymores cut fan-shaped windrows through the packed mass of intruders. The survivors staggered around as the riflemen went to single, aimed shots.

"Surrender, you dumb bastards!" Brubaker almost begged. It was like a turkey shoot. Dead Horus guards lay mounded in front of the glowing portal.

Then the strange, almost musical note sounded again, energy gushed from the ring, and the force field formed anew. A fresh wave of masked figures stumbled forth.

Brubaker stabbed the control for the next ring of claymores. His men frantically slammed new magazines into their rifles. The slaughter started all over again, amplified as more squads rushed in to add their firepower.

When it was over, the hall was almost echoingly silent. Dead enemies lay piled waist-deep on the access ramp.

The hammering finally left Brubaker's ears. His hands were still shaking from the adrenaline surge.

"Sarge, why did they stay bunched up like that while we shot the piss out of 'em?" one of his men asked.

These were, after all, the same warriors who'd kicked major ass on the recon team and later on the expeditionary force. Maybe these guys had had an extra-bad trip through the StarGate. Brubaker's passage hadn't been any picnic. He'd heard fellow Marines refer to the transit as the "puke chute."

Or perhaps the invaders had just never encountered terrible resistance—or such concentrated fire.

Glancing around, the sergeant realized that none of his comrades had even been hit.

Brubaker licked his dry lips and tried to shape them into a grin. "Maybe," he suggested, "that was the Army arm of the Horus guards."

The men laughed, but no eyes left the StarGate. Was it going to cycle again and spill out a new crop of lambs for the slaughter?

Minutes passed, and Brubaker felt the familiar letdown that came after combat. An adrenaline rush used up the body's resources. When it passed . . .

"We ought to get up there and check," he finally said. "Some of them might still be alive."

He detailed a team for the gruesome task of examining the shredded bodies. It was enough to make hardened veterans pale. But the searchers turned from wading among the corpses and pierced Brubaker with shocked eyes.

"Sarge, they're old men," the corporal in charge faltered.

"And women," another Marine added.

"These masks"—one of the searchers crushed a hawk shape in his fingers—"They're made out of, like, aluminum foil."

But it was the corporal who reached the final, damning realization. "And *they were all unarmed*!"

The defenders stood frozen in awful silence. Brubaker heard one of the younger kids retching.

Then the StarGate began to cycle again.

"Get out! Get out of there!" Brubaker screamed.

It was like one of those slow-motion nightmares. The men were drained by combat and still unstrung form their shattering discovery. They were sinking into the mounded dead like kids on a snowbank.

They tried to scramble away, but the hawk-masked Horus guards were materializing behind them.

These were the real thing, moving with agility and strength to engage the guards with their blast-lances.

And Brubaker couldn't trigger the claymores with his own people in the kill zone.

"Bastards!" he cursed, snatching up his own rifle. "Scum-sucking—"

A bolt from a Horus guard vaulting off the heap of dead caught him in the face.

In the golden halls of the downed starship, militiamen stirred fearfully behind their barricades. The improvised fortifications had been raised to bar the Urt-men from the interior of the vessel. Now the strangers seemed to roam the ship at will, trying to understand its mysteries. But the guards and most of the barriers still remained.

Baki, Skaara's deputy at the ship, knew that the belching sound echoing down the corridors was the Earthmen's warning of an attack coming through the StarGate.

He'd heard gunfire, explosions, then a ragged cheer rang out. Moments later, the sounds of combat reverberated again. Then came a long silence.

Baki finally sent one of his men to see what was going on.

The runner had just reached the entrance to the StarGate pyramid when a new combat cacophony broke out. This time the sound of rifles blended—then was overwhelmed—by the crash of blast-lances.

Baki's messenger came dashing back into view seconds after he'd entered the pyramid. The man's eyes were wide with fear as he ran down the hall. Then the hawk-masks appeared in the opening behind him. . . .

"We have to help the Earthmen," Baki cried from his vantage point atop the barricade. He leaned into the corridor to gather his men—

And a blast-bolt from behind jolted his lifeless body down into the hallway.

Gunshots a couple of blocks away jolted the tense silence in the house. "You're really going to go out into that?" Wa'bet asked her husband.

Ged nodded, carefully working the magazine into his M-16. Desert heat had warped the thin metal, making the fit difficult.

Frankly, Ged was just as glad to keep his attention on his work. He didn't want to have to see his young wife, her face too thin, her belly great with child. Wa'bet's accusing eyes were swollen, too, from furious tears.

"We have to impose order," he said. "Skaara has

called out all the militia. I'm one of the trusted men. That's why I have the rifle."

"Can't you give the gun to one of the others?" Wa'bet begged.

Ged finally looked at her. "No," he said.

He stepped out of his door, the rifle slung over his shoulder. One look told him he'd delayed too long. His neighbors were gathered in the middle of the street, blocking the way. He recognized Hormose, who tooled the leather harnesses for mastadges, and Anpu the silversmith.

"Why are you leaving us defenseless?" Anpu demanded. "There were thieves in the lesser market. A man shot them."

"I've been called," Ged replied. "You heard the criers."

"So did the thieves," Hormose said.

"We have valuables to protect," Anpu whined.

"Then call whoever shot the men in the lesser market," Ged said impatiently. "Or stay gathered out here until the militia—"

"I hear the warriors are fighting among themselves!" a shrill voice cut him off.

"What if someone else comes with a gun?"

"You can't leave us!"

Before Ged could move, the crowd engulfed him like an amoeba. For a while a little epicenter of resistance marked his location. Then it disappeared.

A bloody hand raised the rifle. "I have it!" Anpu shouted. "Now we'll be safe!"

Reddish plumes rose among the buildings as Skaara led his riot squad down the street. Some fool had just tried to kill them, but had used a smoke grenade instead of a fragmentation weapon.

Skaara shuddered for a moment. But for that error . . .

He forced his mind to other matters, tiredly sorting through reports. He'd led these, his most trusted men, back and forth through the city, quashing chaos wherever it had raised its head.

Unfortunately, chaos had more heads than he had men. Too many of his followers hadn't come out at his call, or hadn't made it to him. After losses Skaara had little more than half the men he'd used to quell the protesters a few weeks ago.

His men looked tired. Some were bruised or bloody, walking wounded. A number had shattered rifle butts. Reluctantly, Skaara had ended hand-to-hand intervention. His people fired if they were fired upon. Several shots had disposed of the inept bomb thrower.

Skaara came to a decision. "We're going back to headquarters," he announced.

The neighborhood around the building that housed the militia's small logistical detail was quiet. But as he entered the headquarters, Skaara could smell cordite—and blood.

Silently, with hand signals, he deployed his troops. They burst into the room Skaara used as an office to find two of his most trusted men dead on the floor, and four strangers trying to destroy the padlock Jack O'Neil had given him to protect the militia's blast-lances.

Skaara decided there was no benefit to be gained from interrogating any of these. "No quarter," he yelled, and his men took care of the rest.

As his men cleared the room of bodies, Skaara knelt over the mangled lock and inserted the key. He opened the heavy wooden door and made a quick count of his energy-weapon assets. "As I thought," he said. "We have just enough to go around."

Daniel Jackson walked with his shoulders hunched and the hood of his robe pulled low over his face. He didn't want anyone to see or recognize him. And he didn't want to see what was happening to Nagada.

After Djutmose and the young politicians of the Freedom faction had flatly refused to help him, Daniel and Faizah had sallied forth to find some reasonable figure and start proving Daniel's innocence.

But reason was in very short supply in Nagada that day.

There were plenty of mobs looking for Urt-men to kill. People were looting and stealing from one another. Militia units with their blood up were firing into crowds or at each other. The only unifying point among them seemed to be a burning desire to string up anybody with blond hair.

They'd wandered about for a while, but as the streets had grown more and more dangerous, Faizah had finally suggested a possible hiding place.

She'd taken them on a tortuous route to avoid burning buildings, firefights, and rooftop snipers. At last they arrived, footsore and weary, in an area that seemed to specialize in small, rundown warehouses.

Their destination had a door secured not by a lock but by a thin rope with a complicated knot. Faizah examined the intricate loops, then nodded in satisfaction. "I tied that. No one else has been here."

She deftly undid her signature lock knot and led him inside a long, dark room. A lamp stood on a shoulder-length shelf by the door. She lit it, barred the outer door shut, then led him deeper into the gloom.

In the flickering circle of light thrown by the lamp he could see urns and baskets. The air had a spicy tang to it.

Faizah brought him to a wooden loft structure built out over a series of jars large enough to hide the Forty thieves. She pointed to a ladder. "Up here."

Daniel climbed while Faizah followed him up with the lamp. They arrived at a platform with about five feet of head room. The little loft was equipped with all the comforts a student could desire—pillows, bedding, and, Daniel was amused to note, a couple of packages of MRE's.

"What is this?" he asked.

Sitting with her feet tucked under her, Faizah shrugged. "Sometimes it's nice to have someplace where you can get away."

Knowing Faizah, Daniel wouldn't be surprised if she'd set up this little passion pit all by herself.

All Daniel wanted to do was fall asleep, but Faizah snuggled beside him. "So tense!" she said, her hand going to unkink the muscles in his shoulder. That led to a neck rub, and a back rub.

"Faizah," he said hoarsely, trying to put his foot down. But he was so tired, so empty . . .

"It's been so unfair for you," Faizah murmured in his ear. As she moved in behind him, kneading Daniel's loosening muscles, he realized her robe must have magically opened. Warm flesh seemed to burn into his back through his robe.

Then she was undoing the fastenings at his throat, loosening his robe.

"What's this?" she said, finding the chain around his neck.

"It's a gift from an old friend back home." Daniel closed his eyes as Faizah gathered in the necklace. "It was found with the Earth StarGate—"

"The Eye of Ra!" Faizah's voice had a wholly different timbre when she held the pendant in her hand. "Not only Ra's symbol—it's Ra's medallion!"

Daniel's eyes opened. How could this country girl identify something that was ten thousand years old?

"Fai—" he began.

But the fingers that had been easing muscles were suddenly pinching pressure points.

Blackness descended on Daniel Jackson in a wave.

CHAPTER 11
KEY QUESTIONS

The woman known as Faizah let the unconscious Daniel Jackson slump to the loft floor as she continued to examine the medallion he wore. She had seen it often enough around Ra's neck in the days of the First Time, in procession with the other gods, in attendance at Ra's throne room . . . from the times she'd shared Ra's bed.

All of Faizah's wide-eyed, youthful mannerisms faded from the beautiful face. She was Hathor again.

How ironic! In all the time I spent among my enemies, preparing them for the slaughter, I discover this just before the death stroke.

Hathor thought back to a night in the Nile valley, millennia before, when she had discovered that this Eye of Ra was more than a mere decoration.

She had gone to offer herself to the god king when she found Ra leaving his chambers with an unwontedly surreptitious air. So she had followed him out of the palace, into the night, to the place of the StarGate.

There he had removed the medallion from his

throat and pressed it to the heart of one of the constellations that decorated the huge ring. The great torus had revolved of its own accord, each of the chevrons automatically falling into place. But they were not lining up with the constellation coordinates carved into the glowing crystal!

The medallion was a special key, coding the StarGate to a destination it would never reach in its normal operation!

A swirl of energy had gouted from the ring, stabilizing into the familiar gateway. Ra had vanished within.

Hathor had not dared to follow. The danger of discovery was too great, and Ra always thought that the best protector of his secrets was the cold, cruel grave.

But Hathor had always remembered the incident, the secret destination. And now chance had dropped the key right into her hands.

"I wish to God I'd never heard of *Ra's Eye*!" Barbara Shore shouted, her voice echoing through the engine room of the out-of-commission starship. Standing beside her, Sha'uri glanced from the gleaming crystal constructions of the actual engines to the copy of an incomprehensible schematic. Peter Auchinloss had discovered some sort of training programs in the ship's computers. But even when Sha'uri managed to translate the symbols, Barbara was swearing.

"So this junk here just refers to what the *readings* should be on the board?" The physicist tapped a disgusted finger on the section Sha'uri had laboriously succeeded in making some sense of.

"It looks that way," the young Abydan woman admitted.

"What a bunch of crap," Barbara complained. "Not what you did, but what it *means*. I thought maybe we'd get some idea of the underlying principles behind these engines. But this is cookbook science. It's like a recipe—'add yeast to the batter, and it will rise.' But it doesn't explain *why* the batter rises."

"Should we work on this some more?" Sha'uri asked.

"Nah. It will just tell us what buttons to push to make the ship lift off. Unless we find a program that tells us how to fix what's wrong, or how to ask the ship to tell us what's wrong, this stuff is useless."

Still, Barbara pored over the copy. "If we just knew what more of these squiggles meant. I wish Daniel were around here. Or even Faizah. That girl is a pain in the ass, but you'd almost think she'd been reading this stuff before."

Sha'uri stood so still that Barbara looked up. "Sorry, darlin'. I know neither of those names makes you really happy right now."

With a nod, Sha'uri gathered up their papers. "I think it must be impossible for things to get much worse right now."

A voice echoed down the huge, virtually deserted engineering section. "Sha'uri! Sha'uri, are you down here?"

"Who's that?" Sha'uri called back.

A young militiaman came in, his bearing stiff and uneasy. "Baki sent me."

Sha'uri nodded. Baki was one of Skaara's friends.

"We received word on the radio." The messenger pronounced the unfamiliar word carefully. "It said—" he gulped. "It said Nakeer has been shot. So has Kasuf."

"My father!" Sha'uri fought a weird, giddy feeling, as if the ground had been cut out from beneath her feet. Her face hardened. "Who did this?"

The messenger wouldn't look at her face. "The name they said," he temporized, "is Daniel—your husband."

The rest of the message seemed so unreal that this announcement seemed like a fantasy. Finally, she said to Barbara, "Something is very wrong."

After hearing Sha'uri's explanation, the physicist nodded. "And it'll take a trip into town to find out what the hell's going on."

Moving like a sleepwalker, Sha'uri followed the others toward the main ground-level corridors. She would talk to Lieutenant Charlton about getting a lift to Nagada. Where would her father be? Would they perhaps bring him to the camp, to the hospital here? Perhaps Charlton could help her get some answers. . . .

She was so preoccupied, she never even heard the hooting of the alarms in the distance.

"Hey," Barbara said, abruptly stopping. "That's the

attack warning. There wasn't any test scheduled for today." She turned to Sha'uri. "Was there?"

The messenger swallowed loudly when she referred the question to him.

They got their answer a moment later in the crackle of gunfire.

"I think we'd better get our asses in gear," Barbara announced.

They arrived at one of the barricaded side passages off the main hall and heard the militiamen there shrilling in panic. "Baki is dead! Who commands now?"

"What do we do?"

"Our orders are to hold this post."

One man, who'd climbed up on the barrier for a look outside, shouted, "The hawk-heads come! Quick! What do we do?"

Out in the hall some Abydans gave one answer. They were pounding toward the StarGate pyramid, firing rifles and blast-lances.

The women climbed the makeshift fortification—most of its components were blasted debris dragged in from outside. It seemed the impromptu counter-attack had swept back the Horus Guards. At least none were in sight.

Sha'uri stared in consternation, however, at the number of militiamen who hadn't joined the fight.

"Where are you going?" the contentious would-be warriors behind her called as Sha'uri began climbing down into the hall below. Barbara moved to join her.

"Hey, it's a woman!"

"The killer's wife!"

"An Earth woman!"

The messenger joined them, not sure what he should be doing.

Sha'uri shouted down the hall, "Why aren't you joining the fight? Do you want to stand here in little packets until the hawk-heads come to gobble you up?"

"It's an Urt-man plot to draw us away!" a voice cried in rich farmer dialect. "Like the way your Urt-man husband killed Nakeer!"

"Kill the traitor bitch!"

"Kill the Urt-man woman!"

The other sentiments on what should be done to them were even uglier.

Barbara leaned forward. "Those guys by the front door don't sound too friendly," she said in a low voice. "There are still Marines in there." She nodded toward the StarGate pyramid, where ripples of gunfire still resounded.

"I think I can trust them more," Sha'uri said. Her fellow Abydans had degenerated to shooting at one another from their barricades.

The women ran for the entrance to the pyramid. The messenger disappeared, felled by a stray blast-bolt.

Just as they reached the torn stone entrance, a pair of combatants reeled into sight. A Marine officer and a Horus guard both clung to the shaft of a blast-lance, wrestling for control of the weapon.

Sha'uri darted forward, seeing the Marine's holstered sidearm. She pulled out the pistol, making the Marine totter. The Horus guard yanked his lance free, leveled, and fired. The Earthman went down. But before the warrior could turn, Sha'uri put two bullets into his chest from the side.

Barbara Shore froze, staring big-eyed at the two dead men.

Sha'uri shoved the pistol into the scientist's hand and scooped up the blast-lance. "If you're going to throw up, do it later. We have to find help now."

The stone hallways only echoed worse. Sha'uri had no idea how the battle was going. Four Marines came hustling up the final incline that led to the spaceship entrance. Two were all but carrying a wounded comrade. His uniform was still smoldering from a blast-bolt.

"Ladies, you're heading the wrong way," the Marine noncom leading the group said. "In about two seconds, more hawk-headed bastards than you ever saw in your life will be storming up here."

"What about the militia who came charging in?" Sha'uri demanded.

"Horus guards suckered them in, then cut them up," the Marine replied, shepherding the women ahead as they climbed the incline. "We were able to use the distraction to break contact. What's left of our people are pinned down. These guys have the StarGate, and they're massing troops to break out."

They reached the main corridor of the grounded

spacecraft, now full of smoke from fires ignited by internecine blast-lance attacks. Miners and farmers cursed at one another as they fired.

The noncom paused. The only way out of the ship was a hopeless battle zone. Sha'uri dashed to the first cross corridor. It was used as a checkpoint for the technical staff. The barrier was open, and there were no guards.

"This way," Sha'uri called. "If we can't get out, we'll have to go up." She turned to Barbara Shore. "You have people working on the upper levels, especially the command deck."

The Marine looked dubiously from his wounded man to the empty corridor. "They'll be able to come after us," he warned.

"I know," Sha'uri told him. "I've done it myself." She bared her teeth in what might be mistaken for a smile. "But we can make it hard for them."

The wounded Marine stopped climbing halfway up the first flight of stairs.

"Isn't there an elevator?" the worried noncom demanded.

"You might just as well hope that this damned thing could fly us home," Barbara Shore said. "It's a broke-down hunk of junk!"

After five flights of being carried, the wounded man's head lolled. Only the whites of his eyes showed.

"He ain't breathing," one Marine announced.

"Carry on," came the order. "We don't abandon our own."

"You'll have to, unless you want the Horus guards to catch up with us," Sha'uri said.

"I'm not going to leave him out for those bastards," the noncom doggedly insisted.

"All right." Barbara Shore poked her head out to check the deck they were passing. "Let's see if I remember this." She approached an apparently blank wall. Her fingers danced over a set of nearly invisible studs set in the wall. The seemingly solid crystal shifted to create an oblong port, revealing some sort of circuit board. There was just enough space to accommodate the dead Marine.

The noncom stared at her. "How—"

"My job is to discover how this thing works," Barbara said. "Some things we've figured out. Now, put him in there and mark the spot." Her voice was ragged as she glanced down the stairwell. "Just hurry!"

They settled into the stiff climb to the levels where Barbara's technical teams were working. Auchinloss and some military computer techs were at work in what looked like a classroom on a dormitory level. People got thicker up toward the top—translators, technicians, and military techs.

From the next level up, they heard a yell and the distinctive discharge of a blast-lance. The Marines readied their weapons. Barbara carried the dead man's rifle. Sha'uri hefted her blast-lance as they charged up the stairway.

It appeared to be a classic meeting engagement—the computer people coming down the stairs, a squad of Horus guards ascending. The Horuses had spotted the Earthers and charged across the deck, trying to catch and contain them.

They weren't prepared for a flank attack from another stairwell.

Caught in a crossfire, they had tried to turn on Sha'uri's party, only to be cut down by her blast-lance.

Auchinloss and his people were glad to see some human faces—a field telephone warning from below had been cut off in mid-sentence. They were less happy facing the fact that they were cut off.

Sha'uri busied herself collecting blast-lances from the dead Horuses.

"We'll need every weapon we can get," she said.

"God bless Jack O'Neil for insisting that our technicians carry combat gear," Barbara said.

"That was really something," a fresh-faced Army tech burst out. "I shot one of those guys."

"Now you know how it feels to be a Marine," another tech said, obviously stating his service. "We're supposed to be riflemen first, button pushers second."

"Congratulations are fine—later." Sha'uri handed out her scavenged weapons. "But we have to hurry now."

"Why? We won!" the fresh-faced kid said.

"We beat one squad—we don't know if there are others coming."

Sha'uri tapped a dead guard's helmet. "They have communicators in these—so their friends already know about us."

"That beggar said he spotted a yellow-haired man around here." Skaara frowned. "So why would he ply his trade in such an empty area?"

"And why wouldn't he stay with us?" one of the riot squad added.

Skaara nodded. "There's the warehouse. How convenient! The door is even partway open."

The squad spread out. "There's no other way in," his lieutenant, Sermont, reported. "Do we rush it?"

"I think that's what we're being asked to do," Skaara replied. "No. We'll try a flash-bang. That may be effective no matter *what* may be lurking in there."

A blast-bolt shattered adobe as one of the militiamen kicked in the door and tossed the grenade.

After the concussion grenade went off, blast-bolts began flying wildly. Four of Skaara's special squad stormed in. Moments later, one of them returned. "You'd better see this," he said.

Skaara entered to find one man lighting an oil lamp. The other two were up in a wooden loft area, working to suppress a smoldering blaze.

One of the firefighters beckoned him. A Horus guard lay outstretched, dead. His blast-lance had already been appropriated.

"I think we've finally found one of those infiltrators Colonel O'Neil was after," Skaara said.

One of his men shifted some of the bedding in the loft to smother the blaze. Skaara suddenly called for the lamp. He examined the objects the bedding shift had revealed.

The first was an Earth-style wallet, with a driver's license for Daniel Jackson. There was even an unflattering photo of him.

As for the rest, they were items Daniel usually carried around on his person—nail clippers, an automatic pencil, keys whose locks could be found only on the other side of the StarGate.

"This is everything he'd carry except for his glasses," Skaara said. "Daniel was definitely here."

"What was he doing with this one?" One of the warriors nudged the dead Horus guard with his toe.

"I'm more troubled about who else was with him," Skaara said.

There was discarded women's clothing all around. He could smell a heady perfume from it.

The same perfume had rubbed off on the rumpled bedding.

CHAPTER 12
HOLDING ACTIONS

Jack O'Neil slammed his last magazine into the submachine gun he carried. That was the problem with going with a non-issue weapon. When this went dry, he'd have to find himself a rifle.

Unfortunately, there were plenty to go around. Too many dead men were spread over the base camp. The smells of combat were in the air—smoke, cordite, blood, voided bladders and bowels . . . and the cooked-meat smell of human flesh exposed to blast-bolts.

The bad taste in his mouth, however, came from the cold little voices whispering in the back of his mind. And the word they were whispering was *defeat*.

Since his arrival on Abydos, it seemed the other side had always managed to grab the edge. His exploration team took shelter in the StarGate pyramid—Ra's people beamed down and nailed them. He built a base around the StarGate to protect it—Hathor landed a huge spaceship to cut off the pyramid completely.

Battle intelligence seemed to indicate that the enemy forces, while superb, were small. So how could this seemingly inexhaustible river of Horus guards come pouring out of the StarGate?

When the Klaxons indicating an attack through the StarGate had begun to blat, O'Neil had scarcely believed it. He'd thought he'd made the transit room too damned expensive for an enemy to storm through.

He'd never find out what went wrong. The people who'd been in that room were dead.

Even as troops moved into positions to cover the entrance to the spaceship *Ra's Eye*, most of the men figured there was some kind of problem among the Abydans. That seemed justified when the brown-cloaked figures came running from the huge airlock.

But masked, kilted figures had emerged in pursuit.

The militiamen never made it to the safety of the American lines. They'd been cut down by the blast-lances of the Horus guards.

O'Neil's men had given a good account of themselves, driving the enemy back. But the Earthers were understandably skittish about landing anything too heavy in the doorway of their only route home.

This wasn't a situation where the Americans could pound the enemy with rockets and artillery to weaken their hold on a position. It would be a Pyrhhic victory if such a bombardment managed to collapse the damned pyramid on top of the StarGate.

But the Horus guards couldn't be allowed to remain where they were. They held a military man's dream—

a tactically defensive position that achieved a strategically offensive purpose.

O'Neil had to regain the StarGate, or his forces would die on the vine, deprived of the supplies a modern military force required.

The last time around, he had managed to force entry by a weak frontal attack against an even weaker enemy. This time he'd been loaded for bear.

But so had the other side.

His attack had been shattered, not from the door, but from the wrecked hangar dock high up in the spaceship. Horus guards—hundreds of them—had used the blown-open deck as a firing platform on the advancing ground troops.

When every available mortar, artillery piece, and tank in the camp had leveled suppression fire at the summit of the ship, the Horuses had launched a counterpunch on the ground. They'd cut through the remnants of the attack force, then crashed into O'Neil's defensive perimeter . . . and breached it.

Up close and personal, energy weapons beat rifles. They sliced through mortar barrels. And if the handheld blast-lance took too long to burn through the armor on an M1A2, they proved horribly effective against the treads—and the tank's weapons.

And, as one harassed sergeant put it, "There's just too many of the bird-headed bastards."

A confused, swirling battle expanded through the camp. There were secondary positions—fighting holes, sketchy trenches. O'Neil did his best to rally his people wherever it looked as though they could stand and fight. He steadied a company-sized formation, mixed Army and Marines. A line began to build.

Blaster fire resumed from the starship's upper deck. And considerably less counterfire was available. He still had mortars, but his artillery positions were ominously silent—overrun.

Colonel Felton, the ranking Army survivor, had been ordered to draw off with his remaining tanks. He'd been patrolling the high desert—which O'Neil had considered a good tactical and political maneuver—it kept their contact and potential friction to a minimum.

I just hope they're not driven all the way out there before this is over, O'Neil thought.

An Apache chopper came swooping down, miniguns blazing, to launch four rockets into the open deck.

For a moment it was like a reenactment of history, when a crippled udajeet had crashed and exploded up there. Gouts of flame—and, if one looked closely, bits of Horus guards—flew out of the opening. Enemy fire from on high stopped.

But blast-bolts tore through the gunship. It corkscrewed wildly, crashing into the lower slope of the pyramid ship.

Then, through the smoke of burning tents, O'Neil glimpsed what seemed like a phalanx of Horus guards advancing on his position.

He glanced over his shoulder, trying to spot the next viable position for a withdrawal.

The base camp's berm—its original outer defense—was frighteningly close.

Once again Skaara stood on the rope bridge between the watchtowers of Nagada. This time he turned his back on the cityscape, with its rising plumes of smoke and hectic flashes of gunfire, to look outward, toward the Marine base camp.

Through his binoculars, a light show flashed over there, heavier and more dramatic. It was punctuated with the dull booming of artillery.

He chewed his lower lip, feeling more like a kid than ever. His father was in an improvised field hospital under the care of Dr. Destin. The proposed medical evacuation to the base camp had been terminated with the attack out there. Sha'uri was out in that maelstrom of fire, too. He hoped Colonel O'Neil was taking care of her.

And he, the cocky mastadge herder, held the greatest physical strength—in terms of actual rifles—in the city of Nagada.

The question was, what could he do with them?

Most of his units had been spread through the city, trying to pacify violence. In the process, they seemed to be burning everything down.

He glanced at the two young men on the bridge with him. Sermont was quiet, almost withdrawn.

Nabeh, one of the original boy commandos, gawked back and forth from the burning city to the flicker of blast-lances on the horizon.

Poor Nabeh would never rise to command. He did not have the intellectual capacity. But he had a loyalty that would shame a number of Skaara's nominal subordinates, who were now out freelancing with their commands.

When Skaara had burst out in frustration, shouting "What will I do?" Nabeh was the one who'd replied.

"You'll do the right thing," he said.

Skaara hoped his friend was right. He'd called the militia away from riot duties.

"If there's fighting in the Marine camp, that can only mean that Ra's people are back," he said, explaining as much for his own benefit as for the others. "We should be there to help. And maybe, *maybe,* our people will turn to fight the common enemy instead of trying to kill one another."

That hope had already been dashed. Massing in the growing darkness below were less than half of the troops he should have been able to expect.

Skaara could only hope they'd be enough.

The last leg of the trek to the command deck on the good ship *Ra's Eye* had been the most difficult. On the one hand, Sha'uri and Barbara Shore had managed to gather in all the technical teams in the pyramid ship's upper stories. But the climbing refugees had also been harassed by increasingly more aggressive Horus guard patrols.

"They're attempting something up here," Peter Auchinloss said. "But it doesn't seem to involve wiping us out."

"More like keeping us away." The Marine noncom, Corporal Vance, looked suddenly sick. "The udajeet landing zone—that busted-up deck. If they set enough people up there . . . well, they'd overlook the whole camp."

As if in counterpoint to their climbing, a low, irregular percussion beat seemed to whisper through the stairwells. "I'll bet that's the lanyard pullers trying to shut the bastards down," Vance said hopefully.

They'd almost reached the command deck when a jolt severe enough to knock them off their feet rocked the ship. Vance cheered up a little. "Something got a direct hit!" he crowed.

A couple of decks down from the command level, the climbers found the beginnings of a defense system being built. Marine and Army technicians were lugging anything large, heavy, and movable into impromptu bulwarks at the stairs.

Sha'uri shuddered to see the spalls and scars on the wrecked cabinets and consoles being piled in place. She'd probably put some of those marks there, with a blast-lance or grenades, while storming these same locations on her last rise to the top.

But if they were first greeted like a relieving army, the newcomers found the atmosphere more and more tense as they scaled the last flight to the command deck.

Barbara and Sha'uri arrived to find a knot of translators on one side of the room. Mitch Storey lay on the floor, his nose bleeding. And Gary Meyers was using his considerable bulk to tear down the barricade Skaara's people had erected around the top-deck connection of the matter transmitter.

"Meyers!" Barbara burst out. "Are you nuts? Take that stuff down, and the bad guys will be able to beam themselves right up here!"

"I've already composed a suitable surrender note to send down." Meyers waved a piece of paper covered in hieroglyphs. "I think we can expect better terms if we submit quickly, before the flood of military types who'll be rounded up when the camp outside falls."

"I see Mitch Storey disagreed with your evaluation," Barbara said.

Meyers drew himself up, trying to play the male in charge. "As the ranking civilian—"

"Not anymore," Barbara interjected.

"You can't seriously hope—" Meyers stepped forward.

Sha'uri sidestepped, aiming her blast-lance at the academic's fat head.

Barbara aimed her pistol at a somewhat lower and more delicate spot.

"This from the guy with all those pictures of conquering pharaohs bashing in the heads of the submitting kings!" she said. "Just step away from there, darlin'—"

But inside the partially demolished barrier, a cylinder of blue fire leapt into being. Someone was trying out the matter transmitter.

"Oh, shit!" Barbara succinctly stated.

Corporal Vance shot up the stairs, digging into one of the heavy satchels he wore bandoleer-fashion across his chest. As he approached the transmitter, his right hand came out with a grenade, his left hand latched onto the pin.

"Don't stick it into the blue light!" Sha'uri cried. "It will tear your hand off and send it downstairs!"

Vance waited until the figures in the transmitter were almost clear before he pulled the pin. The grenade handle clattered to the floor as he tossed the weapon. "Down!" he yelled.

Gary Meyers made a mess, vomiting where he lay on the deck.

That was understandable, though, considering the mess Vance's grenade made of the assault team trying to beam in.

Crouched on the interior berm that separated the motor pool from the rest of the base camp, Lieutenant Charlton did his best to add to the perimeter's rate of fire. The problem was, there were just too many damned targets out there, and not enough rifles on top of the wall. A Marine dropped into position beside him, resting his M249 light machine gun on its bipod.

A couple of bursts cleared up the local target problem admirably.

Then the weapon ran dry, and the gunner retreated behind the sand wall to load a new drum.

That might have been a wise decision. Blast-bolts flurried around Charlton's position, turning the sand into patches of greenish glass.

"You guys just about ready?" the lieutenant called over his shoulder to the men manhandling fifty-five-gallon fuel drums up the inside of the berm. A combat engineer made a noncommittal noise as he finished setting the demolition charge to the side of a barrel.

"I hope that was an affirmative grunt." In the near distance Charlton could see the enemy massing for a new attack. This was the thrust that would take them over the wall.

The young officer sighed. He'd held this position as long as he could. Anything that could roll out of here had, taking precious men toward the rally point. There was nothing more to defend.

The Horus guards came on, almost undeterred by Charlton's skeleton defense.

"All right, *now*!" the lieutenant shouted.

The fuel drums went over the top and rolled down the berm's sloping side. One of the Horuses fired a blast-bolt, igniting one of the barrels prematurely.

Charlton hugged the ground against the concussion and the sudden wave of heat.

He slithered back down to his retreating command as the other improvised bombs went off.

Okay, they had to abandon this position as well.

But at least they were exacting a heavy real estate tax for every foot the invaders took.

CHAPTER 13
"BOOGIE OUT OF DODGE"

Crouched in a "hasty"—a quickly scratched fighting hole atop the main berm of his ruined camp—Jack O'Neil watched as the exodus of vehicles from the motor pool ended. Judging from the sudden rush of flames over there, young Charlton was either pursuing a scorched-earth policy . . . or he'd been overrun.

Long shadows flickered grotesquely against the sand wall. Even the radio operator silently monitoring transmissions looked up as Charlton and his scratch force ran to join O'Neil's troops.

"I think my farewell present will keep those bad boys busy for a little while." The lieutenant climbed to his commander's position with a hangman's smile on his thin face. "It's the extra-crispy recipe for southern-fired hawk."

Joining the two men in the hasty, the young officer peered off into the darkness in the direction of Nagada. "Where the hell is the local militia?" he muttered. "Skaara has to know there's trouble out here. You'd think he'd get up off his ass—"

O'Neil cut off his subordinate. "From what we heard before we lost radio contact, there's big trouble in Nagada, too. I suspect the civil disturbances Kasuf and Nakeer were trying to avoid have just escalated into a full-fledged civil war." He shook his head. "If so, we can't expect much of anything in the way of aid from Skaara—no matter what he'd like to do."

Charlton's face set in worried lines. "It's just that if we had enough warm bodies on this line, we could make the position look too expensive for the Whorehouse guards to attack right away."

"Where did you pick up that endearment?" O'Neil asked.

The lieutenant shrugged. "Just another insult yelled in combat." He returned to his theme. "I'm sure those birds are stretched pretty thin. If we forced them to back down, we could arrange a more orderly withdrawal in the night."

"You forget, those masks have night-vision equipment that's better than our goofy goggles," O'Neil said.

"This way they'll see we don't have enough men to hold the line." Charlton looked worried. "I know we're trying to get most of our remaining forces to the rally point. It's just that this plan is—well, risky!"

"And therefore better suited for a brave young lieutenant instead of his crotchety commander?" O'Neil inquired.

"I just worry about the men. If you go, Colonel Felton ends up in command."

The radio operator abruptly spoke up. "Message from the pickets, sir. We're being joined by a force from Nagada."

"All right!" Charlton said sotto voce. "I just hope Skaara's brought enough dancers to the ball . . ."

Both sides were disappointed at what they found. The newcomers were neither fresh nor numerous enough to dissuade an attack by the Horus guards. And the Abydan militiamen were visibly shaken to see the forces they considered their powerful allies so gravely reduced and literally pushed to the wall.

Skaara's youthful face looked more like a death's-head mask. "The city is falling apart," he admitted. "But the more serious danger is still here."

"I suggest you fall back on the mines," O'Neil said formally. "That is our designated rally point. You'd better start your movement now. I think the enemy is beginning to stir."

Skaara nodded and returned to his troops.

Charlton's voice was quiet as he said, "He was coming to ask us for help—but he offered all he could."

The mass of Abydans began to stir. Most of Skaara's people set off for the mines. But in ones or twos, a significant proportion were veering off toward the city.

"You could have warned him," Charlton began.

O'Neil cut him off. "Here it comes," he said tightly.

The Horus guards had regrouped and were once again moving out. Given their ability to pierce the dark, they had surely spotted the Abydan militia. It looked as though Skaara's offer of help might only have served to precipitate the final assault.

The men have been briefed. O'Neil reminded himself. *They know what to do.*

With fuel fires still raging off to one side, there was no way the Horus guards could advance in the darkness. They looked even less human, stippled by the flickering flames—like some bad dream out of humanity's childhood.

The advancing tide passed the three-hundred-meter mark—an inconspicuous stake.

"Open fire," O'Neil ordered.

Single shots rippled out as the Marines carefully chose their targets. Light mortars chuffed. Grenade launchers fired. Horus guards dropped, but the losses made about as much difference as pinpricks to a charging rhino.

Two hundred meters.

Blast-lances were now crashing in answer to the patter of gunfire. O'Neil crouched lower, adding his own shots to the fusillade. His stomach muscles tightened . . .

"Now!" He gripped the radio operator by the shoulder.

The man was already shouting into his mike. "Battery Four!"

Out in the desert, the four-gun Marine artillery battery O'Neil had secretly emplaced in case of disaster tore down its camouflage nets and began firing.

The guns were zeroed in to drop their shells a hundred meters from O'Neil's position. A slight error in elevation, and yet another force would become the victim of friendly fire.

Blasts ripped the night—tore through the ranks of advancing Horuses. They might be gods on their own world. But here on Abydos they had been reduced to the level of statistical targets.

In the desert artillerymen pulled their lanyards. A second salvo, a third, a fourth.

It was too much for the hawk-headed guards. They recoiled . . .

The fifth salvo was a starburst, the signal to break contact and run for the mines.

O'Neil launched himself from the fighting hole. "Time to boogie out of Dodge."

Daniel Jackson awoke to a pounding head and a strong urge to barf. He was hanging upside-down, on some sort of coarse material. That explained the head. And he was moving, which might contribute to the nausea.

Funny. I'd expect at least I'd feel physically better after being seduced.

He didn't even have pleasant memories.

Then he discovered his hands were tied.

"Wha—" The word came out more like a croak. "What's going on?"

He was feeling a little more aware now. The rough cloth was a homespun Abydan cloak. He was being carried on someone's shoulder—a fairly big man, he would guess. Certainly, the guy had no problem with Daniel's weight. He managed to maintain a steady marching pace.

Someone on the far side of Shoulders, as Daniel instantly dubbed his carrier, was engaged in a brief conversation.

No one spoke to Daniel.

By craning his neck, Daniel realized he was able to get a view of wherever they had come from. It didn't help much. All he saw was sand dunes, illuminated in a rushing reddish glare.

"Hey!" A drunk-sounding Abydan voice came from ahead of them (behind him?). "You're heading the wrong way! Didn't anyone tell you? The Earthmen have run for it, toward the mines. All you'll find at their old camp is hawk-heads. Thousands and thousands! They'll go to the mine tomorrow and kill them all. Might as well go home—"

Shoulders dumped Daniel ingloriously to the sands and advanced. As Daniel pushed himself to hands and knees, he heard the noise of a scuffle, a scream, then an ominous *crunch*!

Feet, do your stuff, Daniel thought.

His feet couldn't, though.

They were tied at the ankles.

Daniel did manage to turn himself around, so he'd face whoever was coming. The murderous Shoulders advanced, a threatening black shadow outlined against a huge fire raging in the Marine camp.

Could the late drunk have been right? Had Horus guards taken over the beachhead from Earth?

Another low conversation. Daniel didn't make out the words, but he was sure the other voice was female. He turned, peering into the red-tinged darkness.

Shoulders threw back the hood of his cloak and fiddled at his throat. The silhouette of his head abruptly turned into that of a giant hawk.

I think that answers one question, Daniel thought.

The big man fiddled again and his normal silhouette returned. This time Daniel caught the sense of the female voice—assent.

Shoulders removed his robe, revealing the full regalia of a Horus guard.

Daniel also heard a flapping of cloth off to his right. He peered. Another one of the boys? No.

"Oh, my God!" he burst out.

"Goddess, actually," the answer came in English.

The face that gazed down at him was vaguely similar to Faizah's, like that of an older, harder sister.

Of course, the last time Daniel had seen this face, it had also been under strange illumination—the blue glare of the matter transmitter.

"Hathor," Daniel finally said.

"Yes," the warrior woman looming over him said, and Faizah simply vanished.

"You should be grateful you're here to be astonished, Daniel," the cool, ironic voice went on. "I had intended to enjoy—then dispose of you. You might call it pique. Few men have ever rejected what I offered you."

And lived, the unspoken completion of that sentence seemed to hang in the air.

Hathor's hand went to her throat and held out the Eye of Ra medallion.

"Then I found you had this. And I thought that as a scholar, you might enjoy a bit of . . . final research."

Her voice abruptly became businesslike. "Now, if you agree to walk along with us, I'll free your ankles."

"Um—okay." Daniel didn't hesitate to give his parole. He might be able to outrun the big guy. But he'd never beat Hathor—or the blast-lances they carried. "Who's your big friend?"

"He was my aide in destroying Abydos," Hathor said nonchalantly. "His name is Khonsu."

It was in some Egyptian poem—Daniel couldn't recall the source. But he did remember one line. "Khonsu the killer is."

The two godlings activated their masks, and conversation was over. Hathor now wore her conventional sign of the cat instead of the Horus mask. How anyone, with her figure, could have been taken as a run-of-the-mill Horus guardsman . . .

Daniel supposed the witnesses had other things on their minds—like surviving combat.

Apparently his captors had donned their masks for communication purposes. Soon a squad of Horus guardsmen appeared, greeting Hathor with deep obeisance. They formed up around the odd trio like an honor guard and conveyed them toward the Marine camp.

Hathor resumed her human appearance as they entered the shambles of the camp. Tents flapped in shreds, a lot of war machinery lay destroyed, and there were dead bodies—Earthmen and Horus guards—everywhere.

"Your friend the Marine has escaped for the time being," she announced, after receiving reports. "I'll let my minions handle the pursuit tomorrow. I have other concerns."

"Forgive me for sounding nosy," Daniel said. "I don't want to go looking into military secrets. But you barely had enough guardsmen to operate that ship over there." He nodded toward the *Ra's Eye*. "So where did you get the army?"

Hathor looked at him, then shrugged. "One of my rivals governed a fairly populous planet. "He retreated there when I established my ascendancy on Tuat."

"Ra's throne world."

"Yes. I forgot you deciphered those childish hieroglyphs." She looked annoyed at his interruption—which could definitely be a life-shortening problem, Daniel reminded himself.

He took his life in his hands again. "So, how did you get the army? Your rival had thousands, apparently, while you had fifty."

Her voice was almost bored. "How did I turn the Abydan fellahin against one another with only two followers? A stroke against the head is usually the easiest."

They reached the golden spaceship. Teams of guards were at work in the corridors cleaning up.

The same activity was underway in the pyramid of the StarGate. More minions appeared and reported, all in low voices. Hathor shared one bit of what struck her as amusing gossip. "It seems your wife is above us, holding out in the upper levels of the spaceship," she said. "Much as I was not so long ago."

Some of her amusement faded. "My people do not think her resistance will be as successful as mine."

The goddess apparently came to a decision. "I regret you won't be able to offer your good-byes. We're going on a journey."

They marched down to the chamber of the StarGate, which Hathor had cleared. Even Khonsu was ordered to go, though he put up an argument.

When the room was empty, Hathor produced the Eye of Ra medallion. "I examined this while you slept," she said. "While the exterior is bronze, there are workings inside made of Ra's special mineral."

"What does it do?" Daniel asked.

"I saw it once," the goddess replied serenely. "I'll show you."

Sure, Daniel thought. *Dead men tell no tales.*

Hathor approached the StarGate with the medallion in her hand. She stopped at the carving that represented the constellation Serpens Caput—the serpent's head. Hathor pressed the amulet to the center star of the constellation and stepped back. The huge gold-quartz ring swung into silent operation, revolving, then stopping as the triangular chevrons clicked into place.

Then Daniel noticed that the place markers were *not* locking on to the usual constellation signs. It seemed that Ra had designed the portal to two different coordinate codes—the constellations, which everyone in his empire used, *and the spaces between the star signs, which was apparently his secret*!

The final chevron fell into place, provoking that odd harmonic which accompanied the formation of the StarGate's energy fields.

Energy gushed forth in the usual way, then settled into that deceptively placid-looking rippling pool of light.

Daniel found his wrist grasped in a strong, competent hand.

"Come," Hathor said briskly, "let's see what Ra was hiding."

She didn't have to pull, however. Daniel was already stepping up to the energy interface with her.

Throughout his youth and through many misadventures, Daniel's stepmother used to complain that his curiosity would be the death of him.

Maybe, Daniel thought, *after all these years, Mom will turn out to have been right.*

CHAPTER 14
HIP SHOOTING

Taking his second StarGate journey to an unknown destination, Daniel Jackson discovered he couldn't be sure whether it took more or less time. It wasn't just the disorientation of being squirted between two widely separated points. The geometry and space of the connecting "tube," or whatever it was, didn't fit the homely three dimensions (or four, including time) that Daniel's senses were accustomed to.

But one thing Daniel could take as a given. No matter where you went via StarGate, you should expect a bumpy ride.

Daniel was flung from the StarGate terminus feeling as if he'd been propelled by a kick in the head through a high-speed funhouse where they played very rough tricks on you.

Yet in a strange, sadistic way the passage felt . . . less bad. He still landed curled into a fetal ball. But this time he remembered to breathe on his own, and he didn't get violently ill.

Of course, Hathor was kneeling over him, shaking

him rather peevishly and telling him to pull himself together.

Maybe that's what makes the distinction between men and gods, he thought. *The ability to take a complete psychic and somatic pummeling as if it were nothing.*

At last the goddess left off the shaking—a wise decision. He'd been a projectile vomiter in his youth.

It took Daniel a moment or two before he really began taking an interest in things again. That's when he noticed the talking head. It was ashy white, somewhat human—but definitely, chillingly *other.*

Daniel knew that Ra had been a symbiosis of a young human male and an unguessably old alien. Apparently, here was the otherworldly side of Ra's family tree.

At last Daniel concentrated on the fact that the floating head was talking. Then he realized he didn't comprehend a word of what the blasted thing was saying.

Still worse, it seemed as though Hathor didn't have a clue, either. "Do you understand this language?" she demanded.

Uh-oh. Neither of them had considered that Ra might install a security system in—wherever they were.

The floating head seemed to be going through a set speech, and getting a bit more irritated with each repetition. The thing was apparently a three-dimensional image—the edges were just a little bit fuzzy.

Hathor finally held out the medallion around her neck and thrust it into the head. That was apparently the right choice. The face looked friendly, although it still spoke incomprehensibly.

Daniel, meanwhile, was investigating the space where they landed. It bore a vague resemblance to the command deck on *Ra's Eye*—about the same way a bedroom closet resembles the Rose Bowl.

The place was big—spacious enough to accommodate a couple of football fields, at least. Including spectators.

There were lots of control panels, all glowing softly. Daniel avoided them. But directly beside the talking head was a slate and stylus in gold crystal—almost exactly like the microcomputers in Hathor's former ship.

Daniel picked up the slate and sketched in the hieroglyph for *where*?

Immediately, a new image appeared. It showed a stylized pyramid apparently floating between stylized versions of suns.

Hieroglyphs floating between each sun symbol gave the names of stars.

Hathor stared. "According to this, we're parked somewhere in interstellar space!"

Her eyes went speculative. "As good a place as any to hide a valuable asset."

She took the stylus and wrote the glyph for *what*?

The image changed. Now a little pyramid hung before them.

"What else?" Hathor inquired sarcastically.

Hieroglyphs flashed at great speed. Apparently, members of Ra's race were faster readers than humans.

The top point of the image abruptly removed itself, leaving a truncated pyramid shape. Daniel gave it a sharp look, recaptured the stylus, and wrote *larger*.

When the image grew three times its previous size, he was sure. Pointing at the hollow pyramid point, he said, "When I first saw that, I thought it was the biggest spaceship I'd ever seen. It's Ra's flying palace! And all this time it was just the dinghy or lifeboat for . . . this, whatever it is."

"It's an immensely powerful starship from Ra's homeworld," Hathor said. "Hidden, but accessible if he needed it. Who knows how long it's been waiting here?"

She snatched back the stylus and began asking specific questions. Daniel wasn't too happy about their drift. Dimensions—huge. Speed—incredible. Ra had been poking around in a "palace" that had barely a quarter of the speed and range of the mother ship. Weapons—lots of them, all powerful.

Hathor thought for a moment, then sketched in the word *crew*?

Daniel had expected another little 3-D movie. Instead, one of the control panels came to life. First came hieroglyphs for numbers—in the hundreds. Then came the glyph for sleep, with some sort of odd modifiers. But there was no animated discussion. The pictures over the console looked *real*. They showed hundreds of figures lying on simple-looking contour couches, either asleep or dead. When they zoomed in, Hathor stepped back, her teeth bared in a grimace.

The crew . . . people were aliens, though they didn't seem related to the initial talking head. They were furred, about the color of cinnabar, with sharp, Wiley E. Coyote snouts and odd, floppy ears.

Staring until his eyes watered, Daniel savored the solution to one of Egyptology's thorniest questions. No wonder no one had been able to find a match for the typhonic beast in Earthly zoology. The original didn't come from Earth.

The sleeping, red-furred alien was the living image of the enigmatic god Set.

"Setim!" Hathor spat the word, ignoring Daniel Jackson's look of surprise. She knew this stiff-necked race of old. They'd been Ra's first servants, inhabitants of Tuat-the-world. They were the builders, the craftsmen—the ones who had probably fabricated the StarGate that had brought her and Daniel to this treasure trove.

Those red devils had also been a nearly insuperable obstacle in the human godlings' quest for power. Only the fact that Ra's bodily form was that of a young male had opened the door for the likes of Ptah, Sebek . . . and herself.

It had taken long, hard years of intrigue, but finally the Setim had made a misstep—and the human-kindred godlings had enjoyed the sunshine of Ra's full favor. Hadn't she fought against them, the rebels of Ombos? Hadn't they nearly killed her? But her campaign against them had finally triumphed. She covered a world in blood, but the race of Set was no more.

Except for these sleepers . . .

What are they waiting for? Sha'uri knelt by one of the barriers blocking the starship stairwells, waiting for the inevitable attack of the Horus guards. The free folk aboard *Ra's Eye* held only four decks with barely fifty people, including noncombatants. A determined rush could probably sweep them up in an afternoon's work.

Why had the Horuses not begun the job?

Sha'uri left her watch feeling tired, hungry—and thirsty.

There was space enough to sleep, though little privacy. More serious was the question of rations. Pooling all their food, including MREs and Gary Meyers' hoard of snacks, they could survive a day or two of siege, perhaps more.

Worst of all was water. They had no supply, except that which was in their bodies. Wise in the ways of a desert world, Sha'uri knew the ways of "recycling." Could the pampered Earthers live with that?

Perhaps they would rather fight and die quickly.

Arriving upstairs in what the besieged were already calling the "living room," Sha'uri found her compatriots toasting one another with a variety of containers—and drinking water!

"How—?" she gasped.

Barbara Shore gave her the feverish smile of the

sleepless worker. "We kept copies of all our technical translations up here—and we had a breakthrough. It's amazing the way life-and-death decisions can really concentrate your mind."

"We started on that old program for initiating circuit repairs," Peter Auchinloss said. "After trial and error and correcting a couple of errors in translation, we made it work. We've even been able to divert the ship's emergency power to plumbing and such—but we're storing all the water we can while it's running."

Barbara smiled. "Now Peter's threatening to patch in some of the outside scanners!"

Auchinloss was as good as his word. By that afternoon he succeeded in insinuating control over enough scanners to create a panoramic 3-D view in the command deck.

What they saw, however, sank the tiny group's morale.

The camp was completely overrun by the enemy. Everywhere they looked, they saw Horus guards.

Most disturbing, though, were the images from the mouth of the StarGate. First, guardsmen began lugging out odd shapes of the crystal-gold material that underlay all of Ra's technology. Others set to the work of assembly. Within hours, familiar forms had begun to appear. The enemy was beginning to import a udajeet flotilla through the gateway.

Auchinloss turned in chagrin from his largest practical triumph. "Back to basics," he said. "It would be a lot more useful to have motion alarms on the decks below us." He frowned. "We'll want to know when we're getting company."

"Well?" General West looked up from the report he'd been pretending to read. On the third go-around, it made even less sense that it had on the first.

The junior officer shook his head. "No change, sir. We've received no shipments from Abydos for fifteen hours now. No messages, either."

"Then we have to assume the Abydos StarGate is in enemy hands. Are the demolition teams at work in Creek Mountain?"

Cold sweat beaded at the back of his neck as he considered hopelessly stranding the equivalent of an overstrength battalion on another planet.

But he was also determined not to allow another incursion by extraterrestrial warriors. If Horus guards showed any chance of success in trying to force Earth's StarGate, West would rather bring the missile silo down on their heads.

His aide nodded. "Proceeding according to the contingency plan, sir."

West's eyes sharpened. "And the counterforce?"

"Armed and preparing for jumpoff, sir—as per the contingency plan."

Jack O'Neil looked more like a construction laborer than a commanding officer as he stood on the upper terrace of the Nagada mine. Whitish dust covered him from head to toe, except where streaks of sweat tricked down like miniature river systems.

But he smiled with grim satisfaction as a bulldozer cleared the last of a seeming talus mound from the mouth of an artificial cavern blasted into the rocky wall.

Here at the rally point, he had cached and buried some of his excess battalion materiel as well as additional supplies he'd solicited from General West. There were tanks, mortars, and plenty of shells. Ammunition. Medical supplies. Food.

He'd opened a little space between himself and the enemy. Their infantry army was now up against the longer range of his tanks, mortars, and artillery. If he hadn't stopped the Horus guards, he'd slowed their momentum, bloodied their noses.

With his shrunken command he could survive on the cached supplies for long enough—he hoped.

The Horus guards couldn't keep maintaining the losses he was giving them. Sooner or later they'd be overextended. Then he could punch back to the base camp, restore contact through the StarGate. . . .

The bastards had to overreach themselves. They *had* to!

The Army M1A2 tank scuttled along the hollow between two sand dunes, its tracks chewing up a cloud of grit. The big war machine came to a stop, turret traversing as it took an azimuth from a forward observer. The heavy gun fired once, then the tank was on its way again, threading through the sandy terrain, always keeping a new dune between itself and the slowly advancing Horus Guards.

"We used to call it scoot and shoot, or hip-shooting in the Gulf," the tank's commander told his gunner. He licked dry lips. " 'Course, in those days, we were moving forward, not back."

Six dunes away, a company of Horus guards flung themselves to the sands at the screech of an incoming shell. The explosive didn't land on them, but two dunes over.

The guard Reshef pushed himself up, trying to brush the grit off his chest and legs. It stuck there, thanks to the pig sweat of this eternal hell of jog uphill, flop down, tend the dead and wounded, jog on.

"Ammit eat this nonsense!" he groused. "I'm an udajeet pilot, not some marching flunky. My place should be in a nice, cool cockpit overhead, blasting those thrice-damned moving guns."

P'saro, whose service involved house-to-house searches and riot suppression, snorted. "These magic fellahin have some special weapon that blows most udajeet drivers like yourself out of the sky!"

He managed a laugh as they stumbled up the next ridge of sand. "Only the ones with experience against the weapon will fly in this campaign. Or so I hear."

Reshef's grip tightened on his blast-lance. He didn't like being in this unit. It had been amalgamated from the ruins of several other formations after the breakout from the StarGate pyramid.

Even though his other outfit had been ground pounders as well, there had been pilots like him, impressed into the infantry. At least they could share complaints.

"Stupid way to run a war," Reshef growled.

"Maybe you want to take it up with the Lady?" P'saro suggested in innocent tones.

Reshef glared at his supposed war brother's back as they toiled upward. Everyone knew how Lady Hathor dealt with complainers.

Not that P'saro was so pleased with their assignment. He was used to working in large cities, with access to plenty of strong drink and willing wenches. Marching off into the waste to play catch-me-kill-you did not strike him as an excellent plan of campaign.

He shook his blast-lance. "Don't think I've used this all day."

"Nothing bloody to use it on," Reshef agreed. "In a straight fight our lances against their *gunnis*, or whatever they call them, we win. Our blasts travel faster, fly straighter, and hit harder than those pellets they shoot."

"You just don't want to be hit with one of those pellets," another guard said. "Especially from one of those fast-shooters."

"I'd take my chances," Reshef insisted, "man to man. But this sort of work, where they hide and throw things in the air to come down on you—"

"Can't fire a bolt *through* a dune," P'saro said. He'd heard about plunging fire from guards who'd fought mountain savages with bows and arrows. Sooner or later, however, the udajeets had helped herd the savages into a situation where the superior range and power of their blast-lances prevailed.

"We'll catch 'em straight up again." He grinned behind his mask. "Then we'll finish 'em."

"Umph!" Reshef said, skidding down a packed-sand slope. "If this doesn't finish us first," he added under his breath.

The mortar team had pushed its luck, staying for three shots in the same spot. Now angry squads of Horus guards were converging like so many killer bees.

Skaara had a squad of his tried-and-true riot breakers. He beckoned to another militia group, the remains of Sek's company, to slow the Horuses. A few grenades should cool their ardor while the gunners disassembled their mortar and packed it out of there.

It would have worked, except for the high whistle that came from the air. Skaara paled. Udajeets were back on Abydos.

What do the Earthmen need us for, anyway? Sek angrily thought as he led his rags and tags to the commanding position of a higher than usual dune.

They had their long guns to play hide-and-shoot—except for those fools who'd been too lazy to get while the getting was good.

A little gurgle of laughter came from Gamen, the gunless wonder of the troop. He was a real guttersnipe, had lost half the teeth in his head, and just loved grenades.

The little guy was running along behind the head of the dune, listening for the *crunch* of feet on sand on the other side. One hand was already in the satchel of grenades he always carried.

They didn't know the udajeet was on them until Sek saw its shadow. Then it was too late. Heavy blasters crashed, and that was the end of Gamen.

The secondary explosions from igniting grenades took two more of Sek's people.

"Why don't you try that with the tanks, you great bastard?" Sek shouted, trying to aim his rifle. But the udajeet was gone.

"Bastards," he said again. Trust the high-and-mighty udajeet pilots to pick on the fellahin. They figured—rightly—that militia wouldn't have any of the antiaircraft missiles.

After the great orgy of shoot-downs during Hathor's invasion, the udajeet drivers had become very selective in their targets.

Sek looked at the four men who remained of his company.

"It strikes me," he said, "that a man could follow this trade much more profitably back in Nagada."

The five men set off for the flanks of the battle, away from the main advance—and toward home.

* * *

Running through the dunes with a pack of enraged Horuses on his tail, Skaara saw the men pulling out.

Like sand through a sieve, he thought. *My fighters either bleed to death—or they just bleed away.*

The Horus guards at the Abydos StarGate were walking wounded, emblazoned with bandages on legs or slings on the arms not carrying their blast-lances. They also had loud voices, useful for hectoring latecomers to the war.

One thing their voices did not comment on was the way Lady Hathor was stripping their world of Edfu bare of guards to prosecute her war here.

But it was all too true that their side was down to the dregs and the rawest recruits. Probably that was why the latest levy staggered like drunkards as they cycled through.

"Call yourselves Horus guards!" shouted one barrel-chested veteran just beginning to thicken in the middle as well. "In my worst, puling days I didn't look as sickening—as you lot. What did they do, take you right out of the creche? Where did you come from? Hey, you undersize specimen, I'm talking to you!"

The short, skinny guardsman turned to his strapping comrade.

Then both leveled their blast-lances and began firing.

Two-armed Horuses were the first targets of choice.

Guards in slings were attacked hand-to-hand by other members of the levy.

The fight ended surprisingly quickly, with the "fresh meat" overcoming their elders before even any word got out over the mask communicators.

The newcomers began removing their hawk-masks. Some hit the tumbler button at their necks to redeploy the mask's material. Others were pulling off plastic replicas. None of the men was tattooed with the Eye of Ra.

With a rush of energy the StarGate cycled again. But this time the emerging figures didn't look like Egyptian gods. They wore baggy chocolate-chip BDUs

A Marine sergeant led his men down the rampway with a queasy salute. "Guess it worked, sir!"

Lieutenant Kawalsky grinned. "I'd say it did. But more important, have you brought the pants for Feretti and me?"

He self-consciously tugged at the waist of his kilt. "I've never gone into combat wearing a dress before."

CHAPTER 15
THE BOAT OF A MILLION YEARS

By the time Lieutenant Kawalsky had buttoned himself into his utilities and donned the other equipment of a twentieth-century fighting man, the StarGate had cycled more troops into the hall. The dead were moved aside, prisoners cuffed.

Kawalsky was ready to arm himself. He shrugged on a backpack-sized box of insulated plastic. An armored cable emerged from the lower rear of the box, connecting with a vaguely gunlike device, also of black insulated plastic. From a slightly bulbous "nose," a fifteen-inch "barrel" ran to a trigger and pistol grip, beyond which extended a rudimentary stock. The weapon had the same weight and looks as a flamethrower—except what should have been the nozzle was plugged with a solid, flanged cylinder of golden quartz.

The lieutenant flicked a safety on the grip, and a thin whine warned that the weapon was charged. He turned to Feretti, who had also donned a uniform and carried one of the new weapons. "Guess it's time to take this show on the road."

The invaders from Earth organized into four-man fire teams armed with two standard-issue M-16 rifles, an M-203 M-16 with a 40mm grenade launcher, and one of the new weapons. They filtered out into the connecting hallway, then to the chamber of the matter transmitter, now cleaned of the rubble that had blocked the terminus at this end.

A squad of walking-wounded Horus guards entered the apse-like room from the end that opened onto the Grand Gallery. They were unmasked, and consternation showed plainly on their tattooed faces as they leveled their blast-lances.

Feretti, in the lead, squeezed his trigger. His weapon snarled rather than crashed, but the energy bolt that hit the leading guardsman did an equally efficient job of frying him. The Horuses froze, staring, giving the rest of the fire team the opportunity to mow them down.

The colonnaded gallery beyond was thronged—pale, emaciated slaves pushed wooden carts of supplies up the gentle incline, which in turn led to a steeper ramp.

Horus guards supervised. They turned at the sounds of the firefight, and the orderly pattern of the procession disintegrated.

The Horuses fought like madmen to contain the newcomers, taking cover behind columns, carts, even the goggling slaves. The crash of blast-lances rang out against the rattle of riflefire and the snarls of the Marines' blast-rifles.

The riflemen kept the Horuses' heads down, the grenade launchers offered a touch of indirect fire, and the energy weapons dueled directly. The combination worked. The Marines cleared the gallery and fought their way to the pyramid entrance against stiffening resistance.

It wasn't accomplished without losses. Kawalsky saw one of his energy riflemen caught in the power pack by an enemy bolt. The battery went up in a flare of incandescence, and the man went down.

But as they slugged it out toe to toe with the Horus guards, Kawalsky at last felt he was fighting on a level playing field.

Feretti grinned, triggering a blast through a wooden barricade. "So what do you think?" he asked. "From now on we call ourselves Space Marines?"

High above, the command deck of *Ra's Eye* echoed with blasts and the occasional *blam* as technicians and Horus guards exchanged potshots. The Horuses still seemed content to keep the scientific contingent pinned down, with the occasional nuisance attack thrown in. The defenders replied only sparingly, hoarding their ammunition.

This morning the water had stopped again, despite all of Barbara Shore's console fiddling. She sat at her desk, ignoring the crash of blast-lances and the isolated gunshots. Two technical translations sat side by side. One had come from Sha'uri, the other from Faizah. Both dealt with similar technical operations from the crew-training programs of Peter Auchinloss.

So why did they seem to contradict each other?

Sighing, Barbara raised her head to look out the "window"—the holographic view piped in from the grounded ship's sensors.

The whoop she let out drowned all the sounds of conflict downstairs. Troops were pouring into the base camp from the open maw of the good ship *Ra's Eye*.

Troops in homely chocolate-chip cammies from the U.S. of A.!

My God, what did Ra's people use this ship for? Daniel Jackson wondered as he roamed the seemingly never-ending corridors of the gigantic derelict. Dragged along by Hathor, he'd seen titanic batteries of weapons, food supplies sufficient for an army, enigmatic devices labeled "colony equipment."

With an almost brazen sense of ownership, she referred to the enormous vessel as "my ship."

That was enough of a name for her. When Daniel had suggested that the sleeping crew might have a better claim, he had come very close to getting killed. She had contented herself with propelling him across a room with whirling kicks.

Daniel had tried to keep his mouth shut after that.

He wished, however, that he knew the real name of the ship. When he inquired of the ship's computer about any logs, he'd been referred to an on-board library instead.

Hathor immediately appropriated the place, soaking up more about the ship's capabilities and how to use them.

"I had the computer identify the nearest star systems," she told Daniel the next morning. "Abydos is actually very close. Ra must have had this ship run out here when he founded the colony—fortunately for your Earth. His flying palace would have taken four years to get there. Had he decided your world was important enough to punish, he could have been there much sooner—and with power enough to obliterate the planet."

Hathor scowled. "But Ra was always too subtle for his own good. Instead of moving on the Earth rebels with irresistible strength, he sent Anubis and some Horuses in secret—with his key to the StarGate."

"I thought you were busy sleeping the sleep of the gods," Daniel said.

"But it must have happened so. Barbara Shore mentioned the bodies found fused into the soil. And the Eye of Ra was found there, with the cover stone." She held up the medallion she still wore around her neck. "Who knows what other tricks this little key may do?"

Daniel decided to derail that train of thought. "I'd say Ra did pretty well by being subtle. He had a ten-thousand-year track record. Performing your grand gesture could have been done only at the price of revealing all his hidden power—and the crew here."

"With the help of the computer, I could run this ship alone, even now," Hathor insisted. In the beautiful mask of her face, her eyes were ugly. "Perhaps I'll direct my ship to Abydos—as a test."

The look promised that straightening out the mess on Abydos would merely be a dress rehearsal for what she'd do to Earth.

Daniel left her to her studies, visiting the taunting door to freedom on the huge command deck, the StarGate.

I've got to figure how to get you to work before Miss Personality moves this big boat, he thought. If Hathor moved Ra's ship, the change in its spatial coordinates might render his only way out of here useless.

Daniel had two possible destinations. The six-figure coordinates for Earth and Abydos were engraved in his memory. But at this blind location he had the same problem as he'd had on arrival at Abydos. He needed the seventh coordinate, the one for his departure point. If only he knew the name of this damned ship! Maybe then he'd be able to puzzle out its location on Ra's wheel of fortune.

Ra's wheel. The ancient Egyptians believed that the sun's wheeling progress through the heavens was Ra's eternal journey, a never-ending boat ride—

Ra's boat! Every Egyptologist knew about the Boat of a Million Years, Ra's solar yacht.

Wild hope filled Daniel as he picked up one of the slate computers. Taking the stylus, he inscribed the hieroglyph for the Boat of a Million Years.

A holographic image appeared, showing a pyramid-shaped craft. It was the same animated show the computer had played when he'd asked what this place was.

Okay, now he knew the name of this ship. Where did that fit on the StarGate? He ran through the thirty-nine symbols that had haunted him for weeks when he'd started with this project. Even worse, Ra could have been subtle again. The coordinates for this place had literally fallen between the cracks of the carved symbols. Suppose the Boat of a Million Years was also represented by the line between two symbols?

That depressing thought stirred a memory. The Boat of a Million Years had been carved on the cover stone that hid the StarGate. Daniel recalled the image to his mind's eye. The boat had floated in midair, between Geb, the god who represented the earth, and Nut, the goddess whose arched back held up the sky.

Between Earth and sky.

Daniel's eye went to the StarGate symbol that represented the Earth. To the right was a sign that looked like a melted capital H. On the left was a symbol that he'd first identified as a throwing stick, an ancient, boomerang-like hunting weapon of the pharaohs.

Or it could look like a stick figure of someone arching his (or her) back.

Daniel leapt to the StarGate, spinning the inner ring and locking on the chevrons. Maybe this was a stupid idea, a StarGate wrong number, and the gateway wouldn't form. Maybe it would send him somewhere fatal.

Daniel shrugged as the low harmonics indicating an otherworldly connection sounded. Things couldn't get more dangerous than the way they were here with Hathor.

And maybe, just maybe, he'd get home.

It had taken the Horus guards two days to fight their way from the captured base camp to the mines of Nagada—a distance Jack O'Neil could have walked if he'd wanted to take a healthy stroll.

And the Horuses had arrived in a bad mood.

Colonel O'Neil had spent those two days doing everything he could to create headaches behind those hawk-masks. He'd bled them with indirect fire. He'd crushed some of them with tank sorties. When the enemy's udajeets arrived, his Stinger missiles had established a respectable shoot-down rate.

Now, however, the enemy was in a position to fight close up and personal. And Jack O'Neil didn't have any more rabbits to pull out of his beret.

He'd just released the last ammunition reserves when he became aware of rifle fire where it couldn't possibly be coming from. Somebody was attacking the Horus guards from the rear.

Had Kasuf made a miraculous recovery and led Nagada's squabbling factions into battle? Radio contact from Lieutenant Kawalsky dispelled that myth. A grinning O'Neil told his men to spread the word: the cavalry has arrived.

As the attack force came closer, O'Neil began to recognize the old West touch. He stared in disbelief through his binoculars at Marines with blast-rifles. There were even a couple of Marine Light Armored Vehicles, carrying bazooka-sized blasters instead of their usual 20mm cannons.

One thing had to be said about General W. O. West. When results were needed, he didn't screw around.

The enemy guardsmen tried to hold, to fight in two directions, but the newcomers were just too much for them.

O'Neil would have liked to order a charge, to get some revenge, but his force was on the edge, too. He kept his people in their positions, acting the part of the anvil while the relief force hammered the Horuses.

The invading force of guardsmen shattered. Then came the pursuit, driving them into the high desert.

"Between them and the sand lice, caravans won't be able to get through," Colonel Felton warned. "These will be hungry days in Nagada."

"The problem is, the Horuses don't know the meaning of the word surrender," Lieutenant Charlton said. "As we rebuild the base camp, we'll have to increase security against terrorist and guerrilla attacks."

"We'll have to do something else that General West isn't going to like," O'Neil said grimly. "All exits and especially entrances through the StarGate will have to take place on a rigid schedule."

The colonel shook his head. "We're not going to have another snafu like this. Anyone appearing in the StarGate out of turn . . . gets wasted."

Skaara found his sister in one of the lower levels of the starship *Ra's Eye,* arguing over diagrams with Barbara Shore. Baffled military technicians looked from the pictures to the equipment they were trying to disengage from the circuitry in the wall.

"We're trying to get a sample of a large-size blast cannon," Barbara said. "There's just some question that we're getting everything."

She shook her head. "*Damn* that Faizah! If she ever gets that cute ass of hers back to work, I'm gonna kick it from here to Nagada. Her stuff always looks plausible, but something inevitably gets screwed up along the way."

Leaving the techs to take as much as they could, she shepherded Sha'uri and Skaara down the hall. "I know you want to see your father, darlin'. And from what I hear about things in Nagada, you could use a militia escort."

"What's left of it." Skaara grimaced. "Now that the worst of the crisis is over, people are acting like worse fools than ever."

"How is Father?" Sha'uri asked. "I got a wild message just before the Horuses attacked—"

"He and Nakeer were alone, talking when they were attacked. Father fell unconscious shortly after being shot." Skaara's voice was tight. "He hasn't revived."

"People do come out of comas." Barbara tried to sound optimistic.

"Who did it?" Sha'uri demanded. "Have you caught them?"

Skaara wouldn't look at her. "There are no witnesses. But our guards saw a man running from the room. A man with blond hair."

"Daniel was there?" Sha'uri said. "Why—"

"He ran away," Skaara repeated. "The next we know, he was seen with Faizah at the Freedom faction's headquarters. Then they went to a warehouse on Spice Lane. We found clothes and some of Daniel's things there."

His voice got lower. "There was also a bed."

Sha'uri merely looked off into the middle distance, saying nothing.

"When we arrived there, we were attacked by a Horus guard," Skaara went on. "We think Faizah was either working for them or actually is one. Some stragglers from the fight in the camp saw a man who looked like Daniel with a squad of Horuses."

Sha'uri's face was the color of parchment.

The usually loquacious Barbara opened her mouth, then closed it. "I—I don't know what to say."

Sha'uri brought her gaze down from the middle distance and looked at her brother. "I want to see my father," she said.

* * *

A truckload of quartz mineral vanished through the StarGate on schedule. The next truck out would be in a half hour, with an incoming truck due ten minutes after that.

So, when the energy fields in the portal began to cycle, the hall went crazy. Alarms shrilled. Technicians were pulled out of the room altogether. Fire teams gathered behind fortifications more reminiscent of Fort Knox than ancient Egypt.

Military policeman Phil Garber fiddled nervously with his M203. Colonel O'Neil had banned the use of blast-rifles around the StarGate—no one knew if the two types of energy got along together. After the horrifying discovery of the claymore victims, the new anti-intruder weapons would be bullets and flash-bangs.

The StarGate filled with the rippling energy of the transfer field. Something emerged.

Because the brown-robed intruder came through in a humiliating pratfall, the fusillade passed right over his head.

Daniel Jackson choked, coughed, and, still on his belly, raised his hands.

"Uh, guys?" he said. "We've got to talk."

CHAPTER 16
BUILDING UP; TEARING DOWN

When I was a little girl and Father picked me up, he seemed so tall I could reach up and touch the sky, Sha'uri thought. *Now he seems . . . tiny.*

It had been a shock to see her father still and gray, his body invaded by tubes. But Dr. Destin had been a kind man. His services and supplies were being donated by the Marines to help run the first Earth-Abydan hospital.

Following Destin's advice, Sha'uri visited Kasuf every day, the first task of her morning. She'd just sit for a while and speak to her father, generally relating the events of the previous day: people who offered or needed help, jobs accomplished or deferred.

Sha'uri had not returned to the base camp after coming to Nagada with Skaara. After one look at the chaos in the city, she had given up translating to help those rendered homeless and helpless by the disorder. In fact, except for her daily sessions with Dr. Destin, Sha'uri rarely spoke English at all anymore. Her conversations with the doctor usually dealt with finding supplies and beds for an ever growing patient population.

They hardly discussed Kasuf's case. What more could be said about her shrunken, still father?

Stepping out of the oil warehouse turned clinic, Sha'uri surveyed the tiny enclave that now made up her world. Nagada was very much a divided city, with gangs of former militiamen or outright criminals constantly fighting to extend or defend their turf. The markets in food and silver both had collapsed. Acquiring supplies was now an equation based on the number of clubs, knives, and guns on a given side.

But in a small patch around the town gates, some semblance of order still survived. The Abydan militia might have dwindled to skeleton strength as a military command, but it was still the most potent force in Nagada. Skaara had sent some contingents—the more doubtful ones—to the mines, trying to restore some production to justify the supplies Colonel O'Neil was sending him.

With the rest of his people—old friends from his herding days and those eager young volunteers who had first joined his cause—he defended the helpless and battled chaos.

Sha'uri saw her brother stride from the barricades that marked the boundaries of the safe zone toward the city gates. It was later than she realized. The sun was fully up, which meant the gates were about to be opened.

Sha'uri fell in step with her brother as he went to join the gate guards. Although he moved with all his usual energy, she could tell at a glance that he'd spent a sleepless night—again.

The cares of his position as the last defender of Nagada had whittled fine lines and hollows on the young man's face. Sha'uri felt a chill as she detected a sudden resemblance she'd never noticed before. Her handsome little brother was coming to look more and more like Kasuf.

"Dr. Destin said you must get some sleep," she greeted him sternly. "What kept you up this time?"

"Our old friend Gerekh was trying to sneak some people in to raid the food stores," Skaara replied. "The leader of the team carried a fortune in silver, but the watchmen didn't stay bribed. There's nothing the silver can buy anymore."

He shook his head at the irony. "It seems that when things reach their worst, people's choices become . . . simpler. We disarmed the thieves and sent them back—more mouths for Gerekh to feed. He's choking on his silver now. And the connections he made in the food trade were mainly in the nearer hinterland—the farm communes that are held or being raided by the Horus Guards."

They reached the gates. A squad of men pushed the huge, creaking wooden portals open while another squad covered them. But there were no enemies outside this time. The small stream of people who entered, farm folk by their accents, didn't carry weapons or much of anything else.

These wanderers represented a new responsibility and worry. They were refugees, driven from their farms by the actions of the Horus guards. The hawk-headed invaders had been pushed into the high desert but refused to surrender, carrying on a guerrilla war. To support themselves, they preyed on the farm folk.

Sha'uri brought the newcomers to the tented awning where they cooked communal meals, then joined in to help serve out the food. Beside her, enthusiastically stirring the pot of grain meal, was Skaara's old friend Nabeh.

A strained-looking, heavyset man pushed into the line. Sha'uri noticed that his robes were the green of a farm Elder where they weren't covered in a coat of mud.

"Burned out," he said to everyone and no one at once. "Important men used to detour to come to my steading for the crops. Paid good silver. Burned out. No house. Crawled my way out through the fields." That explained the mud. "But I have important friends in Nagada."

One of his "important friends" was a Nagadan Elder who'd gotten himself murdered over some shady business. "He'll be happy to help me out. Used to come and visit when the city weather got too warm."

She'd seen it happen often. People whose lives had fallen apart tried to carry on as if everything were normal, having normal little chats with no one in particular.

This gentleman, however, was blocking a line of hungry people.

Sha'uri broke up a fresh loaf of bread and spread some fruit preserves on the pieces. "Why don't you have some bread and sit down?" she suggested. "I'll bet you could use something to eat."

"My wife always puts up our preserves," the man said, glancing around for his better half. He was alone. With the way the Horuses were going, chances were likely that his wife had been in the house when it burned.

"Wouldn't like me eating other people's preserves. Yes. We finally got a good orchard going—"

The line was becoming unmanageable.

"I'm sorry, Elder. Could you step out of the way for these people? They're very hungry."

"Not the way to treat a person of my rank," the man harrumphed. He drew himself up, preparing to bawl out a supposed scullery maid, and actually looked at her for the first time. The man gawked. "It's Kasuf's daughter, isn't it? How many feastings—"

"Please, Elder." She couldn't remember the man's name.

The Elder turned nasty. "This is what happens. Your home burned. Your wife—" He looked around again, momentarily lost. "And you're insulted by some child who marries a murderous Urt-man. That fellow with the freakish hair. Killed Nakeer—your own father."

Sha'uri stood quivering. Nabeh grabbed the man's arm and gave him an ungentle shake. "Listen, old man. Sit down or go away."

Muttering, the man left.

With a deep breath Sha'uri released her hold on the pistol butt she was gripping beneath her shawl. This was not the small weapon that had served her so well in the past. That had disappeared from the home she'd shared with Daniel. Skaara had found her another one. In the Nagada of today, one needed to go armed.

Just as one needed to pretend things were normal.

She had come close, so terribly close, to shooting that fat fool right in the middle of the food line.

If this kept up, she'd soon be walking around and talking to herself as well.

"So what surprises did you find hiding in that batch?" Barbara Shore asked of Professor Gary Meyers.

The bulky man shrugged helplessly. "Faizah was very good—"

"Hathor," Barbara corrected tartly. Daniel Jackson's news had hit the technical section like a bomb. "She certainly had the gift of tongues."

Meyers reddened.

"I mean, she was masterly at the art of technical disinformation," Barbara clarified. She pointed at the technicians clustered around one of the command center's consoles. "After boiling her bullshit out of the training program, we think we can get this bucket's long-range sensors powered up."

As usual, the Egyptologist's eyes glazed over at what he had been heard to call "the science stuff."

Barbara returned to the business at hand. "So what can you tell me about your reading there?" The translations in question had been handled by the crack team of Faizah and Meyers.

"I can't tell you what's right or wrong," he admitted. "I'm afraid I'm not very good at this, you know." Meyers shrugged, a changed man since the dogs of war had peed on his shoes. "I marked a couple of passages—parts she really worked hard on." He gave Barbara a wan smile. "I suppose whatever she says to do, you should do the opposite."

Barbara couldn't resist the chance to tease. "So, come on, Gary. What was it like?"

"What?" Meyers responded suspiciously.

"What was it like to date a goddess? I mean, as an Egyptologist, going out with the embodiment of good sex—"

"I feel sorry for Daniel," Meyers replied irrelevantly.

"Say what?"

"*She* went after him, and now he's in trouble. Whatever you want to call her, she was very good." He gave Barbara an embarrassed smile. "She'd laugh at my jokes, as if they were really funny." Meyers shrugged his heavy shoulders. "And I really miss her back rubs."

* * *

Corporal Tom Vance watched as Mitch Storey poked around the innards of the gunnery control console. Although the Marine wasn't a technician, he'd been seconded to the research team after spending the siege of the command deck with them. A strong back and a good attitude went a long way with some of the stuff they were doing now.

Vance watched in queasy fascination as the console circuitry squirmed and shifted like a live thing in response to Storey's probing.

"Just like the sensors," the technician growled, removing a gold-quartz test instrument. In moments he'd restored the console to operating condition.

"This end works fine. The controls are simple enough: you squidge around on this doo-jigger to aim—"

He ran a hand over a glowing panel. Overhead, the scanners' view shifted to a schematic representation. The picture of a helicopter gunship flying by on patrol turned to a weirdly faceted geometric symbol. As Storey's finger moved, a stylized eye followed the chopper icon.

"It's simple point-and-shoot, with either your gunnery teams or a computer doing the complicated stuff. Hit here, and that helicopter would be wasted—if we had any juice."

"Hey, Storey," one of the other techs complained, staring up at the ceiling. "Stop screwing around with the sensors. We think we can get this thing up and running."

Storey pressed his hand against the panel, which went dark. Overhead, the image of the helicopter reappeared to fly on, unaware of its brief role as target.

"The chopper was completely safe, as long as these lights weren't on," the technician finished. "That's our problem. We took one of those blast cannons apart—nothing wrong on that end, either." He scowled. "The screw-up is somewhere in the middle. We know this bucket has power—it's just going to all the wrong places."

"There must be training manuals for the engineering people," Vance said. "Don't they suggest anything?"

"Not the ones we've translated," Storey replied. "Then again, this may be something that can't be handled by pressing a few buttons and looking at the dials."

"You mean, they'd go out in something they couldn't fix?" Vance stared in disbelief.

Oh, and tell me you play mechanic whenever your car acts up," Storey retorted.

"Actually, I do—'cause I got one that dates back to before they started putting those damned computers under the hood."

"I guess that's as good an analogy as we could hope for," Storey said with a grin. "This clunker has a short somewhere in the electrical system—and we don't know enough about cars to track it down."

"Damned shame." Vance stared down at the console. "I wouldn't mind giving someone a taste of those headlights."

Daniel Jackson paced the perimeter of his cell, running one hand along the rough walls of golden quartz. The base camp's jug had been demolished in the attack of the Horuses. So Daniel had been imprisoned in what had probably been an equipment locker aboard the good ship *Ra's Eye*.

An entrance appeared in the far wall. Colonel Jack O'Neil and his intelligence chief, Colonel Felton, entered.

"O'Neil! It's about time," Daniel exclaimed impatiently. "This dipshit here—"

The army colonel glared, not used to civilian impertinence. "You'd do well to moderate your tone, Dr. Jackson. Working for the enemy during wartime is considered espionage, and could carry the ultimate penalty."

"I wasn't working for anybody!" Daniel turned beseeching eyes to O'Neil. "You don't believe this crap about me shooting Kasuf, do you? I hear you were given the murder weapon. Didn't you check it—"

"For what?" O'Neil inquired. "I'm afraid Abydan criminology isn't on to fingerprints yet. We have samples from several militiamen, some of the kitchen staff, Skaara, Sha'uri, and some of yours. Not to mention a few from 'none of the above.' " He shrugged. "I'm just surprised that Kasuf didn't get his hands on the damned thing."

"Too bad. Maybe I could've convinced your pal it was a suicide attempt." Daniel shot a sarcastic look at Felton, then turned again to O'Neil. "So why am I in jail?"

"We don't have anywhere else for you to go," O'Neil replied. "And we're still trying to find out which side you're on. By your own admission, you were with the infiltration team and the enemy leader—"

"Like I really had a choice about that!" Daniel burst out.

O'Neil paid no attention. "You could start by giving us a report on what this Hathor person is up to."

Daniel stabbed a finger at Felton. "That's all I've been talking about! What's he been telling you?"

Felton bristled. "We'd prefer some hard data, please, instead of comic-book science fiction."

"My respected Egyptological colleagues at least thought I was *Twilight Zone* material," Daniel replied with dignity.

He turned desperately to O'Neil. "Look, we've been through a lot that could be considered comic-book science fiction. Read my lips. Hathor has gotten her hands on a spaceship that makes the one we're in right now look like a pimple. How big is it? That flying palace Ra used to travel around in was this thing's nose cone. It's full of very high technology from that extinct race whose last survivor was Ra—or half of Ra.

There are weapons aboard this mother that could fry Kansas."

Daniel began to pace the room again, waving his arms. "The ship was parked in interstellar space. According to Hathor, it was fairly close by. So you've only got a couple of days at best—"

"She just gave away this intelligence. And then somehow you managed to escape from her," Felton said.

"The thing had its own StarGate. I was able—"

"But you can't take anyone *to* this StarGate." Felton's voice dripped with dubiousness.

Daniel lost his temper. "I *told* you, the gate had a set of secret, coded coordinates."

"So you have no proof of this . . . this fantasy."

"Well, gee, I'm sorry I didn't smuggle out microfilms with full blueprints of the goddamned thing. Silly me. I was in a hurry to warn you." He threw out his hands. "Where do you think I've been the last few days? Skiing Aspen with the lovely Hathor?"

O'Neil frowned, not happy with having his verities attacked again. "While you were gone, we went through one hell of a war, while Nagada all but suffered a social collapse—again, by your own account, stirred up by Hathor's subversive activities. We're rebuilding the camp and the expeditionary force with weapons that finally give us a level playing field—"

"So what are you saying?" Daniel demanded. " 'Don't bother me with facts, I'm busy winning this one for the Gipper'?"

He followed O'Neil to the door. "Fine. Win your war, but remember this. Hathor is on her way with a juggernaut—a ship that can kick major butt. Even worse, I think she looks on Abydos as just the practice round."

O'Neil turned back at the new tone in Jackson's voice.

Daniel looked frankly scared. "If she nails us because you're not ready—who's going to warn Earth?"

CHAPTER 17
OFF THE SCREEN

Barbara Shore stood on a completely renovated command deck, every console shining and complete. Under her orders, young men and women in metallic, skin-tight uniforms proceeded down through the complicated pre-liftoff checklist.

"Engines, all green," said the craggily handsome second-in-command, his voice all business.

"Navigation, all green," an exotic-looking brunette reported languidly from the console that was her responsibility.

Then the smooth coordination broke down. Barbara glanced in annoyance to the shaggy figure hunched over one of the consoles.

"Sensors?" Barbara asked. A nagging moment of silence passed. *"Sensors?"* she repeated.

Gary Heyers turned from the console. He opened his mouth, but a metallic shriek came out.

Barbara Shore leapt up from the desk where she'd dozed off. The navigation console was open, in the process of being examined. The sensors panel was also open, but its circuits were now operational.

They were what was causing the screaming. Barbara stumbled to the console, slapping the flashing panels.

Above her, the ceiling had shifted into a schematic view of the ambient space around the planet Abydos. A floating globe represented the planet, with a tiny, winking stylized red pyramid on its bosom—*Ra's Eye.*

So what was that phosphorescent green blob of light at the edge of detection range? Barbara fiddled with the alien controls, asking for an extrapolation of the unidentified object's course. It seemed to be heading straight for Abydos—but according to the computer, it would be a clear miss.

Barbara continued to manipulate the columns and panels of light. She squinted at the unfamiliar display, trying to gauge the item's magnitude. It took a moment, since she had to convert from ancient Egyptian measures to their modern equivalents.

When her calculations finished, her lips formed a silent whistle. Something on the order of a trillion and a half cubic meters. The oncoming piece of space debris would look small compared to a mountain, but it would make a damned good-sized hill.

"Hell of a time for something like this to blow in from deep space," Barbara muttered. "It's too much like Daniel Jackson's killer star vessel for this physicist's peace of mind."

She was about to start logging the information when the sensors blared a warning again. The green blob was deviating from the computer's dotted projection. For a second she swore at all balky computers everywhere—then she saw that the readouts floating in front of her were reporting a new speed.

Barbara's eyes went wide as her face went pale. No asteroid decelerated and changed course by itself. Her eyes glued to the ever changing readouts as the intruder came deeper into their sensor net, she fumbled for the field telephone that had been run up to her office.

For the umpteenth time that day, Daniel Jackson urged himself to patience. He had to put his case and his warning calmly. Then, a few minutes later, he found himself pacing his cell, raging like the proverbial lunatic.

He had to get out of here! Although Felton had spent several interrogation sessions with him, the flow of information had been one-way. The colonel had answered no questions about conditions in Nagada, or for that matter, on the base. All Daniel had to go on were his fleeting observations while being marched into the pokey and the few words that Jack O'Neil had let slip in their brief interview.

O'Neil's words had not, to put it mildly, offered the most encouraging picture. And, considering the murderous reception Daniel himself had gotten at the

StarGate, the war situation must still be pretty tense, even if the good guys were winning.

If circumstances were rocky in the Earthlings' enclave, they must be crazy back in town. How was Sha'uri doing? How was Skaara? Was Kasuf still among the living? Evidently, he was still considered the number one (and only) suspect for the shootings of the chief Elders.

Thinking back on it, Daniel wouldn't be surprised if people had seen him walking with Hathor to be greeted by that patrol. She certainly hadn't put him on his feet because man-mountain Khonsu was getting tired.

Wheels within wheels—that was the game that Ra had taught his assistant godlings. Hathor had proven an adept pupil. She'd played Daniel—and everyone else on Abydos—with consummate artistry.

She had me screwed from the moment she turned up in my office that morning, Daniel thought. *I was already dead. I just didn't know it yet.*

That was the past, to be learned from but not dwelt on. Not now, when there was so much that had to be done!

First, he had to arrange a departure from this glorified closet. Next, he had to get to Nagada and clear himself. Then came the hard part—seeing Sha'uri, getting her to believe in him again, attempting to make up for the pain he'd caused her.

From his days as the academic boy wonder, Daniel had always known he could be an arrogant little snot.

But his experiences on Abydos had, he thought, mellowed the old sharp edges on his personality.

Not true, he now knew. Nonetheless, he'd managed to inflict some pretty cruel slices on Sha'uri lately. That had to be amended.

The problem was that part of his three-step plan would require serious investments of time—and he didn't have any to spare. Sooner or later the Boat of a Million Years would arrive, and Hathor would finish up the work of destruction she'd originated.

Perhaps then his warnings would be believed. But it would be far too late.

Daniel found himself on his feet again, pacing. Well, it was exercise—at least he'd be physically set for the long walk to Nagada.

Now was the time to tackle the other steps . . . like somehow opening that damned locked door . . .

The panel vanished. Barbara Shore and Gary Meyers stood in the opening.

"We figured it was time for you to go," Meyers said.

"Something really huge has just entered a parking orbit around Abydos," Barbara amplified. "That means it isn't a meteor. I'm going to give O'Neil the official report, but I figured I'd take care of you before that little pow-wow."

"Are you guys sure about doing this?" Daniel asked. "I mean, you're probably under military discipline . . ."

Barbara shrugged. "Nobody here but us us dumb

civilians. However, if you want to help us get the ship's gunnery station working—"

"Let him go," Gary said.

Daniel was already out the door.

Barbara Shore stared curiously at Jack O'Neil. She'd expected a song and dance from this guy Felton. But she had never seen the Marine colonel so painfully eager to disbelieve a report.

"Is this some sort of joke, Doctor?" Colonel Felton insisted ponderously. "I imagine word has gotten around about Dr. Jackson's warnings. If you think things have gotten too boring of late—"

"No, sir," Barbara said in her best military style. She aimed her attention at O'Neil. "The ship's sensors *are* working, they did detect an enormous mass heading our way, and the mass has been maneuvering. That scared me enough to call the duty officer and pass it on to you—and to roust all our technicians and get them monitoring everything on the command deck.

"Before Colonel Felton called me down, we got some additional information from the sensor net. The object is constructed of the gold quartzose material we all know and love so well. Its shape is that of a pyramid, and it's huge—nearly two thousand feet tall, and more than three thousand feet on each side at the base, which means it would cover more than two hundred acres."

She took a deep breath. "To put it another way, we've got something the size of Disneyland coming down on our heads. Unless we get the gunnery system up and running on *Ra's Eye,* I have no idea what we can do about that sucker."

O'Neil's face went gray, but his voice was calm and formal. "Doctor, I apologize for doubting your report and wasting your time."

Barbara shrugged. "My people have their jobs to do—and their instructions. They're supposed to call directly here if there are any developments—"

The field telephone rang. O'Neil snatched it up. "O'Neil. What?" The colonel listened intently, adding the occasional monosyllable.

"Well, sir?" Felton asked when his superior had hung up.

"I suppose you could call it a bit of comintel," O'Neil said. "The communicators on the derelict's command deck are picking up some message traffic between the oncoming ship and the Horus guards. Hathor is not happy at all with the way things have gone here. She aims to redress the balance, and has ordered all her people on the planet to an immediate assault on the mines."

"Impossible, sir," Felton responded. "The Horus guards would have to gather their forces, then march for miles through heavily patrolled territory—"

"If what I've just heard is true, they're already massed at jump-off points within range of our patrols. And while the defenses at the mine are excellent, they were not made to withstand the kind of pounding this newly arrived ship can doubtless deliver."

He started out of the office. "We've got to warn Lieutenant Charlton and the garrison at the mine. Doctor, forgive me for sticking you with a long climb. I hope you have some success with the weapons systems." O'Neil was grim. "Because I think you're right. We're going to need them."

In the radio tent, Lieutenant Charlton's voice emerged from the set slightly staticky—and full of disbelief.

"Why would the remnants of the invasion force attempt today what their full number couldn't achieve last week? We're better dug in, we have energy weapons—"

"Listen," the intelligence officer hurried on, "the enemy is expecting overwhelming aerial support. *Spaceborne* aerial support. Do you copy? Over."

"Roger that," Charlton responded. After a brief background mutter, the young officer was back on. "I just passed the order to button up and hunker down. We have more than enough cover here. Over." His voice sounded slightly nervous, but optimistic.

"You say this bogey is approaching from the west? Wait one."

A louder comment came from the background.

Charlton's voice was a bit faster and slightly higher pitched as he got back on. "We have the bird under visual observation—an essentially pyramidal structure, occluding large patches of stars."

He broke off. "What the—?"

A heavy, staticky *crash!* came over the receiver. At the same time in the radio tent, dull thunder seemed to rumble in the distance.

"Oh, my God!" Charlton blurted.

"Settle down! Over," Felton ordered, ignoring the contravention of broadcasting decorum.

"That ship let loose a blast in the desert—like a lightning bolt, only straight—Jesus!"

"Watch your language," the Army colonel warned. "Over."

"Shit!" Charlton burst out. "They just knocked one of our choppers out of the sky. This thing is a lot bigger than I thought. We all expected it must be coming at the same altitude as *Ra's Eye* used during its attack. But that bolt looked like regular lightning from 'way up in the sky."

Again the radio roared and buzzed with static while the men in the tent also heard a booming detonation in the direction of the mine.

"—poor bastards!" a shocked Charlton swore when his voice came back.

"This is the net!" a scandalized Colonel Felton reminded the young officer. "Calm down and report what you see. Over."

"I've got a twenty-foot gap in my line, thanks to that goddamned thing up there! Half an infantry platoon, bing! gone! melted! On the outskirts of it there are people—oh, God, that guy's whole body is smoldering!"

More bolts lashed out, degrading the signal. Then,

even as the blasts continued, Charlton's voice came in more audibly. ". . . big bastard is down at the other end of our line, still pounding the piss out of us. Nothing we have reaches that high. The Avenger rockets are gone, and so is one of our LAVs with the heavier blaster. Whenever an energy weapon comes into play, that area gets plastered."

Charlton's delivery was hectic, as if he were trying to get as many words as possible out before he got destroyed.

Then unexpected hope came into his voice. "Wait! It's turning away!"

But although the bombardment of the mine defenses ceased, the monster ship's fusillade seemed to intensify as it traversed a path toward the high desert. New reports came in, terror-stricken or coldly factual, as energy weapons cut their way through O'Neil's patrols, opening a lane of advance for the assembled Horus guards.

O'Neil turned from the high-tech Ragnarok outside to Colonel Felton. "Ask Charlton if he can get out of there before they hit him again."

"Charlie Mike Actual!" The Army colonel spoke Charlton's call signal into the microphone. "This is Mike Bravo Foxtrot. What are your chances of staging a withdrawal? Over."

"This is Charlie Mike. Situation's bad." Beyond Charlton's voice they could hear the noises of troops being shouted and chivvied into line. "I looked into it, but we'd be sure to be caught out in the open. I think—" His voice grew a little grimmer. "I think we'll be able to hurt them more if we maintain our positions. Over."

"I concur," O'Neil said, but the words tasted bitter in his mouth.

Then the reception went bad again as the Boat of a Million Years returned to attack Charlton's positions. The young lieutenant's radio politesse disintegrated almost as quickly as his defenses.

Felton again fought a losing battle for making nice on the communications net.

After several seconds of almost continuous static, the lieutenant's voice came out of the speaker. "Oh, shit! Here come the Whorehouse guards!"

Colonel Felton was getting good and steamed. He must have thought the junior officer was deliberately ignoring his commands. "There's no need for profanity, Charlie Mike. Over."

At the same time the younger man's frantic orders were being broadcast along with his report. "The fucking wire is *gone*! Just shoot! Shoot the sons of bitches!"

Beside himself, Felton snarled into the microphone, "Listen, mister. This is the net, not a toilet. You're looking to get yourself written up!"

Finally, Jack O'Neil burst out. "What the hell are you going to do, Felton? Give him a posthumous reprimand?"

The Army man stood, jarred into silence. Obviously, he'd been paying so much attention to the form of

Charlton's report, he hadn't really been thinking about the content.

The speaker rang with the sounds of close combat. The crash of blast-lances seemed almost quiet after the devastating blasts coming from the spaceship.

Charlton's voice came through clearly. "Shoot, damn you! *Shoooot!*"

Thunder roared again, then there was silence.

"The poor bastard!" Felton blurted.

Then, with a look of horror, he clapped his hand over his microphone.

CHAPTER 18
TO PLAY THE GOD

Aboard the Boat of a Million Years, Hathor stood enveloped in a cloud of virtual reality. Reproduced around her was a miniature simulacrum of the ground below the starship.

Where Hathor walked, the starship moved. Where Hathor pointed, the starship discharged its secondary batteries.

It was a heady experience for the goddess. She felt like a giant presence, bestriding the field of battle.

Yet at the same time it was frustrating. The interplay between commander and ship fell far short of perfection. It was as if Hathor were attempting some incredible feat of precision work with her hands imprisoned in large, awkward, unyielding gloves.

When Daniel had escaped, Hathor had intensified her efforts to develop some sort of interface with the computer that ran the ancient craft. That computer had files allowing it to understand Hathor's court speech. At least she didn't have to write each order for the control device's execution. But faced with a flood of requests for directives, Hathor had in the end decided to proceed with most of the ship working on automatic systems.

She often found herself wondering how the ur-Ra had dealt with the monstrous ship in all its complexity when the last of his (its?) fellows had perished.

Perhaps that had been the reason Ra had used this vessel's pinnace as his portable palace. Doubtless, it had been a simpler entity to master.

There was, of course, an alternative to all this jury-rigging and computer interfacing. Hathor could simply lift the field holding the ship's crew in stasis. But every time the thought even crossed her mind, it was swept back by a wave of revulsion.

It would take more than a little inconvenience to make her free that brood of red-furred monstrosities.

She surveyed the miniature battlefield below her, bringing any knots of resistance under close scrutiny. Would it be worthwhile to neutralize them with another blast?

"Lady." The voice of Khonsu seemed to come from the rift of the mine itself. "The enemy's defenses are failing. Do you intend to cease firing? Shall we deal with them hand-to-hand?"

An odd note surfaced in her deputy's voice—not exactly awe. It was more like worry. Abruptly, Hathor was jolted from her mental throne of godhood. She had the power, true . . . but in her hands it was presently administered in a clumsy form.

The Boat of a Million Years was not built for work

on planets. It handled progressively more sluggishly the deeper it was brought into an atmosphere. But from the height where she was working, the necessary scale of the simulacrum made her finger too large a pointer. Her single-handed gunnery was sloppy, blasting her servants as well as her foes.

"Move forward," Hathor ordered. "I shall be watching."

Hathor refrained from any more firing as her people closed in to capture the remaining points of resistance.

"Lady, we are taking many captives," Khonsu reported. "Should we eliminate them?"

"No," she said decisively, her voice echoing inside his hawk-mask. "Let the fellahin be separated from the Earthmen. They know their duties already. Set them to work mining the quartz mineral."

A mighty warship and a rich cargo would both be useful weapons when she returned to Tuat the throne world.

"Utilize the Earthmen to load the mineral onto your udajeets. You'll have to ferry the loads up to me on the ship."

The airlift was an unfortunate necessity, since the monster ship could never land. But it would be interesting to receive Khonsu's assessment of the wild Earthmen's potential as slaves.

"Lady, must we bring some of the new slaves up to you to unload the cargo?"

She conferred with the computer. "It will not be

necessary," she replied. "Automatic devices can take on your loads."

Lieutenant Charlton's last memory was the unearthly beauty of final defensive fire, the deadly glowing networks that tracer bullets weaved for themselves in concentrated fields of fire. He'd expected it to be his *final* memory, considering the stunning blast of energy that had lanced down near his position.

Instead, he'd awakened to find himself with a couple of sergeants and a good portion of the survivors of his command watching him.

"What's this, Sarge?" he asked a grizzled veteran.

"Example time, I think," came the reply. "They want us to load that wheelbarrow thing with these rocks." He nodded at a generous pile of quartzite ore. "Three of us, and three straw bosses."

A trio of Horus guards strolled up to them. One jerked a thumb at the wheelbarrow. The noncoms watched the officer. "Do we do it, sir?"

Before Charlton could answer, a cocky young rifleman stepped out of the crowd. "Hey, don't you clowns know about the Geneva convention?"

Charlton suspected none of the guards spoke English. But one took exception to the tone. The Horus' blast-lance came down, and there was one less prisoner.

"No!" The young officer stepped forward, his hands out. This, it appeared, was a different form of defiance. But compassion wasn't a burning offense. The guards merely beat Charlton to his knees—quickly, humiliatingly—and very painfully.

Daniel Jackson had clung to the summit of a dune, watching the progress of the Boat of a Million Years as it cleared the way for the Horus guard attack. It had been like watching the Moon suddenly set off in a homicidal frenzy.

Whole formations of troops had been wiped out with as little ceremony as a human would use in stepping on an anthill.

Daniel knew there were still friends and foes scattered across the sands between here and Nagada. He jogged on through the darkness, hoping he could handle whatever he found. The snarl of engines warned him at almost the last moment. He scrambled aside just before being run down by a convoy of Humvees. They were heading back toward the base camp, running without lights. One of the vehicles stopped, and the Marine gunner leaned over his twin machine guns, raised his infrared goggles, and said, "You're heading the wrong way, chum—the Old Man is pulling back all outlying units into a smaller perimeter."

"I've got business in the city," Daniel replied.

The Marine shrugged. "An okay place, if you like snake pits. Except for the front door, where that Skaara guy runs things, they've got gangs running the whole joint. Battles in the streets over turf that may not exist by morning."

He gave an apprehensive glance at the sky and lowered his voice. "You hear about this killer spaceship the Whorehouse guard has helping out? Damn thing knocked us flat at the mines. They captured a bunch of our guys and have 'em doing the rock-pile rag! Even loading it onto those hawk-head planes! Then they fly it up to the ship!"

Daniel frowned. Hathor could have all sorts of logical reasons to seize the mines. On his way to being jailed, he'd seen the energy weapons Earth technology had built. *Cutting off our supply of quartz would make good sense to Hathor,* he thought.

But there was only one reason he could see for Hathor to start stockpiling the wonder mineral. That would be if Abydos ceased to exist.

He hoped his thoughts didn't show on his face as he waved good-bye to the gunner. But some of Hathor's vague threats about whole worlds began to echo in his head.

Daniel began to jog, then run toward Nagada.

It's just too goddamned much, Colonel Jack O'Neil thought as he surveyed his shrinking defenses from the best vantage point in the area—through the fused-open hangar doors of Launch Deck Four. He'd pulled in his mobile forces from the high desert once it was evident that the Horus guards had gotten through. His patrols watching Nagada had also been brought back.

There seemed no good news from the city itself. O'Neil's night-vision goggles registered high infrared radiation from Nagada. The place was burning. Whether from aerial attack or internal arson, he couldn't guess.

Troops of all sorts had to swerve widely in their approach to the base camp to avoid the captured mine, where the Boat of a Million Years loomed like some sort of monstrous cloud over a wound in the earth.

A defense line was stabilizing to block any advances toward the camp, and patrol action was picking up. The Earth troops were firing their blast-rifles only sparingly. Prodigal use of energy weapons tended to get a force targeted for one of those baleful gouts of destruction spurting from the hellish form overhead.

O'Neil watched in pain as another blast lashed out. His people on the front lines were especially vulnerable. Their position would, paradoxically, improve as the lines were pulled closer and closer to the camp.

Merely from his own observation, the colonel could see that Hathor's aim was lousy.

By the time the battle reached the camp, she'd probably have to cease firing.

Otherwise, O'Neil figured, Hathor would be jeopardizing the very things she was fighting to capture—the salvageable spacecraft—and the Abydos StarGate.

Oddly, O'Neil felt at peace with himself. He'd sent a full report to General West through the StarGate, warning of the enemy's new spacecraft and giving his best estimates of its abilities.

He'd also begun evacuating his troops.

The wounded were the first to go. O'Neil had then tried to remove the technical team, but almost to a person they had resisted the idea. "If this is our last shot, we want it to mean something," Barbara Shore had said. "We're gonna bring back this tub's technology if we have to rip it out of the walls before we go!"

O'Neil had put Colonel Felton in charge of getting people through the StarGate in a timely fashion. The Army officer might be a bit of a stick, but he was efficient.

That left Jack O'Neil with the job of getting enough warm bodies out of the desert to him . . . without weakening the defenses so badly that the enemy could get in and disrupt the withdrawal.

O'Neil felt tired. He was a fighter—he hated the idea of having to run. But so many of his people had been sacrificed on this world already. Most of them had died fighting against impossible odds. The fact that in the end victory had been pulled from defeat didn't make them any less dead.

A grim smile tugged at the corners of the colonel's mouth. Not so very long ago, he'd have welcomed the chance to go down fighting. Back then it seemed like the answer to all his problems.

Now he had a life again. He wanted to live. But he was a warrior first and foremost. If he had to give his life, he would.

He just hated the idea of taking other people with him.

"Watch yourself, sir!"

Mitch Storey couldn't believe he'd just yelled that at the commander of the expeditionary force here on Abydos.

But Colonel Jack O'Neil stepped aside as Storey and a couple of technicians steered a pair of dollies precariously piled with technological loot along the deck.

As the clock inexorably ran down, the technical team members began to look less like researchers and more like vandals as they charged through the ship *Ra's Eye,* trying to record and transmit as much of its astonishing mechanisms as they could.

Already, a steady stream of photos, diagrams, and translated material was flowing through the StarGate. Now the tech people were becoming more ruthless. Memory cores were being yanked out of computers. In some places whole computers were being torn out. Where the pieces were too big to remove, circuits would be dissected in place while everything was minutely recorded.

Barbara Shore was down with the engines, an area they had been very leery of screwing around in. Those hulking mechanisms were putting out a tremendous amount of power—somewhere. Now a special team was measuring components, checking for a dozen types of radiation, shooting film and stealing every conceivable file from the engine-room computers.

Storey hoped it would be enough to let them create a duplicate drive when they got home.

Professor Pete Auchinloss had completely gutted the dormitory classrooms. In the end, with the help of some requisitioned muscle, he'd taken every single teaching computer he could find.

Storey wasn't exactly sure he agreed with all this slash-and-burn scientific investigation.

But even he found himself getting annoyed at one of the more timid technicians who was trying to remove one of the circuits controlling the metamorphosis of a wall.

"You need both the circuit and what it controls," he said, stopping his trolley load. "Have you isolated what that is?"

"Ah, more or less," the other man said, indicating an area about four feet square. "It's the size that's the problem."

"No, it isn't." Reaching into the front dolly, Storey brought out a blast-lance. "Stand back, now."

With the weapon's head almost touching the wall, the bearded technician cut loose the indicated area.

"Just give it a moment or two to cool down," Storey told his dumbfounded coworker. "Then add it to the next load of stuff coming through."

Beyond the gates of Nagada, Daniel Jackson saw a city in flames, topped by a sooty, red-flaring pillar rising high into the sky.

Daniel halted in his tracks. He wasn't exactly a religious man, but he recognized hell when he saw it.

Incredibly, there was activity on the catwalks. People ran back and forth, shouting down into the compound below. A knot of figures clustered on the wood and rope bridge. Was that Skaara up there? And Sha'uri?

Daniel sucked in a deep breath. "Hello, the gate!" he cried as loudly as he could.

"Gate's closed!" one of the guards yelled back. "Try again tomorrow—if it ever comes!"

"I bring word from the Earth camp," Daniel responded. He threw back the hood of his Abydan robe. "And I want to talk to my wife," he added in English.

The shouting on the towers and catwalks gave way to gasps as Daniel was recognized. Within the organic noise of surprise, Daniel also heard the sharp metallic *clicks* of firearms being readied.

Nobody said this would be easy, he thought.

He stood with his hands out, showing empty palms.

"Put up those rifles!" Skaara's voice cut across the confusion. "And open those doors. I'll hear what he has to say."

A voice rose in protest—Sha'uri's. But she was pitching her arguments for her brother, not for the whole area. Even the sound of a hostile Sha'uri had an odd effect on Daniel's heart rate.

By the time the gates had screeched their protesting ways open, Skaara had reached ground level. He faced his erstwhile brother-in-law, matching his empty-handed pose.

Daniel, however, could not ignore the pair of snipers with their rifles trained on his head, ready for the least hostile move.

"I'm not going to bite you," Daniel finally said. "You think you can get those gunmen to aim somewhere else?"

A single word from Skaara, and the pair desisted. Things might be bad in Nagada, but Skaara obviously had bloomed into a real leader.

Maybe it's because he's the only hope these people have, Daniel thought.

"I appreciate you not having me shot on sight," he said. "Are your radios still working? Have you made out anything of what's happened tonight?"

Daniel gave a concise report of what had happened during the night—and what the huge ship signified.

Then, not knowing if any of his story had been spread, he gave Skaara a brief account of what had happened to him from the day of the assassination attempt.

"I'd hoped that Sha'uri would also be here. She really ought to hear some of this."

The look Skaara gave him said, *Don't ask for what you can't get.*

"She didn't want you to come in," he said. "When I insisted, she left."

Twenty pounds seemed to settle in Daniel's chest.

"There's nothing to blame her for. Did they tell you at least that Faizah was actually Hathor?"

Skaara nodded. "That did not make it easier for my sister."

Daniel forced his hopes aside. "What's happening with these fires?"

"One of the many rival chieftains set some blazes to burn out an enemy—and his efforts have spread far beyond his plans. So far we've kept the flames from our enclave, but—"

"And Kasuf? How is he?"

For a long moment Skaara gave Daniel an enigmatic look. "Come," he finally said. "I'll show you."

They walked into a large whitewashed building—a hospital, Daniel realized as he came inside. Most of the big structure—a former warehouse, Daniel figured—was devoted to open wards.

There were, however, a few private rooms for the very serious cases.

Daniel couldn't repress a gasp at Kasuf's still condition. He took a lax, cool hand in his. "Old friend," he said, "it grieves me to see you in this case. And that's not just because you're the only one who knows I didn't shoot you—"

"B-but you weren't," a papery voice interrupted Daniel. The hand he held squeezed faintly against his, and Kasuf's eyes opened.

"The one who shot us wore a ridiculous yellow mop on his head. He was a bigger man than you—a Horus guard, with Ra's sign tattooed on his face."

Daniel stared at this sudden reprieve, hoping that Skaara had heard all that the whispering voice had said.

Kasuf's son, however, stood in the doorway.

"Dr. Destin," he called. "Doctor!"

CHAPTER 19
FORLORN HOPES

Dr. Terrance Destin couldn't explain what had brought Kasuf out of his coma. "I'd like to say it was one of those miracles of modern medicine, but I don't know where the credit goes." He nodded at Daniel. "Perhaps it was Mr. Jackson's voice—the voice of the man accused of attacking him." The doctor shrugged. "Or maybe he was just ready to reenter the world again."

At any rate, Skaara agreed that Sha'uri ought to hear what their father had to say.

Daniel stood on one of the watchtowers, staring out into the night, when he became aware of a presence behind him.

"So," Sha'uri finally said in Abydan, "you're not a *political* traitor."

"No," Daniel said, not trusting himself to turn. "Just a fool who didn't know when he was well off." He took a deep breath. "Nothing happened between her and me. I won't kid you and say it was impossible.

She nearly did seduce me—she just found something she wanted more."

"Ah," Sha'uri said with heavy sarcasm. "And now that you've come through your ordeal, you've returned, so things can go on as before."

Daniel shook his head. "I've come to tell you that *nothing* is as it was before. Your city is burning down, the Horus guards hold the mine—and a bunch of your people, Skaara tells me. That thing out there—"

"Thank you, I've heard enough." Behind him, he heard Sha'uri turning away.

Daniel felt a stab of anger. He whirled, catching Sha'uri by the arm. "Listen," he said, "I love you, dammit. I want to make what was between us good again. But I don't have the time. That thing out there has the power to reduce Nagada to a smear in the landscape. Look at it. *Look at it!*"

He dragged her to the parapet. They watched for a long moment as gouts of energy poured from the Boat of a Million Years, pounding the Marine positions. "Those are brave men out there. But they have nothing that can withstand those bolts. All too soon they'll be driven into the StarGate. Then Hathor will control the gate, and no one will be able to get off Abydos."

"Then go," Sha'uri said roughly.

"No," Daniel said. "I want *you* to go. You've been marked for death because of the rebellion—you and Skaara, Kasuf, and many others. Skaara and I are willing to fight. But the ones who escape will need a leader, too. The people trust you. They'll follow you."

"And you think that we'll be welcome on your wonderful world?"

Daniel didn't answer for a second. Then he finally said, "I think Jack O'Neil is an honorable man. And I don't think your people should die because you're angry at me."

He let Sha'uri go. "Hate me if you want. But I hope to save your life—and as many lives as possible."

The dull rumble of Hathor's blast-bolt attacks continued through the night, like unending thunder without the promise of rain. Sha'uri had roused the refugees and explained the situation to them. Those willing to leave were even now assembling their scanty belongings.

A worried-looking Dr. Destin had approved Kasuf for travel and had even agreed to accompany him on a mastadge-drawn litter.

When Sha'uri saw her brother, she discovered that he, too, had been making preparations. He carried a blast-lance and stood among a knot of runners. "When Hathor sees your people, she might think we're coming to aid Colonel O'Neil. We need to create a diversion, and Daniel has suggested a good one. We're going to attack the mine."

"You're going to attack—with that thing up there?" Sha'uri demanded, her eyes going to the Boat of a Million Years. "That's hopeless!"

Skaara looked at her calmly. "Not if it draws off Hathor and your people escape. For some reason

Cat-head Hathor has the prisoners digging up the quartz. If it's so important to her, she'll have to deal with us."

"Kill you, you mean," Sha'uri said bitterly.

Skaara shrugged, not arguing with her. "I've sent messages to some of our old comrades. We'll need every fighting man we can field for this attack. A number are joining us. They'd rather end fighting the Horuses than one another."

He hesitated for a moment, then said, "We sally forth within the hour. Daniel goes with us."

When Sha'uri didn't speak, her brother merely nodded. "No need to wish us luck."

From the berm surrounding the base camp, Colonel Jack O'Neil watched the line snaking through the company streets and into the golden pyramid of the cruiser *Ra's Eye.* Slowly, group by group, the line advanced as those at the head transited through the StarGate. The men shuffling forward were often wounded, always tired. And every man who managed to escape meant that much more contraction on the part of the colonel's defense line.

O'Neil shuddered as another torrent of energy lashed down from the bulk overshadowing them, illuminating the whole battlefield for a moment. The men just in from the perimeter flinched at the sudden radiance. O'Neil understood. They'd been the targets out there.

The colonel focused his binoculars on the point of

impact. Hathor's big guns had scored another near miss as an infantry company executed a quick retreat. Another stretch of desert property large enough to accommodate a tract house had been transformed into a pit of fused greenish-brown glass.

While his Marine's soul hated every step of this retreat, O'Neil was glad that the men had lived to get away.

At least for this blast.

Standing at his side, Lieutenant Adam Kawalsky seemed to pick up O'Neil's thoughts. The lieutenant had an interest in military history, especially that of the Corps. Not surprisingly, he used a historical perspective. "I was too young for Vietnam. But now I know how it must have felt for the men pinned down in Khe Sanh."

"Or the Alamo," contributed Feretti. The other remaining survivor of the first Abydos incursion had a rather fractured sense of history.

"Not a good comparison," O'Neil reproved. "The troops there didn't survive."

"Besides," Kawalsky pointed out, "they weren't Marines."

"Yeah." Feretti nodded, scanning the battlefield with his glasses. "That's probably why the poor bastards lost."

O'Neil cast a glance overhead. Too much time had passed since the last gift from the heavens. Why wasn't Hathor blasting them?

Astonishingly, new starfields disappeared in the

sky overhead. The Boat of a Million Years was shifting position. O'Neil followed its progress tensely. Was this the start of a flank attack? Was Hathor pulling back in hopes of blasting his forward echelons more freely— without threatening the StarGate?

No—the vast bulk in the sky was pulling too far away.

"Where the hell is Hathor going?" he growled, staring upward.

"Sir, I'd say that thing was heading back to the mines," Kawalsky said.

"And, sir, we've got a column coming at us," Feretti suddenly reported. "It's coming from the direction of Nagada, but they're not using the road."

O'Neil quickly wheeled and aimed his binoculars. Although Nagada was not directly in sight, it was easy to zero in on its position. He just had to aim for the reddish pillar of fire in the distance.

A quick scan thorough his night glasses revealed a large infrared concentration coming their way. O'Neil frowned, trying to make some sense of what he was seeing.

The Horus guards had been getting a bit bolder under the aegis of their pyramid in the sky, patrolling aggressively and keeping the pressure on O'Neil's withdrawing troops. But for the most part the Horuses hadn't been attacking. They'd restricted their thrusts to picking off stragglers and overrunning positions that had already been thoroughly blasted by the Boat of a Million Years.

Frankly, O'Neil didn't think the Horuses had the stomach for a full-scale assault. So why were they advancing without the cover of their monstrous air support? Somehow, he'd never think of Hathor as a commander very worried about killing her own people with friendly fire.

The colonel raised his binoculars again, trying to get some idea of the enemy's intentions. Should he commit what was left of his artillery in the hopes of dampening the Horuses' resolve? Or was this a feint to make him reveal his gun positions for a bunch of blast-bolts from on high?

O'Neil was about to order the battery fire when he looked hard into his field glasses. Something was wrong—then it struck him. The figures advancing were too covered up. Infrared showed exposed skin. Clad only in pectoral necklaces and kilts, the Horus guards showed plenty of that. But their battle-masks cut off their heads.

The infrared image O'Neil was getting showed hands and faces. Either it was an elaborate charade, or . . .

"Get a patrol out there," he abruptly ordered his radioman.

"Sir?" Feretti said uncertainly.

"I don't think that's an attack," the colonel amplified. "I think they may be friendlies."

In minutes, he was getting the report from a corporal out in the field. "It's a refugee column from Nagada, sir, led by somebody named Sha'uri. She's talking in English, asking you for passage to Earth."

O'Neil watched the long, ragged collection of people toiling their way across the sands. Of course Sha'uri would have avoided the road. It led to the mines, which were in enemy hands. And between the fires and the Horus guards, there probably was only one safe destination around for the small portion of the Abydan population in her care.

"Sir?" the radioman asked. "Corporal Sanders wants to know if he should try to turn them back."

O'Neil straightened. "Hell, no," he said abruptly, turning to his history-minded aide. "We might be bugging out of here like we did in Vietnam. But no way are we leaving the people who sided with us hanging in the wind."'

"Get the motor pool. I want everything we have with wheels ready to move—immediately."

He was about to cause one hell of a logistical problem, but that would be Felton's headache.

All O'Neil had to do was maintain security while *everybody* got away.

Daniel Jackson aimed his blast-lance and burned a hole through a Horus guard's pectoral necklace. In spite of being in the biggest fight of his life, Daniel felt queerly at peace.

Sha'uri had rejected him, and he was in the forefront of a suicide attack. He couldn't exactly say that all was well with the world. Perhaps it was just that the world seemed well lost.

Skaara had led the advance on the most obvious

route, the old mining road from Nagada. Incredibly, they hadn't encountered any Horuses until they rounded the switchback that led down into the ravine of the mines themselves.

Daniel and the contingent of Abydan blast-lancers he'd joined charged, weapons flaring. The Horus guards dropped their quirts and unlimbered their weapons, but they were overwhelmed in a moment. Following the momentum, the militiamen charged downhill until they encountered another knot of men in the darkness, this one larger. Daniel himself had aimed his lance, poised to fire, when he yelled in Abydan. "No! No! Hold your fire! These are friends."

They faced a bedraggled collection of prisoners, both Abydan and Earthling, pressed into mining duties. White dust clung to robes and BDUs alike.

One of the Abydans stood with tears in his eyes. "When the others told the hawk-heads how things fared in the city, the Horuses said that none would dare come out to rescue us."

"Well, it looks like they were wrong," Daniel said. He moved along to the American contingent asking in English, "Anybody in charge here?"

"I guess I am—just barely," a weak voice replied.

Daniel had to look hard for a moment at the battered face before he recognized Lieutenant Charlton. "You came along at a good time. The guys were covering for me—"

"Man who can't do his work gets killed," one of the

Marine ex-captives explained. "The bastards made that pretty clear."

"But our friends in the funny hats didn't like the fact that the men were looking out for me, and decided to make an example of us," Charlton went on. "I think they were going to toss us off the top of the mine."

"Okay," Daniel said. "Everybody in favor of making them pay—raise your hands."

By now Skaara and the main body had joined them. Anyone with weapons to spare shared them out. The blast-lances recovered from the defunct Horus guards were also distributed; then the enlarged force continued downward.

The Horus guards were actually pretty thin on the ground for the number of prisoners they were overseeing.

But when hope raised its ugly head . . .

In the forefront of the fighting, Daniel several times saw Horuses suddenly drop in their positions with a pickax through the back, or being battered to the ground by men wielding shovels. He also saw the sickening spectacle of work gangs being blasted down just seconds before they could be freed. In some cases he saw men walk into the blast-bolts so their buddies could take down the guards with their bare hands.

From the floor of the valley came a labored whistling sound. It took Daniel a moment to recognize—until he connected it with the shape rising into the air. The twittering was the sound of a udajeet with overloaded engines. The antigravity glider must have been heavily laden with quartzite ore, because it literally wallowed in the air as it spun to turn its guns on the upper mine galleries.

Daniel aimed his blast-lance at the cockpit, sending bolt after bolt before the pilot could fire on the advancing tide of troops. His fire was quickly joined by others. In seconds the udajeet was wheeling helplessly downward to crash and explode. Two more udajeets rose, not bothering to attack. They just wanted to escape. Neither passed the gauntlet of the mine terraces.

Men came climbing up from the lower levels. The Horuses down there had been overrun. Judging from the blast-bolts, the only resistance remaining was on the far lip of the mine, in what remained of the Earthlings' prepared defenses.

Daniel began climbing again, aiming to come around on the flank of the Horuses positions. Even as he joined the battle, he saw squads of masked guardsmen rushing across the dunes to reinforce their brothers. The forces were locking in the deadly embrace of hand-to-hand combat when the sky went dark overhead. Then a lash of unfettered energy fell on the combatants.

Rebels, Earthmen, and Horuses alike were blasted. Daniel found himself knocked flat on the rocky lip of the ravine. Just a little bit farther, and his troubles would have been over.

The two sides recoiled apart at the almost godlike scourging. Daniel raised his voice over the terror-stricken cries. "Don't fall back!" he cried in English and Abydan. "It just gives Hathor a free target! Keep after the Horuses! She can't keep blasting her own men!"

Skaara joined him, and together they managed to get the attack moving forward again.

Daniel didn't know how they succeeded. It was like advancing into an incinerator. It was the former prisoners who turned the tide, swelling the front lines, ignoring Hathor's gigantic energy flail in their intentness to settle scores with the Horuses.

Then the Boat of a Million Years was turning away from them, stabbing gouts of energy down into the desert.

What the hell could be out there?

But Daniel didn't have time to wonder. A Horus guard, his blast-lance shattered in half, leapt from behind some rocks and tried to club Daniel down. The guy was too close for Daniel to shorten the grip on his own lance and blast him. So he swung the shaft of his weapon crosswise across his chest and tried to parry the guardsman's blow.

Things didn't work out the way they usually did in Robin Hood movies. The shock nearly tore the blast-lance from Daniel's hands. The Horus rammed into Daniel, taking them both to the ground.

Daniel's blast-lance was still across his chest, held there by the weight of the guardsman, who was trying to strangle him. Hands like steel clamps tightened around his throat as he tried uselessly to push the masked figure back.

So this is it, Daniel thought, faintly wondering as his view turned red, then black at the edges.

Then there was a searing flash across his eyes and a loud explosion in his right ear. The Horus flopped ingloriously off him.

And Jack O'Neil was helping Daniel to his feet, a 9mm Beretta pistol in his hand.

"Thought you could use a little help there, on the way to your ride."

"R—ride?" Daniel slurred, staring around. The only Horus guards he saw were busy running for their lives. Everyone else was piling into a wild assortment of vehicles before the Boat of a Million Years managed to blast them all.

"Yes. We've already picked up Sha'uri and her refugee column. She told us about this diversionary attack you talked Skaara into. Of all the stupid—"

"It let Sha'uri get away. I'm not such a Delta Foxtrot Bravo," Daniel said. Going into battle without the annoyance of having to survive had been a bizarre comfort for him. But now, having to deal with hope—he hung back as O'Neil led the way to a waiting Humvee.

The Marine turned back, frowning at him. "What they hell are you waiting for, an engraved invitation?"

He grabbed Daniel and hauled him along, tossing him into the vehicle's rear compartment, already full of fugitives.

Their jouncing trip across the dunes was indescribable, combining all the worst aspects of a

StarGate transit with the ill effects of being jostled by elbows and kicked by combat boots, with the attendant smells of unwashed humanity. The driver was apparently attempting to outrun the pursuing starship while selecting the most spectacular bumps and rough spots as he leapt and dodged among the dunes.

But, of course, the Boat of a Million Years couldn't be outrun. In fact, it always seemed to be right over them, blasting something in their near vicinity.

And then there were those pesky collections of Horus guards they kept driving through.

At one point Daniel found himself having a conversation with Jack O'Neil's knees. The colonel had taken the gunner's position on the mounted M240 machine gun. He hosed bullets at everything that moved at the rate of two hundred rounds per minute.

"Sorry about the bumpy ride," O'Neil said, squeezing off a burst at something outside. "We're not just racing Hathor, but her whole army. It'll be tight, getting back to our perimeter before it's overrun."

They came bombing through the open and blasted gates of the camp and swerved with wild abandon through empty streets. The shimmering skin of the grounded spaceship *Ra's Eye* grew closer. Then Daniel got a glance of Horus guards—lots of them—and O'Neil's machine gun began thumping again.

The rescue convoy returned just in time to save another group of troops—the Marine defenders drawn up in front of the entrance to the ship—and the StarGate.

"Come on, Jackson," he heard the colonel say. "Last stop."

Scowling in frustration, technician Sam Gomfrey glanced from his watch to the fire-control relay he was supposed to be removing. Time was running out. The research team was already supposed to be downstairs. He'd wind up personally carrying this sucker through the StarGate. It wasn't his fault that a faulty diagram had left him searching in completely the wrong conduit.

Lateness was why Gomfrey did something that normally would have horrified his tidy technician's soul. He chose a shortcut.

Instead of going for his tools, he unlimbered the blast-lance he'd taken away from a dead invading Horus guard and kept triggering it until he'd sliced the control node free of the wall. As he slashed away, his weapon's heat and energy discharge caused other circuits in the conduit to curl and twist as though they were live things trying to get away.

Gomfrey finished his cutting job, swearing as he burned his fingers picking up the cannibalized circuit. He glanced at the irregular outline he'd cut in the wall, at the writhing circuits, and shrugged.

"Close enough for government work," he said.

In conduit *Sb*-26, the circuits shocked by Gomfrey's rough blaster work cycled through their various biomorphic shapes. One of them, a balky multipurpose unit that had resisted the efforts of even the great technician god Ptah suddenly shifted into its power-shunt mode.

Energy began flowing through entirely new networks aboard *Ra's Eye*.

Mitch Storey was panting after the climb from ground level to the command deck of the defunct starship. Sure, he understood that Barbara Shore needed a trustworthy person to check that nothing had been left behind. But did it have to be him?

The only thing more annoying was to notice that Corporal Tom Vance, who was accompanying him, didn't seem to be breathing heavily at all.

A quick search showed that the place had indeed been cleaned out according to plan—apparently, it just hadn't been noted in the rush. Storey's response was brief and profane. "Well, we won't have to carry anything," he said, heading for the central stairs. "But we'll have to haul ass if we expect get out on time."

"You go on ahead," Vance said, something catching his eye. He'd spent enough time among the consoles here to spot something out of the ordinary. There were lights blinking on panels that had never lit up before.

And a lot of those lights were on the gunnery control console . . .

From the first rank of Skaara's attackers, Daniel Jackson now found himself among the last ranks of the StarGate's defenders. The Marine guards had conducted a stubborn retreat, first into the gold-quartz halls of the spaceship *Ra's Eye,* then into the stone passages of the StarGate pyramid itself.

The bombardment from the Boat of a Million Years had ceased as soon as the last of the rescue convoy had arrived. Apparently, Hathor still preferred not to damage irreplaceable assets.

She was perfectly willing to spend Horus guards, however. Under relentless pressure the Earthlings had been pushed about halfway down the Great Gallery. Daniel was well into the zen of combat, not worrying what the future might bring, when he was suddenly seized from behind.

"Sorry, Doc," Lieutenant Kawalsky muttered in his ear as he hauled the battling Egyptologist out of the battle line. "But the colonel wants you—now."

The hall of the StarGate, recently packed with retreating troops and refugees, now stood almost empty as Daniel walked in with his escort. His promise to go gracefully with Kawalsky at least had protected his dignity. Just as well. Daniel wouldn't have liked Sha'uri to see him being frog-marched in. Skaara was also on hand, as were Mitch Storey, Barbara Shore, Jack O'Neil, and a couple of military types.

Skaara told Daniel quietly, "Father has already gone on ahead through the StarGate. Dr. Destin believes he should survive the journey."

Sha'uri said nothing as Daniel came in. O'Neil evidently picked it up, glancing at the scholar with a sudden expression of comprehension.

"I understand that you might prefer to be out fighting than in here," he told Daniel. "I'd rather be on the firing line myself. But I have a report to make to General West, and frankly, I need you to comment on the capabilities of this Boat of a Million Years. We'll probably be the last group to make it through—"

"But, Colonel," Barbara Shore protested. "I told you one of my people hasn't shown up. Actually, he's one of your people—Corporal Vance."

"We can't wait forever," O'Neil said. "Mr. Storey, would you please activate the StarGate?"

Before Storey could move, however, the inner ring of symbols began moving by itself, altering the combination that led to Earth.

"What the hell—?" Storey said, staring.

Daniel whirled on O'Neil. "Maybe now you'll believe me when I tell you that Ra's medallion also serves as a StarGate key," he said.

"Sure we believe you," a pale Barbara Shore said. "Now that she's used it to lock us all in."

CHAPTER 20
ON TARGET

The StarGate's inner ring came to a stop. Everyone stared at the gleaming toroid.

"There doesn't seem to be any connection," Barbara said.

"*She* doesn't want us to go anywhere," Daniel said. The venom in his voice made it clear whom he had in mind. "Either she'll be coming here, or she'll send some of her bully boys."

As if on cue, the StarGate began to pulse with the energy of an impending transit.

Daniel leapt into action. He dumped his blast-lance and pushed by a surprised Marine security type, grabbing a pair of grenades from the man's web belts. Holding them up, he stepped up to face the steadying energy lens forming within the ring.

"Everybody just get into the next chamber," Daniel said calmly.

"Jackson," O'Neil said sharply. "You know as well as anyone here that StarGate transits are only one-way. You can't throw those grenades through."

"Oh, the grenades are just backup," Daniel assured him grimly. "We're going to have a little experiment in basic physics. I'm going to stand right in the way here—and we'll see what happens when two bodies attempt to occupy the same space at the same time.

"Jackson!" shouted a horrified Barbara Shore.

"Daniel?" Sha'uri said worriedly.

But Daniel didn't get a chance to make his sacrifice. A slim figure in dusty BDUs shoved him out of the way. "The colonel needs you," Lieutenant Charlton said. "Make this count."

They got the barest glimpse of a masked Horus guard starting to materialize. About half of his body was overlapped by Charlton's. The guard recoiled in horror when he realized what was about to happen. There was no way he could stop.

An intolerable glare filled the chamber, and the whole pyramid seemed to shake around them.

When they could see again, the StarGate's torus was empty of energy . . . and Lieutenant Charlton had disappeared.

"Vaporized?" Mitch Storey said in a quiet voice.

"I think maybe there was some sort of bounce-back effect," Barbara Shore offered shakily.

"Well, it looks as if whatever happened has left us with a free StarGate," O'Neil said. "See if it works, Mr. Storey—and get us home."

No StarGate setup had ever been undertaken more quickly. Everyone in the room leaned forward as the usual steps of the cycle—crescendoing tone, energy backwash, and finally the formation of the energy lens—took place.

They held back long enough to let the ladies go first. Then, in no order other than how close they were to the portal, everyone in the room pelted through the gate.

More than seven hundred feet above the chaos in the hall of the StarGate, Corporal Tom Vance sat in front of a control console on the command deck of the starship *Ra's Eye*.

He had faithfully reduplicated everything Mitch Storey had shown him about operating the gunnery controls. The sensor view of the ceiling was in schematic mode. The symbol depicting the vast bulk of the Boat of a Million Years covered most of the representation.

Vance moved the stylized eye of the aiming system until it was dead-center on the huge ship's ass.

"For all my buddies gone," he snarled. "Take *that*!"

Aboard the Boat of a Million Years, Khonsu stood silent as Hathor lividly berated him for the failure of the commando raid she'd just ordered through the StarGate.

"What do you mean, something went wrong?" she demanded.

"I believe the transit was somehow interrupted," he replied. "My belief is that our team was entirely lost."

"And on what do you base this theory?" Hathor inquired acidly.

"This came back through our portal, Lady."

"Nothing comes back through the portals—" Hathor stopped as she realized what her deputy was holding out. Subtly twisted awry, as if it had undergone some incredible pressures, it was a portion of a Horus mask.

And inside, as neatly cut off as the mask had been, was a portion of the former wearer's head.

Sometimes even a warrior goddess has to stare in shock.

Hathor was absorbing one unprecedented occurrence as another took place. The enormous mass of the vessel they were aboard suddenly kicked upward in a drunken lurch. Both Hathor and her liegeman staggered as automatic systems swung into action. One set of burnt-in procedures steadied the craft and brought it higher. Another activated sensors, searching for the aggressor. Reports began echoing through the empty reaches of the command deck—all of them in the incomprehensible tongue of the ancient race that had spawned Ra.

"Computer!" Hathor cried. "Make those reports in my tongue!"

The gabble turned into comprehensible speech. "Automatic defenses have detected source of energy attack."

Hathor stared. The Earthlings had somehow managed to operate the blast-cannon aboard *Ra's Eye*?

The automated report continued. "Main batteries targeting aggressor craft."

Too late Hathor realized the import of what the computer was saying.

As the automated defenses announced, "Firing," she shouted. "No!"

It was too late. A lambent gout of energy flared from the projectors of the huge ship's main battery. It struck the pinnacle of the ship *Ra's Eye,* and for a brief moment the golden quartz resisted the incandescent blast. Then it was gone, as was the command deck—and Tom Vance.

But the deadly thrust of energy continued on, vaporizing the rock of the Abydos pyramid, stabbing down below the surface—and striking the still active StarGate.

Hathor and Khonsu both stared numbly at the hellish interaction of the blast's raw power and the StarGate's subtle energies. The space around the blasted pyramid became subtly . . . *wrong.* Even the light seemed somehow twisted as structures, people, and the ground itself took on an unearthly blue radiance and seemed to wink out of existence. In seconds the spot where her army of Horuses had been massing turned into the epicenter of a huge, gaping cleft extending deep into the planet's crust.

Shock waves of titanic proportions buffeted even the massive Boat of a Million Years. More automated systems snapped into operation, analyzing the situation and taking the huge starship to a safer distance.

The two humans aboard watched the planet's final convulsions on the long-range scanner. Abydos became a shattered, volcanic hell, the site of the former StarGate marked by a continent-long seam, luridly glaring with lava.

Khonsu glanced at the still, beautiful mask of a face beside him, staring at the carnage she'd caused.

The Lady exceeds her legends, he thought. *Where she once covered a world with blood, she has now murdered a planet itself.*

In the missile silo of Creek Mountain, Colorado, Earth's StarGate spewed forth the last evacuees from the Abydos debacle. General West and the Marine M.P.'s in charge of security had seen some bizarre sights in the past hours, including a very upset mastadge that had become massively incontinent after its transit.

But no one had seen StarGate travelers emerge from the energy lens so closely in time that they seemed a single mass landing atop one another in what looked like an impromptu orgy.

"Jeez," muttered one of the guards, "you always hear about cluster fucks, but I never expected to *see* one . . ."

Daniel Jackson managed to push himself off Sha'uri, who crawled away, rising to her feet without a look in his direction.

Barbara Shore disentangled herself and turned to the StarGate lens, which had not vanished after the transit but remained, roiling much more wildly than anyone had ever seen it reacting before.

"It's not done," she said. "Perhaps Vance—"

The film of energy across the ring suddenly coruscated with painful brightness, and something flew from the gateway, nearly braining the physicist where she stood. Whatever it was impacted against the security barriers with the force of a cannon ball.

Back on his feet, Jack O'Neil investigated. "Looks like a piece of stone," he reported. "It's dressed on one side, but vitrified—you can still feel the heat radiating from it. Something seems to have melted onto it as well."

He looked to the other side of the still steaming chunk. "Golden quartz."

"I think that's one of the ceiling stones from the hall of the StarGate," Daniel said quietly. "Hathor must have fired straight down at us." He turned to General West. "I suspect that if you try the Abydos coordinates on our StarGate now, you won't get a connection."

"You think the StarGate was destroyed?" West demanded.

"More likely, the world is gone." Barbara Shore sounded sick.

For a second West's poker face cracked. Daniel was surprised to see regret—mixed with a certain satisfaction. "I sincerely hope that Abydos is not in as much danger as you suggest," he said. "Although it would be a relief, I admit, if Hathor lost the Abydos StarGate as a means of reaching us."

"Sorry, General, but she'll be reaching us anyway," Daniel said. "Give her about a year. That's how long it will take that big bastard she's riding to arrive in the solar system."

He raked everyone in the room with a cold glare. "And Earth had better be ready."